WOLFBLADE

'LOOK OUT!' RAGNAR shouted, throwing himself forward. Haegr moved, not a heartbeat too soon. Moments later their flimsy shelter exploded in a shower of shrapnel. It was like nothing Ragnar had ever seen, but that did not surprise him, he already had a good idea of what had caused it. A glance confirmed it – a halo of light surrounded a figure of glowing whiteness. It would have dazzled Ragnar had his protective second lid not dropped into place to protect his sight.

'Psyker!' he shouted, snapping off a shot as he continued to roll. The bolter shell flew true but was repelled by the aura around the cultist. Things are going from bad to worse, Ragnar thought.

A WARHAMMER 40,000 NOVEL

WOLFBLADE

By William King

For Radka

A BLACK LIBRARY PUBLICATION

First published in Great Britain in 2003 by
BL Publishing,
Games Workshop Ltd.,
Willow Road, Nottingham,
NG7 2WS, UK

10 9 8 7 6 5 4

Cover illustration by Geoff Taylor

A CIP record for this book is available from the British Library

ISBN 13: 978 1 84416 021 1
ISBN: 1 84416 021 1

Distributed in the US by Simon & Schuster
1230 Avenue of the Americas, New York, NY 10020

See the Black Library on the Internet at
www.blacklibrary.com

Find out more about Games Workshop
and the world of Warhammer 40,000 at
www.games-workshop.com

IT IS THE 41st millennium. For more than a hundred centuries the Emperor has sat immobile on the Golden Throne of Earth. He is the master of mankind by the will of the gods, and master of a million worlds by the might of his inexhaustible armies. He is a rotting carcass writhing invisibly with power from the Dark Age of Technology. He is the Carrion Lord of the Imperium for whom a thousand souls are sacrificed every day, so that he may never truly die.

YET EVEN IN his deathless state, the Emperor continues his eternal vigilance. Mighty battlefleets cross the daemon-infested miasma of the warp, the only route between distant stars, their way lit by the Astronomican, the psychic manifestation of the Emperor's will. Vast armies give battle in his name on uncounted worlds. Greatest amongst his soldiers are the Adeptus Astartes, the Space Marines, bio-engineered super-warriors. Their comrades in arms are legion: the Imperial Guard and countless planetary defence forces, the ever-vigilant Inquisition and the tech-priests of the Adeptus Mechanicus to name only a few. But for all their multitudes, they are barely enough to hold off the ever-present threat from aliens, heretics, mutants – and worse.

TO BE A man in such times is to be one amongst untold billions. It is to live in the cruellest and most bloody regime imaginable. These are the tales of those times. Forget the power of technology and science, for so much has been forgotten, never to be re-learned. Forget the promise of progress and understanding, for in the grim dark future there is only war. There is no peace amongst the stars, only an eternity of carnage and slaughter, and the laughter of thirsting gods.

PROLOGUE

ALL AROUND WAS deathly still. The old trees, with grey bark, and leaves long since killed by pollution, loomed out of the shadows like tormented ghosts. In the darkness around him, Ragnar could sense armed men on the move. He was not afraid. They were his men, sworn to follow him, and die at his command if need be. He wondered where the thought had sprung from. There would be no deaths among his men this night – at least not if he could help it.

He looked to the soft ground underfoot. Although he was moving quietly there was no way he could avoid leaving tracks. The weight of his armour ensured it. After weeks of fighting amid the wreckage of the hives of Hesperida, he was almost among nature again. Almost. The area must once have been a park or forestry dome, before the cultists had begun their uprising. It would have been a place of pleasure where the wealthy came to experience what the surface of their world had once been like. Now it was an area of death, the great geodesic dome was shattered, and the foul air of the tortured planet could now enter. Everywhere there were splinters of armour glass from the collapse, some of them almost as large as a man.

The night air was a peculiar mixture of stenches: the rot from the dead trees, the spores of the fast growing fungi that blotched their sides, industrial toxins, the faint scent of animals that had passed by not so long ago. And everywhere and always there was the faint insidious stench that Chaos left when it inhabited a world's surface for any time; it was the smell of corruption, rich, sweet and sickly.

Abruptly it came to Ragnar that he knew the source. Some of the trees were still alive – the blotched ones, the palest, the greyest, the most degenerate looking. They were not being killed by some parasite, he realised. They were being changed by it, or into it. It was the only way any living thing could survive in an environment so rapidly altered.

For some reason, he thought of Gabriella, and the Navigators, and he smiled grimly. It was the first time such thoughts had entered his mind in decades. He shook his head; he needed to concentrate on the task at hand. There were enemies out there in this tainted night, enemies who badly wanted him and his men dead. And right now their only defence was stealth.

Ragnar was not sure what had gone wrong up in orbit, but something had. The last he had heard was a brief scrambled burst on the comm-net that told of the arrival of a massive enemy fleet. Then everything had been lost in static. It was almost as if it were a signal informing them that the enemy offensive had begun. The cultists had attacked en masse supported by heavy weapon fire, and strange sorceries. Ragnar had made his men hold their posts as long as possible, but he had known from the very beginning they were fighting a rearguard action, and that eventually their position would have to be abandoned.

Several times he had tried raising central command, but something had shut down the whole net. Whether it was sorcery or some freak climatic effect, it did not matter. There was no way his superiors could know what had happened, and there was no means of attracting support. In any case, he did not need access to the comm system to know that none would be forthcoming.

The roars of Chaos Titan weaponry and the sounds of battle drifting on the wind told him all he needed to know. The enemy were mounting a massive offensive all along the front. His Blood Claw scouts had brought back word that the two adjacent sections of the line, held by Imperial

Guard and Planetary units, had already crumbled. His men and the local levies supporting them were now a salient pushed into the body of the main enemy advance. And they would soon be cut off.

In the face of the sledgehammer falling on them, there had been no choice but to give the order to retreat. It had not been a popular one. For Space Wolves the most honourable death was in battle, and it was not in their nature to give way before the enemy.

Ragnar grinned. A Wolf Lord did not need to be popular, he needed to be obeyed, and Ragnar was. It was not his duty to throw lives away needlessly. It was his duty to defeat the enemy. However, if that was not possible, he would preserve as much of his force as he could so that they could return and overcome the foe another day. They had held out as long as they could, giving their men a chance to find their way back through the ruins of the great dome while they still had the chance. In fact, they had done the work of ten times their number in throwing back the enemy assaults.

It had not been easy. They had spent most of the time in deep bunkers amid the rubble, riding out the storm of artillery fire, keeping their heads down, and knowing that the enemy would advance as soon as the barrage finished. Perhaps sooner, for the warlords of the Dark Gods of Chaos were careless with their followers' lives. They had emerged from their dens to throw back probing attacks, and one massive wave assault that had been repulsed by the thinnest of margins. When night fell, Ragnar knew it was time to leave. He had given orders to arm the booby traps that filled their position, and he watched as the first squads began to melt away into the night. Even now, somewhere behind him in the darkness, the rearguard waited, keeping up sporadic fire on their enemies so that they would think the position was still held.

He wondered how much the noose had tightened around their necks. If the encirclement was complete the scouts would soon encounter enemy pickets and patrols. They had orders to report back without engaging, but it was always possible that the sons of Fenris would somehow manage to start a fight.

He had done his best to impress on the Blood Claws in particular that now was not the time for violence. A mistake could lead to the death of their entire company. At the time, they had appeared to recognise the gravity of the situation, but who could know what they might do out in the field?

Ragnar pushed these thoughts to one side. He had done all he could, and matters were out of his hands. He should focus on things he could influence. He sniffed the air. He caught the scents of his comrades, along with something that made his hackles rise – the taint of madness and murder that he was so familiar with. Deep within him something stirred. He felt the urge to snarl and rend. His worries about the scouts returned. If the stink of Chaos could still affect him after all these years, what about those youths…

No point worrying, he reminded himself. They were as well trained as he had been. They knew what to do. He just had to trust in that.

The ground shook under his feet as more high impact shells slammed home. He froze, instinctively, seeking to blend in with cover. Those hits had come from close by. Had the enemy spotted and targeted them? It was hard to see how they could have done so by conventional means, but then Chaos did not have to use conventional means. They had sorcerers and daemons and all manner of divinatory enchantments to call on. Ragnar had seen evidence enough of that in his career never to doubt it.

Their own position was supposedly warded by the spells of the Rune Priests, but they had been cast days ago, and such things had a way of untangling when most needed. Ragnar breathed a prayer to Russ and forced himself to start moving again. All around him his warriors did the same. With the pack mentality of the Wolves, they had instinctively waited for his response. Now they loped into action again.

Step by tortuous step, they progressed through the shadow of the great warped trees, grey ghosts in a grey landscape, towards fleeting sanctuary. Ragnar was not even sure that there was a sanctuary any more. What the scouts had reported earlier might no longer stand. Battle was a fluid situation; lines that seemed solid had a way of melting like tracks in sand before the tide. Perhaps the men behind them had been over-run by the advancing tide of evil. He would not know until he was much closer. Once again he cursed the battle that raged overhead. Without access to the comm-net and the divinatory orbital sensors, they were blind as well as deaf. At least, he hoped battle still raged overhead. If the Imperial Fleet had been defeated, then they were cut off, and they were all dead men who did not know it yet.

He glanced skywards at the strange stars through a break in the clouds. They glittered and twinkled oddly, their light filtered by pollution. Some of those lights might be ships, he thought, and some might even now be firing weapons of unimaginable power at foes shielded by titanic energies. There was no way to tell. All he could do was watch and hope.

How quickly the situations change, he thought. A week ago everything had seemed well in hand. His forces had cleared most of the surrounding blocks of territory and were poised to strike at the heart of the enemy – the great citadel where the rebellion had its headquarters.

The appearance of the enemy fleet and an unexpectedly large number of enemy forces had thrown all careful calculations out of kilter. Ragnar told himself not to despair. He had been in worse situations.

He had been in such tight spots that this seemed a mere feast day revel. It was strange though, how faded memories of long past dangers never compared with feelings engendered by current threats. He had seen enough men die to know how long the odds were. No matter how well trained or experienced, there was always the chance that a stray bullet would find you. Even odds of a thousand to one did not seem long when you had been in a thousand fights.

Where were these thoughts coming from, he asked himself? They should not normally occur to a commander with an Imperial field force at his beck and call. He was not normally like this. And he felt worse than a normal commander would, because his scent transmitted his mood back to his pack, and they in turn reflected this.

Was he under some sort of attack, he wondered? Was there some chemical in the air, too subtle for his detectors and his nose to pick out? Or was some daemon-worshipping sorcerer at work? Not all spells involved bolts of fire or the summoning of hell-spawned fiends. He was shielded against obvious attacks, and knew how to resist a direct probe at his mind. But this could be something more subtle, he thought, a flank attack on the citadel of his mind. He began to recite a litany of protection, softly, under his breath.

Immediately he felt better, although he was not sure whether it was from the comfort he took in his words, or the potency of prayer itself. Sergeant Urlec moved up beside him. There was acrimony in his scent. The sergeant had taken to questioning many of Ragnar's decisions in private. There was friction between them, and Ragnar recognised its source. It was the tension that rose between the younger Wolf and the older one, as to who would lead the pack. This friction was grafted into every Wolf's geneseed from the ancient days of the First Founding.

Ragnar had been like this once, and he wondered when the challenge would come. It was strange to think of himself as the elder in this situation. He had come early to his lordship and was probably younger in years than Urlec although that had no bearing on the way either of them viewed the situation.

'Scouts report enemy up ahead,' said Urlec. 'Looks like we are cut off!'

'Did they say that, sergeant?' said Ragnar. Both of them spoke so quietly that only another Space Wolf could have picked up their words, and only then if they were very close. Urlec's scent became more acrid.

'No, Lord Ragnar,' he said grudgingly. 'They only said the enemy were present.'

'Then there's no evidence of encirclement yet, sergeant,' said Ragnar, his hackles rising as he spoke the contrary words. 'Just because there are enemy there, we are not necessarily cut off. Send the scouts forward and tell them to feel out the enemy position. In the meantime, tell the rest of the packs to slow their advance. We don't want to blunder into a firefight in the dark.'

'It's already done,' said Urlec, with some satisfaction. Ragnar fought an urge to growl. Of course Urlec had done it. He was competent. That was why Ragnar had promoted him when Vitulv had died. He only wished the man was not so smug. He did not need this contest of wills and wit with his senior sergeant right now. There were more important things to worry about.

Ragnar forced his breathing to slow. The problem here was his. The folly of Urlec was just one more obstacle to overcome in order to preserve his company. The man would be dealt with later, but right now, Ragnar had to live with with his presence and his attitude.

'Very good,' he said, knowing that Urlec could read his mood from his scent. Briefly he considered once more the possibility of psychic attack. Perhaps this was more than instinctive hostility, perhaps it was some form of sorcerous assault. Ragnar wished Brother Hrothgar were present to perform a divination. But that was like wishing for a fleet to carry him to the moon. Hrothgar had been summoned to command days ago and had not been heard of since. It was a pity. Perhaps a sending would have been able to find out what was going on back there.

Ragnar slowed his pace, as he and the sergeant began to encounter groups of Wolves hunkered down in cover. They were taking things seriously at least. They knew that potential disaster lay ahead of them, as well as behind. He threaded his way through them, silent as a shadow. He made less noise than Urlec although he was the larger of the two. He wanted to get as close to the frontline as possible, and get the word direct from the mouths of the scouts as they returned.

He reviewed his options. One good thing about fighting on this ground was that he was familiar with it. Over the past few weeks he had scouted it himself several times, getting to know the terrain. He had wanted to be prepared for any eventuality, no matter how remote a retreat had seemed at the time. He knew that the dome was full of rolling downs, depressions and ridgelines that could provide cover for defence and attacks. That the hills were sculpted and artificial did not matter – they looked as natural as anything on his home world of Fenris. He knew there were two winding valleys, like canyons that snaked through the park and many sculpted streams and waterfalls.

Right now they were moving along the inside of those valleys, using the cover. On the other side of the elevation, flanking troops of scouts could make sure no ambushers took them by surprise from the ridge tops. This was the easiest line of retreat but also the most obvious for an enemy familiar with the terrain. He had chosen it because they needed to be swift as well as stealthy, and he trusted the ability of his men to keep out of sight of their opponents. He hoped that his trust would prove justified.

Why the constant doubts, he asked himself? He knew the answer. They were not the objects of some psychic attack. They were the products of what was happening. It was easy to have complete confidence in yourself and your men when you were winning. It was a lot harder when things were against you. He did not think it was a coincidence that Urlec's subtle challenges had begun when things started to go against them. He supposed it was only natural, but he did not like it.

Get used to it, he told himself, you cannot always be on the winning side. Not unless you were the Imperium anyway. It was a joke among the human military that the Imperium always won, even if it took a thousand years. Individuals, regiments, armies might be lost in meat-grinder campaigns but in the end the forces of the Emperor were always triumphant – they had to be, they were just too numerous for it to be any other way.

Part of him knew this was mere conceit. In the great cosmic scale of things, the Imperium was relatively young, despite its ten thousand year history. There were races out there that had been old when humanity had just begun to look up at the stars from the caves of a single world. Ragnar himself had seen the remains of civilisations that had once covered as many worlds as humanity did today, and perhaps had been even more powerful. 'Look upon my works ye mighty and despair', as he had observed once on the plinth of a toppled statue on a far off desert world. It had been erected by humans during the long gone Dark Age of Technology, but the sentiment could have been directed at any of the extinct races of the times before man.

He forced his attention back to the task at hand, pushing forward to the best cover at the front of his retreating force. He waited for the scouts to return. Urlec hunkered down beside him and waited too. There was still a look of challenge about him, but he said nothing. Ragnar wondered whether the man was right to doubt him. He doubted himself, and Urlec would sense that weakness and pounce on it. It was the Wolves' way.

He caught the scent of the scouts returning. They caught his and moved towards him, sure-footed in the darkness. Swift, confident and full of the blood lust of the Space Wolves.

'What have you seen?' he asked.

'The enemy are there, lord. They have moved to encircle us with at least two companies of heretics. Some of the accursed Thousand Sons are there too, at their head. They have set up wards, and work evil sorceries. The place stinks of them.'

That did not sound good, Ragnar thought. Ordinary infantry men would be easy to overcome with speed and surprise, but the Thousand Sons were Space Marines like his own men. No – that was not true, they were very different in important ways.

They were Marines who had betrayed the Imperium at the dawn of its history and sworn themselves to the service of the Dark Gods of Chaos. They were ensnared by the subtle sorceries of the daemon god Tzeentch and were given over to the study of his dark spells. They were ancient, inimical and steeped in the most profound and subtle evil. And they were deadly fighters. Ragnar had fought them on dozens of occasions, and it seemed that he was destined to cross their paths throughout his career. Some of those encounters had changed the course of his life.

'Anything else?' he asked.

'There are gaps in their line. I do not know if they are aware of them, or whether it's a trap,' said the scout. He sketched out a map in the dirt, perceptible by the scent trace of his finger more than by the lines drawn. 'Here and here are gaps where their patrols have no line of sight. I could crawl between them and not be noticed.'

'Unless they have some spell waiting to be triggered by our presence.'

'Such was my thought, Wolf Lord,' said the scout, squatting.

Ragnar considered his words. It did not matter if it was a trap. They were caught between hammer and anvil. They could not wait where they were, for the dawn would reveal them to their foes. They could not go back, for soon their old position would be over-run. They needed to push through the gap and try to make it back to the safety of their own lines.

'The slaves of Horus,' Ragnar asked. 'Do they look towards us, or towards the Guard regiments behind?'

'They seemed to be mostly concerned with us, milord.'

Not surprising, Ragnar thought. They would not want to leave a fortification full of Space Wolves behind them when they moved on. That would leave the chance of a break out, or having their supply lines harassed. They would want their foe dead if they could achieve it.

'It was odd, my lord. I know nothing of such things, but I sensed that they were concentrating their spell energies in our direction. Certainly their witch lights flickered towards us.'

'I think if they were targeting us, we would have known it by now,' said Ragnar. He was surprised when both Urlec and the scout nodded agreement. 'Whatever evil they work, no doubt it is aimed at our former position.' Which we abandoned just in the nick of time, thought Ragnar. He offered up a prayer to Russ that the rearguard had already vacated the strongpoints. Whatever the Thousand Sons were planning it would not be pleasant, he was sure.

He thought about the darkness in his thoughts. He recognised it now: it was the effect of an evil spell cast in the vicinity, the seepage of wicked energies filtered into the sane and normal world by the forces of dark magic. It affected the mood of any living thing around it, sometimes so subtly it was not noticed until it was too late. The realisation raised Ragnar's mood. If you knew what you were fighting, you could resist it much better.

Another thought occurred to him. If the feeling was intense here, what would things be like in the abandoned strongpoint? Far more intense, no doubt.

'How many Thousand Sons?' he asked.

'I counted a dozen, wolf lord, but there may be more.'

'Not many,' said Ragnar. 'For a full company of Wolves.'

If the mages were wrapped up in their ritual and did not even know they were there, there was a chance they could strike a heavy blow before the enemy was aware of it.

How swiftly things change indeed, thought Ragnar. One moment feeling beaten, and the next considering swift attack. Such were the fortunes of war.

'I need to know where every one of those bastard offspring of Magnus are,' said Ragnar. He sensed he had the full and undivided attention of the scout and Urlec now. 'I want them all dead before dawn.'

Approval radiated from them now, albeit reluctantly from the sergeant. 'Pinpoint them all. Urlec, spread the word among the men. When I give the signal we're going to remind the Chaos loving scum of the Scouring of Prospero.'

Both men nodded and set about their business. Ragnar considered his options. If the Thousand Sons were lost in evil rituals, his men could have the upper hand. What they needed was to destroy the mages, and then cut through the enemy along the line of least resistance. If things went well, they could interrupt the ritual and make it back to their own lines. If things went badly, they would at least drag some worthy foes down to hell with them.

Was he doing the right thing? Perhaps it would be best to try and find a gap in the enemy lines and go through it. He shook his head. No, this was the bold way – the Space Wolf way. The enemy obviously did not know they were here. Surprise was too great an advantage to throw away. The wait for the scouts to return seemed interminable. Every minute brought dawn closer. Every heartbeat increased the chance of discovery. Ragnar forced himself to relax, to wait, and let go of things he had no control over. He checked his weapons lovingly, a ritual that never failed to ease his mind. He fingered the pommel of his frostblade, which brought back memories of Gabriella and the Navigators and his long ago stay on the heart world of Terra.

He let his mind drift towards those ancient events for a moment, and then he snapped back. The scouts were returning. 'A dozen, wolf lord, I am sure of it. They seem to be standing in some evil arcane pattern unless I am mistaken. Lines of witchfire leap between them, and they chant in some foul tongue.'

Ragnar nodded, and spoke swiftly, giving orders to the scouts to pass to the squad leaders. No sense in using the comm-net, even locally, at the moment. It might well be compromised. Word would have to ripple through the dark in the ancient ways, carried by sight, sound and smell. He sniffed the air, testing it. He could catch the change in the pack's scent. Word was being passed, men were readying themselves for the advance. In his mind's eye, Ragnar could picture them moving closer to all those thirteen points. Suddenly there was a flicker of light overhead, not as bright as a flare but intense nonetheless. Ragnar recognised it as a starship's shields going into overload and its power core going nova. High above them a ship full of men had died. He would have given a lot to know which side they belonged to. Irrelevant, he told himself. Keep your mind in the here and now.

The warriors of his bodyguard were close around him now. They were the best of the best. He had put himself at the spearhead of the attack for he knew it would make little difference now whether he lived or died. He had done all he could with the plan. Now it was a matter of fight or die.

Swiftly and silently, they slithered through the dark, bypassing sentry devices, stepping over trip-wires. Most men would not have spotted them, but for Ragnar and his warriors, the stench of Chaos gave away their position. Suddenly up ahead, through a gap in the undergrowth, he caught sight of a glowing object. He paused and raised his hand. Immediately his men halted.

He studied what he could see, taking it all in with a quick glance. There was a tall, pale staff of yellowed bones, fused together at the joints. At its tip was a skull like that of a horse, only it was horned and had a faint suggestion of the humanoid about it. The skull glowed faintly and lines of fire sprang from it, speeding off to other places where no doubt similar staffs stood. On the bones, crimson runes glowed. The staff radiated an aura of power but what stood beside it commanded most of Ragnar's attention.

He could see a tall man, garbed in glowing armour that was like an ancient baroque copy of Ragnar's own. Every centimetre of the armour was either etched with runes like those of the staff or sprouted tiny cast metal daemon heads which leered and moved with a will of their own. The warrior's arms were spread wide, and Ragnar's keen ears caught the words of some ancient spell being chanted in the tongue of daemons.

All around the man stood Chaos cultists. They were normal men, though some were marked with the stigmata of mutation. All wore the patched uniforms that indicated they had once, in a better day, belonged to the Planetary levies. They looked gaunt and filled with fear and exaltation, but their weapons were serviceable. Their leader, wearing the shoulder markings of a lieutenant, looked as if he wanted to say something to the Chaos Marine but did not dare. The wicked warrior dwarfed normal humans just as Ragnar or any of his men would have done. The mage's voice droned on, almost imperceptibly rising, the words tumbling out faster now, as if nearing a dark climax. The air was charged with alien presence and a feeling of dread began to fill Ragnar.

He had no idea what foul ritual was being worked here, but the time had come to stop it. He sprang up and aimed a shot at the sorcerer. The bolter shell smashed into his armour sending him tumbling headlong into the dirt. Ragnar thought he caught sight of a faint flicker of chain lightning along the armour after he pulled the trigger, but did not let it bother him.

'Charge!' he bellowed, gesturing with his unsheathed frostblade. The men of his guard rushed forward. All along the line he could hear the sporadic sound of bolter fire as other squads engaged the enemy.

Ragnar let out a howling war cry that echoed in the woods around them, magnified a hundred-fold. He emerged from the bushes, cleaving at the nearest enemy and separating him from his head with one mighty blow. Moments later he was among the cultists, hacking and chopping, sending another soul to greet its dark masters in hell with every blow.

His men all did the same. They emerged from the tree-line like a thunderbolt, and cut through the enemy as if they were mere children armed with wooden swords. The initial engagement was not a battle; it was a massacre. Ragnar could see their lieutenant frantically demanding that his troops stand their ground. He put a bolter shell through the man's brain, and his attempts to rally his men ended forever.

'Ah, I might have known the fabled Wolves would show up and spoil everything,' mocked a beautiful voice that carried across the field of battle. 'It has always been your way.'

Ragnar glanced around to see that the Chaos warrior had risen from the ground and had unsheathed a darkly glowing runeblade. When he lashed out Ragnar saw Red Eric, one of his bodyguard, go down. The Chaos blade had cut right through his armour as if it were not there.

It was an impressive feat, for Eric had been a seasoned warrior of no little skill. The Chaos warrior's next strike cleaved through Urlec's chainsword, and then, with a blow from his armoured fist, he managed to knock the sergeant from his feet. Now the Chaos warrior stood over him, aiming a downward thrust. 'I suppose I should thank you for interrupting the tedium of the ritual, and for letting me offer up some half-way worthy souls to my patron. You are certainly more worthy than the mewling, puking defenders of this paltry planet, although if truth be told that is hardly a recommendation.'

Ragnar turned and raced towards the Chaos warrior, intercepting his downward arcing blade with his own. 'I don't care what you think,' he said. 'I don't care what your patron thinks. I just want you dead.'

'Spoken with all the arrogance of a Wolf! But you are no match for the High Mage Karamanthos,' said the Chaos warrior. He spoke with a dramatic flourish, like an actor, and appeared to expect recognition. Even if Ragnar had known him, he would not have given the daemon worshipper the satisfaction.

'It's a pity you don't have the strength to match your overbearing ego.' Sparks flared as their blades clashed. The red runes brightened. They fought over the prone body of the dazed sergeant.

'Don't I?' said Karamanthos mockingly. 'Perhaps it is you who doesn't.'

Ragnar's weapon grated down the runesword with a terrible scream of tortured metal. As it reached the guard of the Chaos warrior's blade it stopped, locked in place. The two mighty warriors stood breast to breast, their strength equally matched for a moment. Ragnar noticed the strange reek of ozone and hot metal coming from the visor of the Chaos Marine. Who knew what lay within that armour, he thought, but he was willing to bet it wasn't anything remotely human anymore. His muscles ached from holding his opponent in place. Perhaps this creature of sorcery had no sinews left to tire. Perhaps it did not feel fatigue. Perhaps it had the unfailing strength of a daemon.

'No, dear boy, you don't,' the Chaos warrior said and made to move its weapon. Ragnar held it in place. His breath was coming in gasps now. The sorcerer seemed to change his mind and began chanting something – a spell no doubt. With an effort of will, Ragnar extruded the claws in his boots. He stepped back and lashed out with his foot, catching the Chaos warrior behind the exposed knee, where the armour's thigh and calfguards met. He felt the blades bite home and saw Karamanthos begin to tip over. Seizing his opportunity he sprang forward, avoiding the Chaos warrior's desperately flailing blade, and buried his own weapon deep in his foe's throat. The chant cut off completely.

Sparks flared at the point of impact and rose into the night sky, accompanied by a dreadful smell of molten metal, corrosion and rot. Vapour, hot as steam, but far more corrupt, rose too. It was as if the spirit of the ancient sorcerer was fleeing its host body. Ragnar lashed at it, but his blade passed through and the thing began to dissipate for a moment. Then it started to cohere and flowed towards the skull tipped staff.

Ragnar howled in defiance and struck the staff. For a moment the vitrified bone, product of alien sorcery, resisted his blade, but then it snapped. The glow faded. The lines of fire winked out as if they had never been. From various points in the distance Ragnar heard screams like those of lost souls in torment. He guessed that disrupting the focal point of this dark ritual had had no good effect on the sorcerers weaving it. He felt no sympathy. Those who trafficked with dark powers deserved what they got.

He brought his boot down on the glowing skull, and smashed it to smithereens. Immediately the sense of dark presence vanished. He howled triumphantly and his men echoed his call. Then he dived forward into the roiling mass of Chaos cultists cleaving them asunder with renewed vigour. He drove them from him like a hero from some primitive saga unleashed once more into the world. His men followed him forward to victory. Howls of triumph along the line told him that the Wolves had overcome.

RAGNAR SAT IN the main camp of the Imperial forces. The walls had taken a pounding but he could see fresh troops gathering, ready to drive back the Chaos worshippers. The comm-net had been restored. It seemed the Chaos fleet had been driven off and the reinforcements they had been sending down to the planetary surface had let up. His men were encamped below, talking softly among themselves. Casualties had been mercifully light but they did not know about the rearguard, who had yet to report in.

Ragnar knew he would have to send out a search party for them, but now was not the time. The support barrage from the Imperial artillery was already pounding the earth around them. Soon, he would requisition some Thunderhawks and begin the search. He would either find the men, or collect their geneseed to be returned to the Chapter. Such was the way of the Wolves.

Ragnar stretched his legs and relaxed while he could. Soon it would be time for battle again. He caught the scent of Urlec approaching, and looked up, wondering what the sergeant wanted this time. Urlec gave him a shame-faced smile and said, 'I wish to thank you for saving my life, Wolf Lord.'

'It was nothing, sergeant. You would have done the same for me.'

'I doubt it, wolf lord. I doubt that I could have overcome the Chaos sorcerer.'

'Perhaps not today, Urlec, but you will learn.'

'I doubt that on the best day of my life I could. He was the chief of the Chaos lovers. None of the others gave our men such problems. I have never seen anybody so fast or strong as you, my lord. And his blade was stepped in evil magic! No normal weapon would stand against it. I am surprised that even yours could.'

Ragnar inspected the blade. 'I am not,' he said.

Urlec stared at the blade as if seeing it for the first time. Of course, he knew of the weapon, but knowing of it and seeing it in action were two different things.

'That is a fell weapon,' he said eventually. 'And no forge on Fenris produced it.'

'You are the right,' Ragnar replied.

'How did you come by it then?' The sergeant asked.

'It was a gift,' he said.

'A gift worthy of a primarch then,' said Urlec.

'And yet it came from no primarch.'

'From whom then, lord? And why would someone make such a gift?'

'From a woman whose life I saved, although there was a price. It is a long story,' said Ragnar studying the position of the sun. 'And now is not the time to tell it.'

But as Urlec moved away, he could not help but recall it.

CHAPTER ONE

'By Russ, I cannot believe that they are bloody well doing this to you,' said Sven. His blunt, honest, but ugly face was angry. He slammed his new prosthetic fist against the palm of his still-human hand. 'There are a million reasons for sticking your head on a spear shaft: vanity, ugliness, brute stupidity and your sheer lack of heroism and charisma, but this is daft!'

'Thank you, wolf brother,' said Ragnar. 'Your support overwhelms me.'

Ragnar tried to smile. He was glad to see his old friend, and more glad still to see he had recovered from the hellblade wound he had taken in the battle against the Thousand Sons. But he could not maintain his usual jocular tone – this was too serious. He was in deep, deep trouble. The assembled

Convocation of Wolf Lords had made that perfectly plain. That all of the Wolf Lords present on Garm had met to discuss his fate was a sign of just how serious things were.

As was the business of confining him to his cell while the rest of his battle-brothers scoured the world of the remaining heretics. Sven was his first visitor in days, and he had snuck in during a brief respite in the campaign. There had been no guards, but visitors to this part of the shrine complex had not been encouraged.

'I mean, so what if you lost the Spear of Russ,' said Sven. 'You did it with the best of bloody intentions, I'm sure.'

'It is not something to joke about, Sven.' That was something of an understatement, Ragnar thought. The Spear of Russ was perhaps the most sacred of all the Space Wolves' holy relics. It was the mystical weapon that the legendary founder of the Chapter had carried into battle at the dawn of the Imperium. With it, the primarch had slain monsters and dae-mons, and had saved whole worlds. It was said that his first act on his return would be to claim his Spear from this very shrine. He was going to find that a little difficult now, Ragnar thought, all things considered. 'What you are saying is very close to blasphemy.'

'I am sure if good old Leman Russ is eavesdrop-ping on our conversation he would agree with me.'

'And how would you know that, Brother Sven?' asked a stern voice from the back of the chamber. 'Does the spirit of the primarch consult with you in secret when he needs a particularly stupid opinion? If such is the case, perhaps you should share it with your battle-brothers? They will be pleased to learn that they have such an oracle among them.'

Both Ragnar and Sven looked around. They were startled to see that Ranek, the Wolf Priest, had entered the great chamber. It spoke something of the old man's stealth that he had managed to approach them unnoticed despite their supernaturally keen senses. He must have come from down-wind, Ragnar thought. He checked the direction from which the recycled air was coming. Either that or we were both simply too preoccupied to notice him. That is a more likely explanation, he decided.

Ragnar studied the old man. He was huge and grim and grey looking. The fangs protruding from his upper lip had an almost tusk-like quality. His hair was so grey it was almost white. But his eyes were keen and piercing, like the cold blue of glacial water off the coast of Asaheim. His eyebrows were enormously bushy, whereas his beard was long and fine. How long had it been since Ragnar first set eyes on him on the long voyage to the Islands of the Iron Masters?

A lifetime ago was the simple answer, no matter how you measured it in Imperial Standard years. In those days his father had still been alive and captain of his own dragonship. His people – the Thunder-fists – were still one united clan. They had not yet been killed or become the enslaved thralls and bondswomen of the Grimskulls. It was before he had died and been reborn, when the limits of his universe were the grey, stormy skies and leaden seas of his home world, Fenris. It was before he had learned how big the universe really was, how strange and dangerous.

It was before he had become a Space Wolf, one of the legion of genetically re-engineered warriors who served the Imperium of humanity in its galaxy spanning wars. It was before he had fought with men and monsters and the daemon-worshipping servants of Chaos. Even before he had known what a green-skinned ork was.

'Well, Sven? Do you want to induct me into the mysteries of your new theology? As a Wolf Priest, I would be honoured to share in your wisdom.'

Sven looked abashed. There were very few things in this universe that could make him so, but this old man was one.

'I am sure Sven meant nothing by his words,' said Ragnar.

'Ah,' said Ranek. 'So you are the prophet's chosen interpreter, are you, Ragnar? He speaks only through you now, does he? He is too far above the rest of us mere mortals to deign to talk with us.'

'That is not what I meant,' said Ragnar.

'Then pray keep your mouth shut!' said Ranek. 'You are in enough trouble already without using your tongue to dig yourself deeper. Now, get out of here, Sven!'

Sven slunk off towards the chamber exit. Just as he was about to pass through the door, Ranek spoke once more, in a kinder tone. 'It does you credit that you came here, lad. But it will do you no good if the Wolf Lords find out.'

Sven nodded, as if he understood. Then he simply departed. Ragnar immediately regretted his going. He was now alone under the stern eye of the priest. The old man walked around him, studying him from every angle, as if he were a puzzle that could be deciphered with enough contemplation. Ragnar stood stock still, determined to show no nervousness under this chilly examination, even if Ranek could smell it coming from him, which he most likely could.

'Well, laddie,' said Ranek, 'you've caused quite an uproar, and no mistake.'

'That was not my intention,' said Ragnar.

'And what was your intention, when you cast the Spear of Russ into the realm of Chaos?'

'I was trying to prevent the arrival of the Primarch Magnus through the infernal gateway he had created in his temple on this world. I was trying to stop the resurrection of the Thousand Sons and the destruction of our Chapter. I believe I succeeded.'

'Aye, laddie, and I know you believe that. The question is whether it is the truth. Magnus is a powerful sorcerer, perhaps the most powerful who ever lived. He could have put that thought in your mind. He could have put others there too.'

'Is that why the Rune Priests have kept me segregated from the Chapter until today, and chanted their spells over me day and night?' Ragnar asked.

'It was. That and other reasons.'

'Which were?'

'You will be told them in good time, if you need to know, and if the Wolf Lords decide to let you live.'

'To let me live?' Ragnar was shocked. He had known things were serious but not this serious. He had imagined imprisonment, exile, even banishment to the nether regions of Fenris or some isolated asteroid. He had not imagined death.

'Aye – a fallen Space Wolf would be a terrible thing to let loose on the Imperium, laddie, and one who has been tainted by Chaos could not be allowed to live. Too much of a threat.'

Ragnar considered this and understood it. The Chapters were small, but their strength came from their ability to fight as a unit. Every man relied implicitly on those he fought alongside. To have a traitor within the Chapter was unthinkable. He knew he was not one but…

Of course, that is what he would think if he had come under some sort of spell. He might well believe himself to be completely loyal until some moment of Magnus's choosing and then...

He knew such things were possible. Psykers could read minds, alter memories, and change people's thoughts and emotions. He had been trained to resist such things but Magnus was a primarch of the Fallen, a being only marginally less powerful than the God-Emperor himself. Furthermore, of all the primarchs, Magnus was the one most deeply immersed in sorcery. So if anyone was capable of such a feat it was he.

Ragnar briefly considered that he might have been corrupted without his knowledge. What now? Could he live with himself if he was a threat to Sven and all his other friends and comrades, and to the Chapter that had become his home?

'You don't think I have been corrupted, do you?' Ragnar uttered, proud of the fact he had kept a plaintive note from his voice. Ranek shrugged.

'For what it's worth, laddie, I do not. From what I have seen of you, not even Red Magnus could power a spell through that thick skull of yours. But we will know for sure. You have been tested as thoroughly by the Rune Priests as Logan Grimnar was before he took the Wolf Throne. The probes they have used are deeper and more subtle than those you encountered at the Gate of Morkai. The Rune Priests will speak their findings before the Convocation at your trial. Only they know what they think, and they will speak first to the Great Wolf and his lords. That is the way it has always been, and that is the way it will always be.'

Ragnar was not at all reassured. His whole life, and the fate of his soul hung in the balance. Ranek looked at him. He stared back.

'Why are you here?'

'I am here to counsel you and speak on your behalf. After all, I am the one who chose you to join the Wolves.'

'You were assigned to this?'

'I asked to do it.' Ragnar felt himself profoundly touched by the old man's faith in him. 'When will the Convocation reach its decision?'

A bell tolled distantly through the corridors of the temple.

'Perhaps it already has. Come laddie, let us go and hear what they have to say.'

Ranek led him into the chamber where the Wolf Lords sat in judgement. Great carved wolfs' heads glared down from the walls above. All the lords were seated in a semi-circle on a raised dais. In the centre was Logan Grimnar, the Great Wolf himself, firmly ensconced in his floating throne. He looked as old as the roots of mountains, and as hard as the armour of an Imperial battleship. His face was bleak as he studied Ragnar. The others all looked equally impassive.

Before the dais stood three robed and masked rune priests. Their glances settled on Ragnar as he entered. Ragnar stood as straight as he could and met their stares. He did not want to appear daunted. Whatever their judgement and whatever his eventual fate, he would meet it like a Space Wolf. He thought he sensed approval coming from Ranek, but he was not entirely sure.

He strode directly in front of the Great Wolf's throne and looked up defiantly. The Great Wolf stared back unmoved and then spoke in his deep gravelly voice. 'Rune Priests of Russ, you have examined this Wolf Brother for the taint of Chaos? What have you found?'

Ragnar could not help but turn his head to look at them. The moment seemed to stretch into eternity as the Rune Priest glanced at him. Then he banged his staff three times on the stone floor. 'We have examined this youth to the very depths of his soul and we have found...'

Ragnar leaned forward. He was holding his breath.

'...that he is untainted by the Powers of Darkness and loyal to his Chapter. The decision he made, he made in all honesty and with only the good of his battle-brothers in mind.'

Ragnar allowed himself to breathe again. So he was not a traitor and a heretic. Nothing had been laid upon his soul. He saw some of the Wolf Lords nod. Others shook their heads and looked angry. Berek Thunderfist, his company commander, gave him a broad wink. Logan Grimnar smiled gravely. Ragnar sensed the old Wolf Priest's relief beside him.

Sigrid Trollbane stood up. 'But, as you all know, there is another matter.' He had a surprisingly deep and cutting voice. 'No matter how pure his motives, this youth has lost us the Spear of Russ! Unless it is recovered and returned to this shrine, Russ cannot return to claim it in the last days. By losing it we have betrayed our sacred trust and forfeited all claims to be the true sons of Russ. Ragnar has betrayed a sacred trust.'

Ragnar considered this. He knew that all was not quite as it seemed. Berek had already explained this more than once. The politics of the Wolf Lords were at least as important as their religious beliefs. He doubted that there was any man among them who did not aspire to sit in Logan Grimnar's place on the Wolf Throne. The only difference was in the timing.

This was more than a simple attack on himself, deserving as it might be. Ragnar could *smell* the hunger and ambition of Sigrid and those who sided with him. Others merely watched, waiting to see how a leadership challenge would go. And others, like Berek, were siding with the Great Wolf for their own purposes. In Berek's case the motivation was clear. One of his men was the accused. Ragnar's misdeeds reflected on him, and undermined his prestige, and Berek was not a man to allow that to happen without a fight.

Berek rose to his feet, every inch a heroic commander. The lamplight turned his hair and beard golden. He moved and spoke with perfect poise and confidence. 'Ragnar performed a heroic action, single-handedly attacking a primarch in a bold attempt to save his battle-brothers. Who here can criticise him for such heroism?'

Ragnar saw some nods, and heard some muted murmurs of approval. Heroism was something that played well among the Space Wolves. They were proud warriors, with a respect for courage. Ragnar saw the ancient head of Egil Ironwolf nod grimly. Nonetheless, Ragnar could not help noticing that most of those who approved were of Berek's faction. Like Sigrid, Thunderfist was positioning himself as the natural successor to Logan Grimnar.

Sigrid smiled coldly. Compared to Berek he was pale. His face was thin and sallow. His eyes were cold, and his long moustaches drooped sadly down his face. Yet there was steel in him, Ragnar knew. No man became a Wolf Lord without it. He also had a chilly intelligence that was lacking in many of his fellows. His voice was mocking as it normally was when he was not bellowing commands on a battle-field.

'Ragnar is brave. Of that there can be no doubt. I salute his heroism. What I question is his intelligence. I also question our ability as a Chapter to prove ourselves worthy heirs to our predecessors. And no matter what his motives, this is Ragnar's fault. It may be that there is a way for the youth to atone for his deeds but some sanction must be taken against him.'

Ranek stood and strode forward to confront the council of Wolf Lords. He fixed Sigrid with his gaze and spoke clearly and calmly. 'A prophesy is a prophesy. It will be fulfilled in its own time, and in its own way, or it is no true prophesy. Russ will return. Russ will reclaim his Spear. Russ will lead this Chapter into the final conflict with the Evil One. Of that there can be no doubt.'

Sigrid was not daunted. If anything, his smile became mocking. 'You are suggesting then, Brother Ranek, that it was somehow Russ's will that this callow youth cast his sacred weapon into the void?'

'I am suggesting that if the prophesy be true prophesy that is irrelevant. In its own good time the Spear will return to us.'

'I can see why you are a great priest, Ranek. I wish I shared the strength of your faith.' Laughter, this time from Sigrid's supporters, greeted this sally. Most of the assembled Wolf Lords looked shocked. Sigrid's mockery of a priest did not play well with them.

'Perhaps you ought to,' said Ranek.

The flash of emotion across the Wolf Lord's face showed he realised his mistake. When next he spoke his voice was more conciliatory.

'You protect the boy because you were his chooser, Ranek, and your loyalty is to your credit. But still I say he must be punished for his actions.'

Sigrid paused and let the implications of the statement hang in the air for a moment. He wanted all present to see the connection between Ranek and Ragnar and Berek. The fault of the one was a reflection on all three. 'And I do not think it sits well for a priest of Russ to claim that all will be well and that the Spear will find its way back to us of its own accord. I doubt that the warp will give up its prize so easily. I agree it would be wonderful, miraculous even, if it did. But what are we to do if the Spear does not come back of its own free will? What are we to do when the Last Days come? All the signs say they are almost upon us. What then?

'And whether or not the Spear returns to us or not avoids the question. Do we really want a warrior in our midst that could so easily cast it aside? We do not need one so careless. Who knows what his next exploit might lead to?'

Logan Grimnar and the others considered this. Ragnar could not help but feel that Sigrid had a point. He had not thought through his actions; he had acted without any thought as to the consequences. He had taken it upon himself to lose the Sacred Spear. He felt like stepping forward and saying so when he noticed a messenger had entered the council chamber. He spoke briefly in the Great Wolf's ear.

Sigrid stopped and all eyes focused on Grimnar expectantly. Nor were they disappointed. Grimnar knuckled his eyes wearily and said, 'Grave news, brothers. Adrian Belisarius is dead and so is our old comrade, Skander.'

Howls of grief echoed around the chamber from some of the older Wolf Lords. 'It gets worse,' continued Grimnar. 'Both were assassinated on the sacred soil of Holy Terra itself. This is a grave matter indeed. I move that we adjourn to consider our response to this.'

All present gave their assent, save Sigrid. Ranek led Ragnar back to his cell, wondering exactly what was going on.

CHAPTER TWO

ALL AROUND THE shrine was silent. In the mighty hall, banners of mourning flew at half mast. Ragnar wondered why he had been summoned to the chambers of the Great Wolf in the quiet watches of the night. It did not bode well. He was even less reassured when Berek and Sigrid emerged from the throne hall together.

Neither looked happy. Sigrid glared at him as they passed. Berek looked melancholic. Neither spoke to him.

Moments later, Lars Helltongue, Grimnar's stone-faced herald, beckoned Ragnar forward. He found himself in the long hall, which was covered in banners and trophies of ancient battles, under the eyes of the Great Wolf's bodyguard. At the far end of the chamber sat the lord of all the Wolves, ensconced on his floating throne, with a scroll in his hands.

He looked up as the young Wolf entered and was beckoned to stand before his throne.

Ragnar knelt briefly and then rose, as a warrior does before his lord. Grimnar studied him, not unkindly, half amused, half annoyed. Then he grinned.

'Well, Ragnar Blackmane, you have set us a pretty problem, haven't you?' He gestured with the scroll. 'You can speak freely here.'

Grimnar was obviously waiting for some response, so Ragnar spoke. 'And what problem is that, Great Wolf?'

Grimnar laughed. 'I would have thought it was explained with commendable clarity at the conclave today, pup.'

Ragnar was not stung by the address, as he would have been had it come from almost any other man. Grimnar was centuries old, compared to him Ragnar was still but a child. 'I would do what I did again, Great Wolf, under similar circumstances.'

'I am glad to hear it. Under the same circumstances I might have done what you did, Ragnar. On the other hand I might not. To take it upon yourself to use the weapon of Russ himself might be considered presumptuous. Some think you should be punished for doing so, others believe that it marks you for great things.'

'What do you think, Great Wolf?'

'I think you are a youth of great promise, Ragnar. Beyond that, I do not know. I do not wish to waste that promise, but at the same time you are a source of dissension among the Wolves. And at this moment in time we can afford no dissension. I fear that if I take no action against you, others might.'

Ragnar knew what he meant. Cold-blooded killings were rare among the Wolves, but other things could happen. In the heat of battle a stray bullet might find him. Comrades might be slow to come to his aid at a moment of deadly peril. Such things were never talked about, even though they happened. And if he was thought to be a blasphemer, or a traitor, they might happen to him.

'What would you have me do, Great Wolf?'

'I would put you out of harm's way, in a place where you might do some good.'

'Exile, Great Wolf?'

'That would be one way of looking at it. Tell me Ragnar, what do you know of the Wolfblades?'

Ragnar sifted through the memories that had been implanted by the training engines when he was an aspirant.

'They are Space Wolves sent to Holy Terra to fulfil our treaty obligations with the House of Belisarius. We provide them with bodyguards in return for the Navigators they provide us.'

'That is true insofar as it goes, Ragnar, but Wolfblades are much more. They train the Celestarch of Belisarius's House troops and lead them into battle.

They act as his strong right arm when there is need. They slay his enemies in open battle and by stealth if need be.'

Ragnar could see where this was going.

'You wish me to go to Blessed Terra, Great Wolf?'

'There is need. Adrian Belisarius, the Celestarch, and a good friend to our Chapter, is dead. One of our battle-brothers died with him, Skander Bloody-axe, an old comrade of mine from my Blood Claw pack.'

Ragnar could see sadness in the old warrior's face. There were few left from that generation in the Chapter now, and Grimnar and this Skander must have been among the last. There were no closer comrades in the Chapter than those who had gone through their initiation and basic train-ing together, and who had been part of the same initial unit. They were almost siblings in a very real sense.

'Yes, Ragnar, I want you to go to Earth. And I want you to keep your ears open. One of the Wolves has died on holy soil, and I want to know what hap-pened. What really happened! I have had reports. I want to know if they are true.'

'Do you seek vengeance, Great Wolf?' It was a pre-sumptuous question, but Ragnar felt compelled to ask it. Grimnar shook his head slowly.

'If it is in the interests of the Chapter, Ragnar, I will take vengeance. If not, I would still like to know what happened.'

Ragnar considered the Great Wolf's words. Obviously, he could not commit the Chapter to wholesale bloodletting on the sacred soil of Terra. Nor could he simply order the assassination of some powerful man there without consequences.

He also knew that whatever the old man said, Logan Grimnar had a long memory, and he would find a way, if need be, to claim the blood price for his old comrade. It was the Fenrisian way.

'I will do my best,' said Ragnar.

'Do so, Ragnar, and let no one know that you are about this business.'

'How will I let you know my findings?'

'There are ways, Ragnar, channels of communication between Fenris and Belisarius. You will be told them before your departure. Also, Adrian Belisarius was assassinated. His daughter is with us on Garm but must return to swear allegiance to his successor. You will see that nothing untoward happens to her on her journey to Earth.'

'You think something might, Great Wolf?'

'If someone could assassinate the ruler of House Belisarius when he is surrounded by guards, then they have a very long arm and a very powerful one.'

'Yes, Great Wolf.'

'You may go, Ragnar.'

Ragnar knelt before departing, leaving the old man deep in thought over his scrolls.

* * *

'IT'S NOT BLOODY fair,' said Sven. 'You lose the Spear of Russ and they send you to Terra. What would they do if you had managed to destroy it? Make you Great Wolf?'

'That is not something to joke about, Sven,' said Ragnar.

'Who is bloody joking?' Sven gestured around his meditation cell with its sleeping mat, armour stand and weapon racks for furnishing. 'I get this! You get the fleshpots at the heart of the Imperium!'

'Earth is a holy planet, Sven.'

'Earth is as holy as a hornweed addict's visions. It's the capital of the Imperium. All the nobs are there and I don't think *they* spend their time fasting and meditating.'

'You might be surprised.'

'I bloody well would be if they did! I can't believe they are sending *you*. What is needed is a man of tact, diplomacy and vision, a man with enough sense not to have lost the Spear of Russ. A man like me! You think if I asked Grimnar he would let me go along?'

'I think if you asked Grimnar he would lock you up. The last thing we need is a brainless ape running amok in the streets of Holy Terra!'

'Then why are they sending you?'

'Because it suits them,' said Ragnar seriously. 'Anyway, I just came to say farewell. It seems the ship is outward bound in six standard hours, and I have to get ready.'

There was a long silence. In the years since they had been aspirants together, Ragnar and Sven had become fast friends. More than once they had saved each other's lives. But now Sven was a Grey Hunter, and Ragnar was something else, destined for a life in limbo as a Wolfblade, perhaps for the rest of his life.

A great gap had opened between them, and it was not just distance. Both of them knew it, despite the banter. Sven would be going to war and battle with the Chapter, while Ragnar was going to be stuck guarding the spoiled aristocrats of the Navigator Houses. Any dreams he might have had for a glorious destiny, of inscribing his name in the annals of the Chapter, would have to be given up. He would probably be remembered as the man who had lost the Spear of Russ. He would be the butt of jokes and maledictions of every new generation of aspirants.

Briefly he considered going to Grimnar and asking to be allowed to stay on, but he knew he could not. His fate was sealed. It was his duty to go to Earth. In a way, it was a punishment for his deeds, and a way to atone for his mistake. But I would do the same thing again, he thought defiantly.

Sven had stuck out his hand, and they clasped wrists. 'Watch your back,' he said. 'Without me to pull you out of the fire, you're going to have plenty of trouble.'

'Most of my troubles came from your blundering attempts to help,' said Ragnar half-heartedly.

'By the time you get back I will have blundered my way to Wolf Lord,' said Sven. 'They'll be singing my praises in the sagas.'

'Why bother with sagas singing your praises when you do it so well yourself!'

'Go on, get out of here! You have a ship to catch.'

Ragnar was surprised to find there was a lump in his throat as he turned to go, but he did not look back.

RAGNAR REPORTED TO Ranek's chamber. His personal possessions had already been sent to the shuttle. He bore only his weapons and such gear as a Space Wolf was expected to carry into battle.

'A Wolfblade, eh?' said the old priest. 'You've found an interesting trail to follow.'

'What do you mean?' said Ragnar.

The old man laughed savagely. 'Earth,' he said. 'Holy Terra. The Blessed Planet. The Seat of the Emperor. The Hub of the Imperium. The biggest snake pit in the galaxy.'

'It can't be that bad,' said Ragnar.

'Can't it? What do you know about such things, lad?'

'Not much but–'

'Earth is the hub of the Imperium. It's the centre of government, the setting of mankind's greatest temples, the home of our wealthiest and most powerful merchant houses. And the most corrupt.'

'What do you mean?'

'I mean, where there is government and where there is money, there is corruption. And there is no place in this universe that has more government and more money than Old Earth. You be careful there, laddie.'

'I will just be a bodyguard,' said Ragnar.

'Is that what you think? Don't be so naïve. You will be seen, quite rightly, as a representative of our Chapter. They will judge us by you, read things into your actions that you would never expect. You will be a living symbol of who and what we are, and don't you ever forget it.'

'I will try not to.'

'You will do more than try, lad. Remember these words and obey them, or I will personally come to Earth and rip your lungs from your chest.'

'Very well, Rune Priest.'

The old man's voice was gentler now. 'There's no need to be huffy, laddie. Just remember what I have said, and do your best. It will be more than enough.'

'What will my duties be?'

'You will be a soldier of the Celestarch. You will obey him as you would your own Wolf Lord. You will fight at his command, and you will die if need be. What else would you expect?'

'What if I am ordered to fight against the Imperium, or my battle-brothers? If Earth is so corrupt?' Ragnar realised he sounded sullen, and that he only asked the question to be contrary. But the reply surprised him.

'What would you do if your Wolf Lord ordered you to commit heresy?'

'I would depose him.'

'If he turned out to be a traitor sworn to Chaos?'

'I would kill him.'

'Having a bodyguard can be a two-edged sword, can't it, young Ragnar?'

Ragnar considered what he was being told. If he understood the Wolf Priest correctly, he was being given leave to assassinate the Celestarch of Belisarius should he prove disloyal to the Imperium. Ranek appeared to read his thoughts.

'Our pact with House Belisarius predates the Imperium itself. Some members of the Administratum dislike it, but they have to accept it. They know that we keep this Navigator House honest. The Celestarchs of Belisarius have been good men and women, Ragnar. They are loyal to us and to the Imperium and we have always been part of the reason for that. No matter what you see or hear on Terra you should remember that, before passing judgement.'

'The Great Wolf said Adrian Belisarius was assassinated, and so was our brother Skander. Who would do such a thing? Heretics?'

Ranek laughed. 'The reports say they were fanatics of some new cult, but many people would do such a thing, Ragnar. It might have been these supposed fanatics. It might have been a rival House, or a faction in the Administratum that supports those rivals. It might even have been an ambitious relative of the Celestarch himself.'

'What?'

'Not everyone follows our code, Ragnar. As I said, Earth is the locus of the greatest concentration of power and wealth in our universe. These things have a way of distorting morality. I repeat: watch yourself.'

Ragnar did not quite know whether the priest meant he should keep a close eye on those around him or on his own morals. Perhaps he meant both. It appeared that he was to face other perils than those of battle.

'Aside from assassins, what other dangers might there be?'

'You may be called upon to lead House troops or perform clandestine actions in support of the Celestarch's wishes. You will be briefed on your arrival by your fellow Wolfblades. Pay attention to them. Some of them have been on Terra longer than you have lived and know of its pitfalls and hazards.'

Ragnar felt his heart sink. It appeared he was in for a long exile. Ranek seemed to read his thoughts.

'Space Wolves can live for centuries, Ragnar. In the great scheme of things a few decades is not much to lose.'

'I would rather be here with Berek's company than playing nursemaid to Navigators.'

'Your wishes do not enter into this, Ragnar. And keep those thoughts about your duties to yourself.

We expect your performance and behaviour to be exemplary. Never forget, some of the folk you meet, many of them very powerful, will judge us by you. And some of them may use your failures against us. We have many enemies among the factions of the Administratum as well as many allies. Imperial politics are a vast and complex web.'

Ragnar did not quite follow what the old man was saying. His training had been in battle and warfare, not politics. It looked like his duties were going to be more complicated than he had expected.

'The Great Wolf said there would be ways of communicating with Fenris should the need arise. He said I would be told them before I departed.'

Ranek gave a grim smile. 'Did he now? I wonder why he would do that... No, don't tell me. Should the need arise, go to Brother Valkoth of the Wolfblades. He will know what needs to be done. But be circumspect. And Ragnar, one more thing...'

'Yes?'

'Many great Space Wolf leaders have been Wolfblades. It does us no harm to have warriors who know how the Imperium works and who have personal contacts within its hierarchy. Use your time on Earth well. Logan Grimnar does nothing without purpose. Remember that!'

Ragnar felt his spirits rise. Perhaps in a roundabout way he was being groomed for leadership. Or perhaps this was just Ranek's way of raising his morale. Whatever the case, it was working.

'Now, en route to Terra, keep a careful eye on Gabriella. She is Adrian Belisarius's daughter, and she may be the target of an assassination attempt herself.'

Ragnar looked at the Wolf Priest's lined and chiselled face. 'You think some of our people might kill her?'

'You are not travelling on one of our ships, Ragnar. We cannot spare them. You will be returning on the courier that brought us the news from Terra. *The Herald of Belisarius* will not be secure. Stay close to the girl and see that nothing happens to her. You may go now.'

Ragnar walked towards the door of the chamber. 'And Ragnar...'

'Yes?'

'See that nothing happens to yourself either. Farewell.'

'Farewell.' Ragnar felt another lump in his throat. He liked Ranek, and trusted him. And he realised he might never see the old man again. Old age or battle might claim either of them. Such were the realities of a Wolf's life, he told himself.

As RAGNAR STRODE down the quiet corridors, he realised how isolated he was. He would be on his own, far from his battle-brothers, for an incalculable distance for an unspecified amount of time, and for the first time since he had joined the Chapter. He felt a pang of loneliness, almost like pain.

Then unaccountably his heart lightened. He would also be free, in a way that he had not been in years. He was setting out on a great adventure, to the holiest and deadliest world of the Imperium. He would look upon the temples and palaces of Terra, and their glittering inhabitants. And it sounded like there would be danger and intrigue enough to occupy him.

Slowly his step lengthened, and he found that he was trotting and then running towards the loading bays where the shuttles waited.

CHAPTER THREE

RAGNAR STRODE THROUGH *The Herald of Belisarius* beside Gabriella Belisarius. Sailors and retainers greeted her formally and respectfully. Many of them flinched when they saw the massive Space Wolf standing at her shoulder. He could tell from their scents that he made some uneasy and others downright afraid.

'Your crew seems scared of me,' he murmured.

Gabriella turned and smiled up at him. She was a severe looking woman: tall, slender, with very long black hair and a face that was all angles. She was beautiful in an inhuman way, and the black dress uniform somehow enhanced that beauty.

Now that she was on the ship – her home territory as it were – she had removed the scarf from her forehead to reveal her third, pineal eye. 'They are a trading crew. They are not used to having one of the fabled Space Wolves aboard. The folk of Terra are a little more cosmopolitan, I think you will find.'

It was obvious that she did not share her crew's nervousness, but then again why should she? She had just spent a decade among the men of the Fang. He wished he could read her moods better. The Navigators smelled different from other humans. There was something alien about their scent. Alien and well nigh unreadable.

Ragnar knew they had been bred for countless generations to guide starships across the interstellar void. They had done so since before the founding of the Imperium. Somewhere, their gene line and that of normal humanity had parted company. Ragnar knew that they were no longer human but they were tolerated by the Imperium because they were necessary. Without Navigators interstellar voyages would take years or decades, if they could be made at all. Travel through the warp was treacherous even with a Navigator. Without one, it could be deadly.

Ragnar considered this, as he considered the woman before him. Their skills had brought the Navigator Houses wealth beyond measure. Belisarius had sent a ship to bring the news of Gabriella's father's death to the Wolves. Granted it had also brought trade goods and a request for a new Wolfblade, but even so the thought was staggering. Ships were enormously expensive. Belisarius had its own fleet, one considerably larger than that owned by the Space Wolves. Ragnar knew this from the histories. They had leased ships to the Wolves on very favourable terms when they were needed. It was one aspect of the ancient alliance between the two.

'What are you thinking?' Gabriella asked, as they made their way to the command deck. She was going to guide the ship home to Terra. The Navigator who had brought it, a cousin, was to stay on with the Wolf fleet as her replacement.

'I was thinking about the alliance between our Houses.'

'It's one of the bedrocks of my family's power,' she said.

'How so?'

'It helps keep our rivals in check. Few would move openly against us for fear of reprisals from the Space Wolves.'

'Few would move openly against you on Terra anyway. It is sacred ground. Bloodshed is not permitted there.'

Gabriella laughed. 'Blood is shed on Earth as it is everywhere else. It is merely done more circumspectly. And we do not have holdings only on Earth.'

Ragnar thought about this. 'The Wolves have come to your aid in the past.'

'Aye, they have, and would do so again, if need be. Who knows, they might even fight on Terra if the need arose. Your Chapter is known to be wild and uncontrollable, a law unto itself.'

'All Space Marine Chapters are. Their privileges and prerogatives date back to before the Imperium itself.'

'Aye, but your brethren have a reputation for being more erratic than the other Chapters.'

'It has never stopped us from fighting well, or from being loyal to the Emperor.'

'I did not mean it as a criticism. Indeed from the point of view of my House it is praise. Our enemies might have swallowed us up millennia ago, had they not thought your Chapter would avenge us.'

'I thought Belisarius was one of the most powerful of the Navigator Houses?'

'It is now, and has been at many times in its history. But these things are cyclical. All Houses suffer setbacks. Such is the nature of trade and competition. In our history there have been many periods where we have suffered reversals, and we have been eclipsed. Leading a House is like guiding a ship: sometimes all it takes is one bad or unlucky decision for you to founder.'

'It has not happened to Belisarius yet. For more than ten millennia we have been your allies.'

'And let us hope that we are for another. Although I have a foreboding that events are taking a turn for the worse for House Belisarius.'

Ragnar wanted to contradict her, but he could see the sadness written on her face. He realised this was a woman who had just lost her father, a father who had been the leader of his House, the Celestarch, a Navigator of Navigators.

They passed more sailors in the wide corridor. Almost automatically Ragnar put himself in a position where he could interpose himself if they proved to be a threat. The humans sensed this and gave him a wide berth.

'There is no need to terrify the crew,' said Gabriella.

'I am here to ensure your safety. Those were my orders.'

She glanced at him. 'Fair enough, but there is no need to glower while you do your duty.'

'I had not realised I was glowering.'

'You Fenrisians never seem to realise. You are so feral. What you think is always written on your face, and what you think about is mostly violence.'

'Before this voyage is out you may be glad of that.'

'Perhaps. I am glad you are here anyway.'

'Why?'

'Because if there is a threat to my life, I think you will deal with it.'

'You think it a serious possibility?'

'Yes. These are troubled times. My father has just been assassinated. Anyone who could get to him could get to me.'

'You seem to take it very calmly.'

'It happens. It happens even within the Houses themselves. Siblings have been known to remove those they think of as rivals.'

'You think they would kill you to remove a contender to the throne?'

'Now you are thinking like a Fenrisian, Ragnar. I
am not a contender for the throne. Not at this time
anyway. The Celestarchy does not pass from parent
to child. Our rulers are selected from a short list of
available candidates by the Council of Elders.'

'They are the oldest and wisest of your tribe?'

'Something like that.'

The door slid open and they arrived on the command deck. Tech adepts hovered over command
altars, linked to the ancient devices by cables that
ran to occipital sockets. The smell of ozone and
technical incense filled the air. Officers in the House
uniform of Belisarius stood to attention as
Gabriella entered.

'Navigator on deck!' snapped someone and the
others bowed their heads reverently.

'Be at ease,' said Gabriella. 'May fortune smile on
us and prosperity wash over us.'

'May fortune smile on us,' responded the crew.
Gabriella strode forward to the centre of the command deck and began communing with the crew.
They spoke a technical argot of their trade, which
was less than gibberish to Ragnar so he took the
opportunity to study his surroundings.

The command deck was large and circular. It
occupied a blister on top of the massive hull of *The
Herald of Belisarius*. There were several large circular
armourglass windows. Through the starboard side

the vast white and blue sphere that was Garm was visible. Swift moving dots told of other sub-orbital craft going about their business.

Various technical altars were arranged around a central holo-pit. Something like a huge throne occupied its own dais on the balcony overlooking the pit. Ragnar recognised this as the Navigator's command chair.

Various personnel presented reports for Gabriella's approval. She listened and nodded before beckoning Ragnar over.

'When we leave orbit, we will be about twelve hours away from our insertion point. The captain will handle the steering of the vessel until then. I am going to get something to eat and have some rest.'

'Very well,' Ragnar said. 'I will accompany you.'

She gave him an amused look. 'I have asked for you to be given the stateroom adjoining mine. Your gear has already been stowed there.'

'Very good.'

THE NAVIGATORS OF Belisarius did well for themselves, Ragnar thought. He was used to the bare cells of military starships. This chamber was more like something from the hookah dream of a Slaaneshi cultist.

The massive bed was bolted to the floor. The mattress was soft. There were chairs carved from single pieces of Leviathan tooth ivory, desks and furnishings from precious scented woods. Faintly narcotic incense perfumed the air. A vast mirror dominated one wall. The controls beneath it indicated that it doubled as a televisor. He had already dismissed the body servants who had hovered around waiting to satisfy his whims. He had told them that all he wanted was something to eat.

A bell announced that the food had arrived. 'Enter,' he called. A row of liveried servants entered bearing silver trays. On each was a collection of enamelled porcelain, which his enhanced senses told him bore all manner of highly spiced delicacies. The servants bustled around the room, arranging a table, spreading tablecloths, and setting heating elements in place to keep the food warm.

An elderly white-haired man, the possessor of a superlatively supercilious expression, uncovered each dish with a flourish.

'Pickled slime eels,' he said proudly. Ragnar nodded.

'Roast haunch of dragonbird in a venomberry sauce. I think this one will tickle your palate, sir,' he said with an ingratiating smile.

'Really,' said Ragnar.

'Boiled naga-goat tripes in leper brandy.' The dish looked as if someone had been sick in it, Ragnar thought. He ignored the rest of the descriptions until the old man tried to move into a position behind him. Without thinking, the young Space Wolf whirled ready to strike.

The servant blanched. 'Your napkin, sir,' he said, displaying a serviette almost the size of a small sheet.

Ragnar glared at him. 'Do not attempt to get behind me again,' he said.

'But how will I prepare you for feasting, sir?'

'I require no help to sit down to table,' said Ragnar. The servant looked affronted.

'But sir, proper etiquette at the Court of Belisarius dictates that…'

'Proper etiquette in the halls of Fenris dictates that a man is left alone to eat when he wishes. Breaches of etiquette require duels to settle them.'

'Duels, sir?'

'Personal insults require the challenge,' said Ragnar.

'I meant no insult, sir. We must all make allowances when two cultures meet.'

Ragnar grinned, showing his fangs. 'Indeed we must. Now I would be obliged if you would leave me to my food and my meditations. Else…'

'Quite, sir, quite.' The elderly servant clapped his hands, and they all fled the room. Ragnar was left alone in his chamber. He surveyed the food and realised that it must have cost a small fortune to bring it all this distance. The selection of wines, brandies and cheeses that had been provided had been brought all the way from Terra. Given the cost of transportation the Navigators charged, it seemed almost a sin.

Nonetheless he sat himself down to eat. The tastes were interesting but he would have preferred plain old Fenrisian seal or caribou meat. Perhaps he would ask about getting some. Just at that moment, he heard a faint panicked call from the adjoining door.

Without pausing to think, he snatched up his bolter and threw the heavy airlock door open. Fortunately it was unlocked or he might have had some trouble. He could see Gabriella on the far side of the chamber. Something glinting and metallic scuttled over the bed towards her.

The situation was dangerous. In this small heavily armoured chamber, bolter shells would ricochet. Ragnar's armour would shield him, but there was every chance they might harm the woman he was supposed to protect. He focused his attention on the thing that stalked her.

To normal humans it would have been moving with blinding speed, but Ragnar was a Space Wolf, and his perceptions and reflexes were superhuman. For him, in combat mode now, it moved in slow motion. The scent gave it away. It was a compound of metal and oil and subtle toxins: a form of robotic spider created by the black arts of some degenerate alien race. Two long needle-like fangs protruded from its front. Camera eyes glittered high on its back.

An assassination device obviously, probably controlled by someone nearby.

Ragnar sprang forward onto the bed, slamming the butt of his weapon down on it. He was taking a chance. If the thing contained an explosive device he might well detonate it, but he was counting on this thing being more subtle: you did not equip such a device with poisoned fangs, if you intended to detonate it. The spider cracked open. Blue sparks shot everywhere. A strong stench of ozone wafted into the air.

Ragnar picked it up in a gauntleted hand and crushed it again.

He glanced around to see if there were any other threats in the vicinity and detected none. He gestured for Gabriella to follow him into his own stateroom where he tossed the mechanical spider into a flagon of water, hoping to short it out permanently.

'Are you all right?' he asked. 'Did the thing sting you?'

The Navigator appeared perfectly composed but her face was white and her pupils dilated. The pineal eye on her forehead had opened. It was much smaller and less disturbing than he had expected it to be.

'If it had, I would be dead now. That is a jokaero death spider. An assassination device that contains zarthax, one of the deadliest poisons in the galaxy.'

Ragnar cursed. He had expected many things but not this use of foul deviant alien technology. Another thought struck him.

'You seem very well informed about such things,' said Ragnar.

'Every child of the Navigator Houses knows about such things. They are commonly used devices. Small enough to crawl through ventilator shafts, stealthy enough to infiltrate a mansion. I was lucky. I had gone to wash my face when I heard it thump down on the bed. I froze and shouted for help. Its camera eyes would have tracked movement. The operator could not have seen me or I would be dead now.'

Ragnar kept his manner all business, but part of his mind reeled. They were *commonly* used assassination devices? Such vile alien works were forbidden throughout most of the Imperium. He supposed that the Navigator Houses would naturally have access to these things but still... 'Whoever unleashed and guided that thing must be on the ship.'

'Yes.'

'We will find him.'

'Perhaps.'

'You do not seem very confident.'

'How could you tell who, on a ship as large as this, could have done it?'

'As long as they are human, I have my ways,' said Ragnar, knowing that the stink of guilt would be on someone, and his nose would pick it out. Another thought occurred to him.

'The attack was well timed: you were in your chamber, and I was supposed to be eating.'

'Yes.'

'Who would know about such things?'

'The ship's quartermaster, the major domo, and many of the serving men. A host of people, in fact.'

'In future, we will share the same chamber.' She considered this for a moment.

'As you wish.'

'Now let us call your security people, and see if we can get to the bottom of this.'

RAGNAR CURSED. A body had been found in an equipment locker near to the stateroom. Controls for the spider were with it. The man had taken poison, from a hollow tooth. It appeared he had been prepared for failure. Ragnar was surprised. This spoke of a level of preparation and fanaticism he had not expected.

'It does not surprise me,' said Gabriella when he told her. 'This sort of thing has happened before.'

'The man must have been a fanatic,' said Ragnar. To his surprise, she laughed.

'What is so funny?'

'That a Space Marine should accuse someone else of fanaticism.' Her face was suddenly serious. 'But maybe you are right.'

'The man must have been one, to give his life up so easily.'

'Perhaps he hated my family. Perhaps he belonged to one of the cults that hate Navigators. Or perhaps he had no motive at all.'

'What do you mean?'

'Perhaps he was hypno-conditioned or psychically brainwashed to perform this action. There are many ways it can be done.'

'We should check the body for marks. Sometimes cultists have tattoos or the stigmata of Chaos on them.'

'I doubt you will find anything,' said Gabriella, 'but go ahead. I must go now to guide the ship. We are less than an hour away from warp insertion.'

'I will come with you to the command deck.' As he spoke, Ragnar stripped the corpse.

'I doubt anyone would attack me while we are in the warp. You know as well as I do that the ship would founder and all of us would be lost.'

The girl was right. There were no tattoos, no stigmata of any sort. Even the scent was perfectly normal for a corpse, save for the faint acrid hint of poison.

'If the assassin is under some sort of mind control why should he care?'

'A fair point. But once we are warp-bound, I will be sealed in a life support throne, alone in the command blister. The place is secure as a fortress. It has to be.'

'Why?'

'It must be able to shield me from anything we might encounter in the warp. I can say no more than that.'

'There is no need to say more.' He gestured for the security men to take the body away and dispose of it. They obeyed. Some of them stuck close by. They seemed embarrassed and ashamed that a Navigator had almost been assassinated while she was in their care. Ragnar understood how they felt.

'How difficult would it be for an enemy to place an agent on one of your ships?' he asked as they strode towards the command deck.

'All our people are carefully screened, particularly those who serve on House ships like this one. Still, no system is foolproof. I would imagine that a truly determined enemy could get someone aboard. Or could corrupt someone who was already screened.'

'That's a worrying thought,' said Ragnar. He was a taken aback by how calmly the Navigator was taking this. She seemed to be treating it as part of every day life.

'It is also possible that someone in my own House wants me dead,' she said. 'It would be much easier for an insider to achieve, than an outsider.'

Someone had already got to the head of the House, Ragnar thought. And he was presumably more securely guarded than Gabriella would ever be. As they entered the command deck, he reflected that this assignment was turning out to be a lot more interesting than he had anticipated, and they had not even reached Terra yet.

CHAPTER FOUR

RAGNAR LOOKED DOWN upon the strange globe beneath him. The hemisphere glittered metallic silver in the daylight. There were patches of red upon it that might have been seas of rust. The lines of the ancient continents were gone. All that was left to suggest them were vague outlines where the density of buildings became even more intense along what had once been shorelines. Now the world wore metallic armour over its entire surface. It seemed fitting somehow.

Ragnar smiled; it was an astonishing feeling. The image was a familiar one. This was the birth world of humanity. He had seen the likeness so often that it was strange knowing that the planet was actually below him now, a glittering jewel set against the black velvet of space. Ragnar felt excitement build up in him.

This was where humanity had first reached for the stars, where the Emperor of Mankind was born and from where he had launched his great crusade. Where Horus had besieged the Imperial Palace and the future history of the galaxy had been decided. This was the hub of the greatest Empire that had ever existed, a seat of government of incalculable power.

Somewhere down there the Lords of the Administratum decided the fate of countless billions. Somewhere down there the Emperor lay half-alive within his golden throne. The primarchs had walked there amid the gardens and plasteel starscrapers. Russ had led the distant forebearers of the Chapter into battle on its soil. This was Earth, old and weighted with millennia of history. Soon he would join the countless trillions who had made the pilgrimage to its surface. Soon he would be part of everyday life down there.

He considered their approach. He knew that they had passed countless fortresses and fleets as they had swung in from the ultra-solar jump points. They had passed the armoured moons of Jupiter and the forge world of Mars. They had been subjected to hundreds of challenges and scans and they had been boarded twice. It had been a long drawn out process but it was only to be expected.

The world down there was better protected than any other planet in human history. There would not be a Second Battle of Earth if the terrible lords of the Imperium could help it. Even now, the sky was filled with satellite fortresses: great weapon installations with enough firepower to destroy battle fleets. The whole of sublunar space was crowded with warships. For once in his life, Ragnar felt insignificant.

Gabriella appeared by his side. She was wearing the full formal regalia of her House, a black tunic with the eye and wolf symbol of Belisarius was embossed on every button. Its epaulettes bore the mark of her status as a master Navigator. On the braided jacket were medals and emblems which doubtless told of her lineage and status. Some of them also contained powerful sensors. She had a dress sword and pistol on her belt.

Despite his polished armour and well maintained weapons, Ragnar felt almost slovenly beside her.

'It's time,' she said. 'The shuttle has docked with *The Herald of Belisarius*. We have been given permission to descend to the surface of the Earth.'

Ragnar felt almost nervous as he strode with her to the airlock. It slid open and a file of House troops garbed in uniforms only slightly less elaborate than Gabriella's emerged. Their weapons looked serviceable and they moved with a precision that would not have shamed an elite unit of Imperial Guard. Their commander moved up to Gabriella and gave her a formal salute. He surprised Ragnar by giving him one too.

'Lady Gabriella, welcome home,' he said. 'The Celestarch Elect sent my men to provide an honour guard. I would just like to say the honour is mine.'

Ragnar suppressed a smile. The officer was young with a wafer thin moustache that crept like a caterpillar along his upper lip. His hair was long. His features sharp, his lips thin. He was exactly the sort of soldier the Space Wolves were not.

'And you are?' Gabriella asked.

'Lieutenant Kyle, milady, at your service, now and always.'

'Well, lieutenant, I would be grateful if you could escort us the twenty steps from this airlock to the shuttle. I am keen to set foot on my home world again.'

'At once, milady.' The two rows of guards clicked their heels and swivelled, forming a corridor along which Ragnar and Gabriella walked into the airlock. Ragnar was about to strap himself into one of the military style bucket seats but Gabriella gestured for him to follow her. He passed through a second airlock into an infinitely more luxurious salon, decorated with the House insignia on the walls. The acceleration couches resembled huge, padded leather armchairs, far more plush than the military gear Ragnar was used to. The airlock swished closed behind them. Ragnar made sure it was sealed before strapping himself in.

'That was very formal,' he said eventually.

'Far more formal than most arrivals, I can assure you. But my father is dead and my aunt must be seen to make every effort to protect me. It was a message that protection is the order of the day.'

'I think the jokaero spider proves that she was right.'

'Indeed. What do you think of our House troopers?'

'They were very well dressed.'

'You do not think much of them as warriors then? You can speak as frankly as you like.'

'I think they would not last twenty seconds against a company of orks. They seem to have spent more time practising marching than fighting. Of course, that is just my opinion. I have not seen them fight.'

'They are merely security guards. You will meet the real warriors later. Perhaps they will impress you more.'

'You do not appear to think so.'

'I find my time at the Fang has changed me, Ragnar. Once I was impressed by men like them. That was before I spent time among Wolves. By the way, we will be met by some of your brethren on arrival.'

'I look forward to it,' said Ragnar. Through the porthole he could see the shuttle had already broken away from *The Herald of Belisarius* and had begun its descent to the surface of the glittering world below.

As they broke through the clouds, he saw they were heading towards what looked like a vast island separated from the rest of the world by barriers and towers at least a kilometre high. A fortress within a fortress, he thought – the fabled island enclave that was the Ghetto of the Navigators.

RAGNAR STEPPED OUT into the light of a new day on a new world. He squinted in the bright sunlight. The air had a faint acrid chemical taint: partially from the exhausts of the shuttle but partially contained within the air itself. A faint shimmer rose from the plascrete. He strode down the exit ramp, in front of Gabriella. Then, he glanced around to make sure all was clear before signalling for her to follow. The honour guard had already begun to line up before them.

Ragnar noticed several small armoured vehicles nearby. An armoured figure, a head and shoulders taller than the locals, lounged against one of them. There was something about his posture that conveyed both an amused disdain, as well as a complete watchfulness of what went on around him. When he spotted Ragnar, he stood upright and strode purposefully forward. Ragnar was not in the least surprised to see that he was a Space Wolf, although many things about his appearance conveyed an impression of difference from the average battle-brother.

As he came closer, Ragnar could see that his hair was short but not cropped, and his moustache had been shaved pencil thin, in the style of the young officer who had greeted them on the ship. A faint smell of perfumed pomade surrounded him. Many strange amulets and pieces of jewellery were attached to his armour.

He smiled affably as Ragnar looked him over. Ragnar did not doubt that despite the man's languid expression, he was studying him too.

'Greetings, son of Fenris,' said the stranger in the tongue of Ragnar's homeworld. 'Welcome to Holy Terra.'

The troopers had begun to hustle Gabriella into the largest and most heavily armoured of the waiting vehicles. Ragnar was about to follow when the stranger spoke. 'Your duties as escort are done, Ragnar. You are to accompany me to the Belisarian Palace.'

The man was obviously a Space Wolf, but Ragnar felt a reluctance to part from Gabriella. Having seen her safely over such a great distance he wanted to escort her for the last small segment of her journey.

'She is safe now,' said the stranger. 'Or at least as safe as any of her kind can ever be on the surface of this world.' He gestured at the sky. Sleek air vehicles hovered above them, doubtless part of the ongoing security operation.

'Her father was not safe,' said Ragnar. A pained expression passed over the other Marine's face. 'Was he?'

'Do you think your presence would have made any difference there, brother?'

'Perhaps.'

The stranger smiled. 'I like to think mine might have as well, but alas duty called me elsewhere on that fatal day.'

There was a brief pause.

'I am Torin the Wayfarer,' he said.

'Ragnar Blackmane.'

'These are not matters that should be discussed openly. There are many with televisors who can read lips.'

'Can they also speak the tongue of Fenris?'

'Ragnar, you would be amazed at what a variety of skills can be found on ancient Terra. I have lived here almost twelve standard years and it still astonishes me.'

Gabriella had disappeared into the armoured car. Ragnar found he had fallen into step beside Torin as they headed for the smaller machine. Up close it looked like a smaller, sleeker version of an ork buggy. Although far more streamlined it had the same rugged look.

Torin vaulted into the open cockpit and Ragnar jumped in beside him. With a flick of a switch, a tinted bubble hood rose into place. Moments later he was pressed flat into his seat by the acceleration as they set off in pursuit of Gabriella's vehicle. It took a few moments for Ragnar to realise that they were following just far enough away to be out of the blast radius of a rocket attack, but close enough to act if there was an attack. For all his easy manner,

Torin appeared to be competent enough. In fact, Ragnar had begun to suspect that he was more than competent. Instinctively Ragnar picked up on the deadliness of the man; it was a lethalness that was all the more effective for being partially concealed by his manner.

'That's a little better,' said Torin. 'The hood should protect us from casual snooping and this car has its own share of divinatory wards. We can speak a little more freely now.'

'Do you greet every ship that comes in?' Ragnar said, speaking loudly over the roar of the engine.

'Only the ones with new Wolfblades on them.'

'There must be few enough of those.'

'You are the first in five years. Any trouble on your way in?'

Ragnar told him of the jokaero spider. Torin did not seem in the least surprised. He simply cocked his head to one side without taking his attention away from his driving.

'Do you have any thoughts about it?' Ragnar asked eventually.

'Could have been anything from a jealous rival in the House to outsiders trying to destabilise a newly chosen Celestarch. Given Adrian Belisarius's assassination, I think it would be best to assume the latter, but who can tell?'

Ragnar could tell from his scent and his manner that he did not want to say more under the present circumstances.

'What's it like here?' said Ragnar. He had begun to study the massive buildings around them. They were far more ornate than anything he had seen on Fenris, or anywhere else for that matter. Great spires prodded the sky. Every centimetre of their ancient facades seemed to have been carved into elaborate patterns. Hundreds of statues lined the arches in their sides. Stone gargoyles and angel-winged saints stood sentry on the roofs. Lush vegetation was everywhere but it had none of the riotous uncontrolled life of the jungles Ragnar had seen. It appeared to have been tamed and cultivated, designed to add one more element to the carefully contrived beauty that surrounded them.

'It's rather like what you see,' said Torin, guiding the buggy around a massive fountain with a flick of the control bars. Water spouted from a dragon's mouth. Some trick of the light made it look like liquid fire. 'Beautiful on the surface, but rotten underneath. Don't ever, even for a second, doubt that this is the most dangerous world in the galaxy.'

'It does not look very dangerous. It appears quite peaceful compared to some of the worlds I have been.'

'Danger does not always come in the shape of orks with bolters, Ragnar. This world is where the elite of the Imperium have gathered. We are talking now of the most ruthless, ambitious, unscrupulous collection of rogues ever culled from a million planets. This is the place they have come to realise their ambitions, and on Terra they can, and will not let anything stand in their way. Not me, not you, not their own kin if need be.'

'I would have thought that on such a world, loyalty would be at a premium.'

'No one is loyal here, Ragnar. Trust no one save your battle-brothers.'

'Not even the Celestarch?'

'Particularly not her.'

'Why?'

'We are just another tool to her. One to be used when cunning, diplomacy and money fail. She feels no loyalty to us as individuals. As we are a link to the Space Wolves, we are an important ally. But we are disposable here, Ragnar.'

'You think?'

'I know. Don't get me wrong, that does not mean she would sell our lives cheaply, or be glad to see us die. But if the circumstances were right, we would be sacrificed.'

'That does not sound right!'

'It's exactly as it should be.'

'In what way?'

'The Celestarch is not responsible to us. She is responsible for House Belisarius and to its Elders. It is her duty to guard and protect the interests of her House, just as it is Logan Grimnar's to do the same for the Wolves.'

'Surely it is Grimnar's primary duty to be loyal to the Emperor?'

To Ragnar's surprise, Torin laughed. 'Ah, it does me good talking to you, lad. I was like you once, fresh from Fenris and the Fang. There are times when I think I have been too long on Terra. Of course, Grimnar's first loyalty is to the Emperor, just as it is the Celestarch's. Just as it is everybody's here on Earth and in the Imperium. But you'd be surprised to see how often people use loyalty in a way that promotes their own interests.'

Ragnar was starting to feel a little uncomfortable with Torin's attitude. It was not unlike some of the behaviour he had seen exhibited by the Wolf Lords. He did not doubt that Sigrid and Berek, for instance, both believed they acted in the best interests of the Chapter, and that their eventual ascension to the Wolf Throne would be assured. 'You are a very cynical man, Brother Torin,' he said.

'Maybe, Brother Ragnar,' said Torin smiling, 'or maybe I am just a realistic one. Keep an open mind until you have seen more.'

'I always try to.' They fell silent for a few minutes. Ragnar watched the magnificent buildings flow past. Generations of craftsmen seemed to have spent their entire working lives carving small sections of those walls. Even to Ragnar's untrained eye, it was evident that the sculpture and fresco were masterpieces.

'When will we reach the Belisarius Palace?' Ragnar asked.

'Soon. You're already inside the Belisarius estate. They own everything in this sector, from the spacefield to the shops to the residential buildings. It's a measure of their wealth.'

'In what way?'

'Land on Terra is the most expensive in the Imperium. For the price of one square metre of any of this, you could buy a palace on a Hive World, or on most worlds of the Imperium if truth be told.'

'The sacred soil of Terra,' said Ragnar.

'The sacred and very expensive soil of Terra, Brother Ragnar. Thousands of lives have been lost for areas the size of a small farm on one of the islands on Fenris.'

'I thought wars were outlawed on Terra.'

Torin grinned. 'Ragnar, look at this car, tell me what you see?'

'A fast manoeuvrable vehicle of more or less standard design.'

'Of more or less standard military design. It's armoured against anything short of a krak grenade. It contains every form of protective counter-measure the Adeptus Mechanicus have at their disposal. It has a beacon for summoning aid from the palace. If Terra were peaceful do you think all of this would be necessary?'

Ragnar considered the point. 'My briefing has begun, has it?'

'Good boy, Brother Ragnar, I knew you were quick.'

'I am not a boy, Brother Torin,' said Ragnar dangerously. Again, Torin grinned.

'No. I can see you are not. Even if you lack a Grey Hunter's colours. I shall not forget that in the future. How did that come about anyway? You are not a Blood Claw, and you are not a Grey Hunter…'

Ragnar felt sure that the man beside him already knew the answers, and was taunting him. 'You must know,' he said grimly.

'Let us assume for a moment that I do,' said Torin guiding the vehicle down a broad highway towards a massive building rising before them. They were on a flyover bridge that passed over a deep chasm surrounding the structure. Looking down, Ragnar could see that things were a little deceptive. The building appeared to recede into the depths below them. He could see lights burning in thousands of windows, and more bridges with traffic on them.

'Not everything makes it into the reports we get, believe me. Let's assume I simply want to hear your own side of the story in your own words.'

'I will tell you when I am good and ready.'

'That is fair enough, brother. We have plenty of time. You and I will be seeing a lot of each other over the next few decades.'

The words had all the finality of a prison sentence. Ragnar realised that his fate was indeed sealed. Like it or not, he was stuck on Earth with this man and less than two dozen of his compatriots. The realisation settled on him with all the weight of the great armoured plasteel gateway that had dropped into place behind the buggy.

CHAPTER FIVE

'WE ARE IN the palace now, Ragnar. Be discreet. Choose every word with care unless you are certain you cannot be overheard,' said Torin. The buggy rolled to a halt in the courtyard beyond the gate. He could see that the guards had already emerged from the large armoured car, and were hustling Gabriella through an arched doorway.

Torin hit the button. The control levers slid into the dash and the tinted bubble roof retracted. Both Wolves pulled themselves out. Ragnar studied his surroundings carefully. They were in a massive atrium. Far overhead, an armour glass ceiling allowed natural light to play down into the hall. From where he stood he could see countless balconies rising up the inside of the building. In each wall was a massive translucent elevator shaft. Although Ragnar knew this place could not be nearly so massive as the Fang, it felt as if it was, and it was disorientating to a newcomer.

While the Fang felt like a base of battle-brothers, this felt more like a bazaar. Humans from all over the civilised galaxy thronged the place. He could see Catachans in green silk and pale Boreans in robes of whale fur. There were metal armoured men from the forge worlds of the Talean Rim. One incredibly obese man reclined on a suspensor palanquin while two beautiful naked girls fanned his shaved head, and sweating servants pulled him through the crush. Retainers in the elaborate uniform of Belisarius passed everywhere on their errands. Many possessed bionic eyes and prosthetic limbs. Some were armed.

The building was the product of a great artistic endeavour. The walls were carved with frescos. Gargoyles clutched glow-globes in their talons. Saints radiated light from their halos as they perched on platforms above the throng. Closer inspection told Ragnar that some of the statues had televisor eyes.

He could see that a great deal of business was being conducted here. Niches in the walls led into halls from which came the sound of haggling and bargains being struck. Goods were traded for other wares. Future contacts were being exchanged. Agreements about the use of ships and fleets and Navigators were being made.

Thousands of scents filled the air: of man and beast, of spice, silk and animal pelt. Machine oil mingled with technical unguent and hallucinogenic incense. To a man with senses as keen as Ragnar's it was a little overwhelming until he started to catalogue the stimuli and get a grip on his surroundings. He followed Torin across the mosaic floor, through one of the archways and into an elevator. Moments later, without experiencing the sensation of motion, they were a hundred floors below, surrounded by walls of armoured reinforced plascrete.

Torin led him through the suddenly quiet corridors. The smell of Space Wolves was much stronger here. This was obviously an area frequented by the battle-brothers. Ahead of them a door slid open and they entered another chamber. This had walls of panelled wood. Furs of the great Fenrisian wolf were strewn across the floor. Alcoves in the walls held scrolls and books. What looked like a real log fire, but which was, in fact, a cunningly wrought hologramic simulation, warmed the room. All of this Ragnar took in at a glance before his eyes came to rest on the man behind the desk who dominated the room.

In his own way, he was as impressive as Berek Thunderfist or any of the Wolf Lords. He was thin for a Space Wolf, almost cadaverous. His face was long and sad and seemed unaccountably mournful. There were dark bags under his eyes, and deep lines in his face. His hair was long and grey. His beard was clipped short and streaked black. His eyes were cold, blue and calculating. They seemed to measure him in a moment, and file their conclusion away deep within a chilly brain. When he spoke, his voice was deeper and more resonant than Ragnar had been expecting.

'Welcome to Terra, Ragnar Blackmane. And welcome to our small band of brothers. I am Valkoth, and I am in charge of the Wolfblade contingent here.'

Ragnar felt no urge to challenge him. 'I have asked Torin to begin your briefing. He will take you to your quarters and see that you are settled in. If you have any questions do not hesitate to ask him. The Celestarch is busy at the moment, but as soon as she has time you will be taken to her to swear your oath of loyalty. Until then you should act at all times as if the oath were already sworn and in force. Behave as if the reputation of the Space Wolves rests on it – for it does.'

'Aye,' said Ragnar.

'I believe there was an attempt on the life of Gabriella Belisarius,' said Valkoth. 'Tell me about it.'

Ragnar did so, and the older man listened carefully, without interruption. After Ragnar had finished, he said, 'Be vigilant. There will be more attempts on Gabriella's life and the life of everyone in our charge.'

Ragnar nodded and Valkoth turned his attention back to the open book in front of him and began to make marks on it with a stylo. It was clear that they were dismissed.

Torin led Ragnar back into the hallway and deeper into a labyrinth of corridors. There were far fewer servants and retainers here and no sign of any Space Wolves, save himself and Torin.

'That was the old man,' said Torin. 'He's something of a scholar but don't let that fool you. He is as fell-handed a warrior as ever lifted a chainsword and as cunning as Logan Grimnar himself.'

Ragnar did not share the common Fenrisian prejudice against scholars. It was obvious to him that what Torin was saying was true. 'Where is everybody else then?'

'You were expecting a welcoming feast, perhaps?'

'No. I just thought there might be more of us about.'

'Actually there are more Wolves in the palace than at any time I can remember, what with the new Celestarch taking her throne, but that is quite unusual. Normally we are scattered hither and yon about the Imperium.'

'Why?'

'Various assignments. Some train Belisarian troops. Some have covert missions to perform. Some are bodyguards to Navigators going into particularly dangerous situations.'

'People keep telling me about training Belisarian troops. As I understood it, the Navigators have no troops.'

'Yes, and no. They have no formal soldiery but they have security guards who perform the same function. And they have mercenary companies under permanent contract who have served them so long that they might as well be part of the House. They are House soldiers in all but a legal sense.'

Ragnar felt like spitting. 'What is the point in having laws if people find ways of getting around them? Civilisation!'

'You sound just like Haegr. You two should get along.'

Ragnar was not entirely sure that he was as righteous as he sounded. At the moment, he felt completely out of his depth and he was retreating into the code of his homeworld. Once again Torin read his mood. 'It's not entirely a bad way to be!'

Just at that moment a huge figure emerged from an archway. He had a double-sized ale tankard stuck on one foot and a massive hambone that had been gnawed clean in one hand. He was quite the largest man Ragnar had ever seen, gigantic even by Space Wolf standards, and the only one who might conceivably be called fat. His tiny eyes were sunk deep above huge rosy cheeks. His armour seemed to have been modified to contain a massive belly, which made it something of a triumph of the smith's art.

'Did I hear someone taking my name in vain?' He bellowed, in a voice that reminded Ragnar of an enraged bull moose. 'Was it you, little man?'

Torin grinned at the giant. 'I see you are trying to start a new fashion in boots.'

The hulking stranger looked down and blinked. 'I left my tankard by the bed when I lay down for a nap. I must have stood in it when I sprang manfully into action to challenge any who mock my good name.'

Ragnar realised that the newcomer reeked of ale. Spots of food had settled in his beard. 'You know I would not do that, Haegr,' said Torin. 'I was merely remarking to our latest recruit that you and he have something in common.'

Haegr blinked owlishly, as if noticing Ragnar for the first time. 'A newcomer from the blessed world of Fenris, where the cold winds scour the rugged earth of all pollution and corruption. I fear you have come to the wrong place, lad. This foul festering sinkhole of iniquity is anathema to our kind, to the manly virtues of the mighty Space Wolves…'

'Haegr is as windy as the world that birthed him,' said Torin.

'Do you mock me, little man?'

'I would not dare. I was simply admiring your new honour badge.'

'I have no honour badge.'

'Is not that the order of the gravy stain, used to mark the armour of the mightiest of trenchermen?'

Haegr reached down and touched the gravy spot on his armour, then licked his finger. 'If I did not know better I would think you were taunting me, Torin. Only I know that no man would dare.'

'Your logic is impeccable as always, old friend. Now I must show Ragnar to his quarters and brief him on his duties.'

'Be sure you let him know that he will be surrounded by effete cowards without the least of the manly virtues. This world is not Fenris, lad. Don't you forget it!'

'I don't think I am likely to,' said Ragnar. 'Everyone keeps telling me about it one way or another.'

'I will see you later then, and we shall quaff ale in the heroic fashion of the Sons of Fenris. Now I must see about removing this tankard from my foot.' He turned and stamped back into his room.

'That was Haegr,' said Torin. 'He's not the brightest man who the Choosers of the Slain ever picked to join our ranks, but he is perhaps the bravest, particularly when it comes to the consumption of ale and meat.'

'I heard that!' bellowed a muffled voice from behind the closed door.

'It was a compliment to your heroic prowess!' shouted Torin, lengthening his step suddenly.

'I would not want to have to beat you again,' shouted Haegr, his head sticking out of the door. His enormous bushy whiskers reminded Ragnar of a walrus.

'I am still waiting for the first time,' said Torin.

'What was that?'

'Go and take the tankard off your foot,' said Torin, as they ducked around a corner.

'He would not really beat you?' Ragnar asked. Torin raised an eyebrow.

'He wishes he could. Haegr is very strong, but his bulk makes him fairly slow. I have yet to lose a bout to him in unarmed combat.'

There was a quiet confidence in Torin's manner that was utterly at odds with Haegr's bluster. Ragnar saw no reason to doubt his words.

'How did he get so heavy? I thought our bodies had been engineered to burn food efficiently. I don't think I have ever seen an overweight Space Wolf before.'

'There is more muscle than fat in there, as you will find if you ever arm wrestle with him. As to his fatness, something went slightly wrong when Haegr made his ascension to Space Marine. It did not show up for a long time; the Wolf Priests merely thought he had a huge appetite. It was only after he piled on the pounds that they realised there was some sort of flaw in him. Not enough to turn him into a Wulfen or get him exiled into the Cold Wastes but one that made him what he is. You will find most Wolfblades did not exactly fit in back at the Fang. That's how most of us ended up here.'

'What brought you here then?'

'I asked for it.'

'You wanted to see the Holy World?'

'Something like that. And here we have your new chambers. It's not much, but it's home,' he said.

Looking through the door, Ragnar could see that once again, Torin was mocking. The chambers were vast and singularly well appointed. They made his suite on *The Herald of Belisarius* look positively spartan. He could see that his gear had already been brought in and laid out for his inspection on a massive oaken table.

'It's not quite what I expected,' he said.

'It comes with the job. The Belisarians like to keep us happy. They do not want anyone buying our loyalty so we get the best of everything.'

'They think someone could buy the loyalty of a Space Wolf? They do not know us very well,' said Ragnar. He resented the implied slur on the honour of the Chapter.

'Perhaps they know us better than we know ourselves, Ragnar. Or perhaps they simply project themselves onto us. Make yourself comfortable. You will be summoned to your duties soon.'

Before Ragnar could say anything, Torin had retreated and the door was shut behind him.

Ragnar moved through the suite of rooms, and tried to drink in the unaccustomed luxury. The fittings were of the finest quality. There were armchairs, couches and desks, a suspensor bed where it was possible to float above the mattress on a repulsor field. There was a wash chamber with a sunken marble bath.

There was a hologramic window which changed views when you passed your hand over a rune. He cycled through views of Fenris, a desert world dominated by massive ruins, the hall of merchants above, a huge structure that might have been the Imperial Palace with an endless queue of pilgrims about it. The air was filled with relaxing scents, low thrilling martial music was piped in.

Ragnar continued to look around for concealed surveillance devices. He unplugged cameras set within the plasterwork of the ceilings. He sniffed out sub-auditors beneath the beds. He found a camera eye in the poison snooper above the table. He did not like being watched and wanted to make sure that the person who had planted these things got the message.

After he had finished going over the room, he lay on the bed and stared at the ceiling wondering what he was going to do. This place was not at all what he had expected. It reeked of suspicion and intrigue and everyone he met had warned him about it.

It seemed he was to assume everyone he met was treacherous, just as they would assume the same about him. It was no way to live, he thought, and then realised that he had no choice. Assassination was evidently a way of life here. People committed stealthy murder for their own advantage. And it appeared that anything could be bought.

Why was it so, he wondered? Surrounding him were riches beyond the wildest dreams of most of the subjects of the Imperium. All of the Lords of the Imperium, and all of the Navigators shared in that huge wealth. Why did they need more? Perhaps it was not riches they fought for. Perhaps it was power. He had seen what the desire for power could do even among the comparatively austere warriors of Fenris.

And what of his new companions? How trustworthy were they? Torin seemed a man of many secrets and his mocking manner was unlike any Space Wolf Ragnar had ever known. He seemed to have become more a Belisarian in his manner of dress, speech and thought. Haegr seemed simple, but Torin had spoken of some sort of flaw that had perhaps resulted in his exile to this place. Perhaps the flaw went deeper than that.

Ragnar forced himself to relax. He was in no position to judge his comrades. He was simply uneasy at having been torn from the routine of his life with the battle-brothers and thrust into the murky undercurrents of this place. He was like a fish out of water. He had been trained to deal with the hard realities of battle, where objectives and enemies were clearly defined. He hadn't been trained in palace intrigue. Perhaps that was why he had been sent here. Perhaps this was something he needed to master. He knew that whatever happened here, he was being presented with an opportunity.

He was in a position to study the dark underbelly of the Imperial political system close up. He was going to do his best to learn from this, and master it. At this moment, Ragnar was alone and ignorant and vulnerable, but it was his task to see that he did not remain that way. He would take his destiny into his own hands. He would learn what was necessary, and he would triumph over his circumstances. This was a test he was not going to fail.

Coming to this decision made Ragnar feel better. He realised that ever since he had lost the Spear of Russ and learned that he must face trial at the Council of Wolves, he had been drifting, uncertain and unsure. That time was over now. Whatever challenges lay ahead he would face them like a true Son of Russ.

There was a knock on the door. He opened it and found Torin and Haegr waiting for him. 'The Celestarch desires the pleasure of an audience with her newest Wolfblade,' said Torin, half-jokingly.

'She sent us to make sure you would not get lost,' said Haegr, licking his lips.

'Actually she sent me,' said Torin, 'to make sure you both did not get lost.'

'You know I know my way about the palace better than any newly arrived cub.'

Ragnar smiled at them. 'I am sorry. I did not recognise you, Haegr, without that bucket on your foot.'

'Are you mocking me, lad?'

'Would I do a thing like that?' said Ragnar.

'You'd better not,' said Haegr.

'I think you're going to fit right in around here,' said Torin, leading them through the maze of passageways towards the distant elevator.

CHAPTER SIX

THEY EMERGED FROM another elevator in a different part of the palace. Ragnar's head was spinning from all the new sights, sounds and stimuli as well as the sheer immensity of the place. But the process of adapting to the new environment had already begun. As they walked they were leaving a scent trail he could use to retrace his steps. The more ground they covered, the more marks they would leave. Even now, he could find his way back to his chamber blindfolded.

The people in this area were better dressed. There were more Navigators, and more ostentatious signs of wealth. Hologramic tapestries of spun golden thread covered the walls; the perspective on the scenes changing as you walked past in a manner that fooled the eye completely. Here were pictures of treaties, and ships against starry backgrounds, and landscapes of a hundred alien worlds. In each landscape the banner of Belisarius fluttered. On each ship the sigil of its power was painted. A Navigator in House uniform played a prominent part in every negotiation.

Most startling of all was the picture of a Belisarian walking beside three haloed figures. One was winged like an angel, one had the long fangs of a Space Wolf, and one had a blazing aura. Ragnar gave it more than a passing glance. Unless he was completely mistaken, the picture showed one of the precursors of the current Celestarch walking beside the Emperor, Leman Russ and Sanguinius, primarch of the Blood Angels.

Ragnar flinched a little at the sight of the spear in Russ's hand. He flexed his fingers. They too had briefly held that holy weapon. Looking at the accuracy of the depiction, Ragnar had no doubt that the artist had seen the weapon. The painting was a none-too subtle reminder of the ancient lineage and the mighty connections of the House of Belisarius.

He took time to study the people around him. The humans looked at them with a mixture of respect and fear, as they passed. Their nervousness was evident in their scent. The Navigators, as always, were much more difficult to read. There was something about them that was as alien and inhuman as an ork. Torin and Haegr gave no sign of being upset by it, but he supposed that they had had many years to get used to it.

Ahead of them loomed a massive archway. The support columns were formed by two starships, surrounded by angels with the third eye of Navigators – an image that some would think came close to blasphemy. In the centre of the arch was embossed the sigil of Belisarius, an eye flanked by two rearing wolves. The guards at the entrance saluted them and allowed them to pass directly into the presence room.

Here too was evidence of power and wealth. The domed ceiling of the chamber was a jewelled representation of the night sky. It was reflected in the black marble of the floor. On a raised floating dais of polished black stone, the present Celestarch rested on a throne of true silver. She was a tall woman, with an ageless beauty, garbed in a long black gown, belted at the waist with a girdle of silver. The buckle of the belt bore the sign of the eye flanked by two wolves, as did the diadem on her brow. In its case, the metal eye was positioned exactly so that the Celestarch's own pineal eye was visible through it.

Two men stood beside the throne. One was tall but stooped, with long fine silver hair and beard. He wore robes similar to the Celestarch's but trimmed with white fur at the collar. The other was shorter and more intense looking with black hair shot with grey and a well-trimmed goatee beard. He

wore the dress uniform of the House with panache
and looked like he knew how to handle the sword
and bolt pistol clipped to his belt. All three of them
bore a distinct family resemblance both to each
other and to Gabriella. They were all tall and slender, with fine boned hands and faces, slightly
sunken cheeks and large eyes. The Navigators
looked up as the three Wolfblades entered.

'Greetings, Torin of Fenris,' said the woman. Her
voice was deeper than Ragnar expected. 'I see you
have brought our latest recruit with you.'

'I have Lady Juliana. May I present to you, Ragnar
Blackmane of Fenris and the Wolves.'

'We are pleased to make your acquaintance, Ragnar Blackmane. Advance so that we may recognise
you.'

Ragnar did so. He strode forward with all the confidence he could muster, determined not to be
intimidated by the wealth of his surroundings or
the ancient lineage of the Celestarch. He realised
the ostentatious display en route to the presence
chamber was designed to impress and intimidate
the visitor. He was not going to let it sway him. He
would judge the Celestarch on her own merits, just
as she must judge him. Such had been the way of
the warriors of Fenris with their chieftains since
time immemorial.

He stood before the dais and looked up at the
Celestarch. If she was offended she gave no sign,
nor did the elderly Navigator. The uniformed man

scowled but said nothing as he witnessed Ragnar's swagger. Ragnar thought he sensed amusement radiate from Torin and approval from Haegr.

'I can see you are a true son of Fenris,' said the Lady Juliana, not unkindly. 'Step on to the dais.'

Ragnar did so, and noticed not the slightest tremor in the suspensor field, as his massively armoured form rested on it. The platform might look as if it floated like a raft in a swell, but it felt solid once you were on it.

'You have come to swear allegiance to us, Ragnar?'

'I have. You have my word as a warrior and Space Wolf that I will follow you and shield you and obey your commands as I would the Great Wolf himself.'

'I can ask for no more,' said the Celestarch. 'Be welcome in House Belisarius, Ragnar Blackmane.'

'I thank you, lady.' A nod told Ragnar he was dismissed, so he bowed and backed off the dais, easily retracing his steps to Torin and Haegr.

'You may go,' said Lady Juliana. All three Wolfblades saluted and withdrew through the archway.

'I think she likes you,' said Torin.

'How can you tell?'

'She kept the formalities short.'

'Who were the other two?'

'The old man was Alarik, the chamberlain, also head of security. The dandy was Skorpeus. He is the Celestarch's cousin and he thinks he is her advisor.'

'Who cares?' said Haegr. 'Let us go and consume vast quantities of beer in a manner suitable for heroes of Fenris.'

'An excellent suggestion,' said Torin. 'Come, Ragnar, let us introduce you to one of the delights of Terra – the taverns of the merchants quarter.'

Ragnar felt like saying he was tired and wished to recover from his journey, but there was a challenge in the gaze of both his companions. Torin appeared to be judging him, and Haegr's manner made it clear that no true son of Fenris would miss such an opportunity. On reflection, Ragnar thought it would not be such a bad thing to do. He was keen to see more of his new homeworld and once his duties had started he might not get an opportunity. It occurred to him that this might be the case for the other two as well. Perhaps they had been assigned to show him around and would be assigned to something else if he left. That being the case…

'Lead on,' said Ragnar. At that moment, the uniformed Navigator Skorpeus emerged from the presence chamber. He was greeted by a hulking figure with a scarred face. The two of them exchanged a few words and then strode over towards the three companions.

'Welcome to Terra, Ragnar Blackmane,' said the Navigator. His manner was smooth and easy, perhaps overly so, thought Ragnar. 'I wish you better fortune than your predecessor.'

'Skander died performing his duty. No Wolf could ask for a better death.'

'Perhaps it would have been better for us all if he had succeeded in his duty which was, after all, to keep Adrian Belisarius alive. It would certainly have been better for my cousin.'

Haegr grunted and spat. Torin said, 'In his place I am sure you would have found a way to preserve both your lives, noble Skorpeus. Doubtless the stars would have warned you to stay away. Perhaps they did… which is why you were not around when the attack came.'

'The stars did indeed smile on me. Although, of course, it saddens me that my cousin did not heed my warnings.'

Ragnar turned to the Navigator's hulking companion. He was listening to the exchange intently and showing no sign of emotion. There was a hard competence in his manner that reminded Ragnar of the elite units of the Imperial Guard.

'Did the stars not also predict that you would become Celestarch?' said Torin smoothly. Skorpeus cast him a patronising smile.

'You think that the Elders' selection of Cousin Juliana invalidates that prediction, do you, Wolfblade?'

'To an untutored barbarian such as me it would look that way.'

Skorpeus's smile widened. He resembled a gambler who holds a trump card and is about to produce it. 'The stars did not predict when I would become Celestarch. Only that I would. It's something you should keep in mind. I will be your master someday.'

'I think you misunderstand the relationship between Fenris and Belisarius,' said Torin. Ragnar noticed a faint hint of anger in his scent. Although he concealed it well, the Space Wolf clearly disliked Skorpeus.

'Perhaps once I take the throne I shall redefine it,' said the Navigator. He strode off with the jaunty air of a man who knows he has had the last word.

'What was that about?' Ragnar asked, when Skorpeus had disappeared out of earshot.

'That fine specimen of Navigator pride and self-love thinks the stars predicted him being on the throne,' said Torin, swiftly walking in the other direction. 'In case you missed it, he is convinced that he should and will be Celestarch. His lackey there, the ape Beltharys, agrees with him.'

'You think Skorpeus would do something to help the process along?'

Torin shook his head. 'He would if he could, but there is no way he could influence the selection of the Elders.'

'Who are they?'

'Don't ask,' said Haegr. 'Drink beer instead.'

'I am curious,' said Ragnar.

'They are very mysterious,' said Haegr. 'And really you don't want to know.'

'For once my vast friend is right,' said Torin.

'In what way mysterious?' said Ragnar.

'Most people never see them. To most of the people in this palace they are as invisible as Haegr's common sense.'

'I hope I am not going to have to thrash you again, Torin.'

'All know that common sense is a quality, Haegr, and therefore noticeable if not perceptible.'

'That's all right then.'

'You mean no one sees the people who select the ruler of House Belisarius.'

'There are couriers who venture into the Vaults below. They are blind. And the Navigators sometimes go down there too. And I think Valkoth has been. Skander had too.'

'Down there? Vaults?'

'Below this palace is a maze, Ragnar. It is fortified, and sealed off from the rest of the underworld by a ten metre thick moat of reinforced plascrete. It fills every corridor and is riddled with sensors and traps and detectors. The Elders dwell in these Vaults.'

'Perhaps they fear assassination,' said Ragnar.

'You're very quick, young Blackmane,' said Haegr sarcastically.

'And perhaps they fear something else,' said Torin.

'What do you mean?'

'Now is neither the time nor place to discuss it.'

'It's one of the Navigators' guilty secrets, is it?'

'Don't mock, Ragnar. It may be.'

'Are we going to talk or drink?' demanded Haegr.

'Doubtless you have noticed that our steps are taking us in the direction of the flitter bays, friend Haegr,' said Torin. 'And doubtless your mighty brain will have deduced that one of those vehicles will carry us to the tavern quarter. Many of us can perform two tasks, such as walking and talking at once.'

'Are you suggesting that I can't?'

'You have proven many times your capacity in those arenas. Even as we speak you perform both with diligence. Why then would I suggest otherwise?'

'There is a slipperiness in your manner, Torin, that I like not. A beating may be necessary.'

'Save your energy for the drinking, my friend.'

'I will consider your advice.'

Torin led them to a vast hangar somewhere high on the side of the palace. From its cavernous interior, there was a panoramic view of the skyline of the city. A number of enormous structures glowed in the distance, every window like a small beacon. The running lights formed streams across the skies. Gigantic trains wended their way between buildings and the endless tide of tens of thousands of people. The taste of pollution tainted the air. Ragnar felt a very long way from the cold wilderness of Fenris.

Torin led them over to a small four-man flitter. It bore the markings of Belisarius, a sleek streamlined insect like vessel painted in black and silver. They clambered in and Torin took the controls, handling them as expertly as a Thunderhawk pilot. He quickly ran through the pre-flight invocations, and the engines hummed to life. Moments later the vehicle slid swiftly out into the night.

Ragnar felt a moment's disorientation as he looked down at the metal and plascrete sliding away below. They were a thousand metres up and rising. Torin was giving his attention to their surroundings and the holosphere gauges. The Belisarius Palace receded behind them. From this vantage point Ragnar could see it was a massive black and silver lozenge with the logo of the House embossed on the side. He knew now that the skyscraper was but the tip of an iceberg: the real domains of the House extended far below the surface to the mysterious Vaults. What could possibly go on down there, he wondered? Why were the Navigators so secretive? What were they hiding?

Another glance showed him that the flitters were all following routes through the sky as distinct as the roadways beneath them. There were vast open spaces occupied by solitary structures that were avoided. He asked why.

'Those are the homes of the other Houses. No one violates their airspace without invitation and clearance. To do so is to risk being shot down.'

Ragnar understood that. Such cordons would be the easiest way to prevent a surface attack and would allow any gunner on the building a clear line of fire at any target – a thing that would not be possible if vehicles crowded the skies above them. It had been what he expected, but he was glad to have his thinking confirmed.

'I thought the Inquisition and the Arbites maintained tight security on Terra.'

'They do, but not everywhere. You are in the navigators quarter now. The whole island is a free zone. The families are left alone and maintain their own security. The Inquisition cannot enter here unless invited or unless there is some flagrant violation of the laws. There is little love lost between the families and the Inquisition.'

'Aye,' said Haegr. 'The black-cloaked bastards hate the three eyed devils. None of them are worth a fart, except one or two of the Belisarians, of course.'

'You don't like it here?' said Ragnar.

'The place disgusts me. I wish I were back on the icefields of Fenris with a herd of elk before me and a spear in my hand.'

'It's funny,' said Torin. 'That time when you saved old Adrian from those fanatics I thought I heard him offer you your heart's desire. He would have sent you home if you asked. Instead you asked for a meat pie.'

'It was a big pie,' said Haegr. He sounded almost embarrassed.

'It was indeed,' said Torin. 'They killed a bull and wrapped it in pastry. Haegr ate it all himself too.'

'It was my reward. I didn't notice you stepping in the way of any bullets.'

'Is it true you trampled several servants to death as you rushed the table?' said Torin.

'No. None would dare stand between me and such a prize.'

Ragnar was amused listening to them. Their banter reminded him of the cheery insults he had often traded with Sven. But he still felt out of place here. He noticed that the flitter had started to descend towards a tightly packed cluster of buildings. The sky above them blazed with light.

'You said the Inquisition does not come here.'

'It would take little short of open war between the Houses to give them reason,' said Torin. 'The Navigators spend enough in bribes to buy a small planet. It ensures their privacy.'

Ragnar was a little shocked by all this talk of bribery. That the heart of the Empire should be so corrupt disappointed him and left him feeling naïve. The others seemed to take it in their stride. Perhaps he would too when he had been here as long as they had.

'Are you saying the Inquisition takes bribes?'

'Nothing as blatant as that,' said Torin. 'You have to understand how the Imperium works, Ragnar. All the High Lords of Terra spend their time intriguing against each other, jockeying for position, prestige and power. That takes money. The Navigators have a great deal of money. The High Lords and many ranking bureaucrats ensure that the trusted allies who provide them with money are not bothered.'

'The whole planet would be better off if we virus bombed it,' said Haegr. 'Except the Emperor's Palace.'

Torin looked at him.

'And the Belisarians, of course,' Haegr added as an afterthought.

'Only you would suggest virus bombing Holy Terra,' said Torin.

'It would improve the place,' said Haegr.

'Don't say that too loudly where someone might hear.'

'What will you do if I do?'

'I will attend your funeral after the zealots incinerate you.'

'Bring them on. I do not fear them or the Inquisition. Haegr fears nothing in this galaxy.'

'Zealots?' asked Ragnar.

'Religious fanatics. Terra abounds with them, as you might expect. It's not all corruption and luxury. Not everyone can afford them. There are billions of people here on the holy soil who have no comfort but their faith. A certain percentage of them take comfort in killing anyone who does not measure up to their idea of virtue.'

'That's one of the reasons why the Navigators prefer to be isolated in the middle of this sludge sea,' said Haegr. 'The zealots hate them, they call them mutants.'

'They would kill Navigators?' said Ragnar.

'Who do you think killed Adrian Belisarius?' demanded Torin.

CHAPTER SEVEN

THE TAVERN WAS packed with hundreds of people. Sailors, soldiers, merchants and their bodyguards from a thousand worlds had congregated here. Music pulsed loudly. Semi-naked women danced on tables, while others brought food and drink to the customers. The interior had been built to resemble a wooden tavern on some frontier world, but Ragnar's senses told him that this was an illusion. The beams overhead were in fact painted plascrete, not wood. The walls were panels overlaid on stone. The fire, strangely enough, was real and roaring.

Many animal heads had been mounted on the wall. Ragnar recognised wolf and elk. Strange how some variant of these creatures could be found on thousands of worlds. Ragnar supposed they must have been borne outwards with the original migration from Earth. This idea brought him back to the realisation that this was where it had all started. This was the home world of the Emperor – this was where humanity had originally come from. It was an awesome thought, although he doubted it was passing through the minds of any of the revellers who surrounded them.

It was a testimony to the cosmopolitanism of the crowd that surrounded them that when Torin and Haegr made their way towards a table, no one paid them the slightest attention. It was not something Ragnar was used to. On any world save Fenris a Space Wolf could expect to be greeted with awe and not a little reverence. Of course, it was entirely possible, looking at this crowd, that the revellers were simply too drunk to have noticed three armoured giants moving through their midst.

Haegr had already bellowed orders for food and drink. The landlord greeted him as if he were a long lost brother. 'The usual?' he asked.

'The usual!' Haegr bellowed.

Moments later a massive tankard of ale splashed down in front of Ragnar. 'Skal!' roared Haegr and raised his stein.

'Welcome to Terra, Ragnar,' said Torin.

'Glad to be here,' said Ragnar, and found to his surprise that it was true. The ale was cold and went down well.

'Not as good as Fenrisian ale, but it will do,' said Haegr. He had already finished one tankard and was proceeding to another. It took a lot of ale to get through a Space Marine's ability to metabolise poison, and Haegr was obviously helping it along with a beaker of whisky. A few moments later what looked like two whole roasted sheep were set on the table in front of him.

'Are we going to eat all of this?' asked Ragnar.

'This is mine,' said Haegr. 'Here's yours now!' His gesture indicated that another dead and roasted animal was about to be delivered to their table.

'This is just a starter for Haegr,' said Torin, and seeing Ragnar's look added, 'I am not joking. Dig in, or he'll eat yours before you can have a mouthful.'

From the other side of the table came a noise like a chainsword going through a side of beef. Ragnar was astonished to notice how much of the meat on one of Haegr's sheep was already gone. Two loaves and a slathering of butter had gone with it. He tore off a haunch of his own and bit into it. It tasted good. The juices flowed over his tongue and down his throat. He washed them down with more ale, some whisky and then some bread.

He looked up and was surprised to see that Torin was using a knife and fork in the local manner, and was carefully cutting his food into small bite sized portions before chewing on it. A translucent goblet the size of bucket contained wine. It was his only concession to the Fenrisian style of feasting.

He smiled at Ragnar. 'Sensorin dreamwine. It contains some powerful hallucinogenic mushrooms. They have quite a kick. I like to test myself on such things.'

Haegr let out a belch like a thunderclap. 'Torin has gone all decadent. I blame the influence of all these effete earthlings. Only my regular thrashings give him any semblance of true Fenrisian hardihood.'

'Watch your arm, Ragnar,' said Torin. 'Haegr almost grabbed it by mistake. Several men have needed prosthetics after dining with him.'

'A scurrilous rumour spread by my enemies,' said Haegr, shredding the second sheep with his teeth. 'I am no ork.'

'Sometimes it's difficult to tell,' said Torin. 'Did your mother know your father well? I am sure I detect a greenish tint to your skin sometimes.'

'The only greenish tint around here is on your skin and it comes from your envy of my manly prowess.'

'Actually, as I recall, you did look a little green after our last drinking session. You claimed that you should not have had that last alligator curry, although I suspect it was the two barrels of firewine that disagreed with you?'

'How could you tell?' asked Haegr complacently. 'You were unconscious at the time. Which reminds me – you still owe me for that bet.'

Ragnar glanced around the room. The whisky had warmed his belly, and the food was going down well, but something made him uneasy. There was a faint prickling of the hairs on the back of his neck. He sensed that he was under hostile observation and tried to identify the source. Many people were looking at them now, but that could be because they were betting how much Haegr could eat. He could hear wagers being made at the other tables if he listened hard.

There was other talk too, about politics mixed in with the usual bar room gossip. Some of the strangers were talking about the death of Adrian Belisarius, and their discussion was becoming quite animated. It appeared the former Celestarch was not the only highly ranked Navigator to have died recently. Evidently there had been attempts on others too. Again and again, Ragnar picked up the word *Brotherhood*. He was about to go over and enquire about it, but a warning glance from Torin told him it would not be a good idea.

'It seems the death of Adrian Belisarius is common gossip,' said Ragnar. Torin shrugged.

'Men will talk about what men talk about.'

Ragnar considered what he had heard. 'Did he really die in a flitter crash?'

'You could say that.'

Haegr grunted something but his words were incomprehensible through his huge mouthful of food.

Despite the friendly hustle and bustle, Ragnar began to feel more and more uneasy. A couple of people eyed him with hostile intent. When he cast his mind back, he recalled that several of those men's friends had rushed out of the tavern earlier.

'It seems we are not popular here.'

'Space Wolves never are on Terra,' said Torin.

'Why?'

'Ask the locals not me! You'd think they would be grateful after all we have done for them.'

Ragnar swigged the ale and considered this. He could just go over and challenge the strangers. Seeing his look the men got up and ducked for the door. Maybe he had been wrong, Ragnar thought. Maybe they were simply curious or disliked offworlders. On the other hand they could be zealots though they certainly had not shown any zeal for sticking around when he looked like he was about to talk to them.

More and more food was being heaped on the table but Haegr and Torin appeared to be having a drinking match, in order to warm up. Goblets of whisky and massive steins of ale filled their table, and both contestants appeared to be able to consume them with little trouble.

Ragnar slowed his own drinking to sips. The atmosphere of incipient danger had not changed – if anything it had increased. A glance told him that Torin, while appearing to drink as heartily as Haegr, was also covertly studying their surroundings. He was subtle about it, and if Ragnar had not been doing the same he would not have noticed it. When their eyes met, Torin winked surreptitiously. Ragnar felt reassured. If there was going to be trouble, he was not the only one expecting it.

A mountain of food appeared in front of Haegr. He smacked his lips and gestured for the waitresses to keep it coming. Loaves, sides of beef, and fish the size of small sharks continued to disappear along with a small mountain of butter and cheese. More men had entered. Some of them brought with them an odd stink of hatred and menace. It was sharp as a knife and as bitter as the soul of a miser who had lost a gold coin. The hackles on the back of Ragnar's neck rose further, but aside from Torin he was the only one in the place who did not give off the odd scent or who showed any sign of unease.

All eyes were focused on Haegr now. Gasps of disbelief and cries of awe filled the chamber as the orgy of consumption continued. Haegr was chewing through whole bones now, grinding them in his teeth and swallowing them down. Torin had risen now to clap Haegr on the shoulder and congratulate him, but Ragnar caught him leaning forward and whispering in his comrade's ear.

Haegr's cheeks were red, and sweat dotted his brow. Although his whole concentration appeared to be focused on his eating orgy, he nodded imperceptibly and quaffed a huge mouthful of ale. Torin did not sit back down, instead he glanced around to seek the source of impending danger.

A man bumped into Ragnar. There was an angry expression on his face as if he resented being jostled. The anger was real, but the cause was not. Ragnar knew from his stink that he had already been on the verge of berserk fury before they had made contact. The man's pupils were the size of pinpricks and a faint trail of drool dribbled from his mouth. Close up, Ragnar caught the acrid unhealthy chemical scent of his sweat. A vein pulsed in the man's forehead. His lips were drawn back in a snarl revealing yellowing teeth.

'Out of my way, off-world pig,' he slurred. Most would have assumed the slurring was caused by alcohol, but Ragnar knew better. This was one of the many side effects of Fury, an alchemical concoction designed to goad men to berserker fits in battle. It had been banned by the Imperial military centuries ago because it made troops unreliable and increased their susceptibility to the influence of Chaos. Still, it had been used by heretics in several of the planetary rebellions that Ragnar had helped quash. He was shocked to discover it being used here on Earth.

He was not intimidated. A man in the grip of Fury could be erratic, incredibly strong and almost immune to pain but that would not make him a threat to a Space Wolf. The man obviously did not see things this way. He slipped something over his hand, and said, 'I said, out of my way off-world pig. Don't make me repeat myself again.'

Ragnar scented more men closing in on him. They all had the same tainted sweat. Ragnar grinned, showing his teeth. If the man was too far gone to back off after that, the consequences would be on his own head. The stranger swung at him.

The blow came in faster than it would have from a normal man but Ragnar blocked it with ease. He caught the man's wrist in his hand. There was a stinging sensation in his arm as a blue electrical arc jumped from the band on the man's fingers to Ragnar's arm.

The man was wearing electric cestii, designed to enhance the power of a punch with an electric shock. If set to maximum, the blast of power could stun or even kill a man if his heart were weak. Ragnar smiled and casually backhanded his attacker. Teeth flew everywhere and bones broke as his foe was thrown across the room. He landed on a table, but immediately struggled to his feet, his resilience obviously enhanced by the drugs in his system.

One of the people at the table was annoyed to have a stranger suddenly strewn across his food. He showed his displeasure by breaking a wine bottle over the attacker's head. That was a mistake – the berserker turned and lurched for his throat. Red wine and blood mingled as they ran down his face. Shouts, screams and warnings rang out as chaos spread and the brawl became general.

Ragnar made out more attackers closing in on him. They were a villainous looking bunch. Many had bionic hands or eyes. Some of their prosthetics had been enhanced with retractable daggers that emerged like nails from their finger tips. Some wore electric cestii, and others carried weighted truncheons. All of them threw themselves at Ragnar with an unhesitating fury that told of the drugs in their system. Ragnar caught the first by the throat, raised him high and then tossed him onto his friends, knocking three of them over.

Another came on in a rush, his claws extended to pierce Ragnar's eyes. Ragnar caught him by his prosthetic arm, twisted for leverage, and pulled. He ripped the mechanical limb clean out of its socket in a shower of sparks, and used it as a bludgeon to knock his assailant from his feet. Then he kicked him in the head.

More blows rained down on him now. Electric cestii sparked against his armour. Sparks flashed and the scent of ozone filled the air as they connected. Ragnar's armour was designed to take far heavier punishment than this, so he ignored it and concentrated instead on smiting his foes.

He lashed out around him with his fists. Each blow dropped a man but a surprisingly large number of them got back up again and instantly came back on the offensive. It seemed obvious that these men had been sent specifically to start this brawl and they were pulling no punches. The drugs left them incapable of hesitating. They would have killed him if they could. In fact, the treatment he had received would have killed a normal man ten times over. Fortunately, Ragnar was a Space Marine. His armour was almost part of his body and his bone structure and musculature had been heavily modified so he could absorb enormous amounts of damage. Still, he had collected a few bruises and cuts. He could feel his skin sting where his ultra-coagulant blood had congealed on them.

He glanced around to see what had become of his companions. Torin was swinging from one of the suspensor chandeliers. He planted his boot in the face of one assailant before letting go and flying into a mass of others. His every movement was swift and certain, every blow decisive. If anything he had less to worry about than Ragnar. He was moving so fast it would be difficult even for a man with a gun to draw a bead on him, and this was clearly his intention.

Then it happened. Up to this point Haegr had ignored the carnage about him as he concentrated on stuffing his face. One of the berserkers dived onto the table, scattering food everywhere, sending wine and whisky and ale splashing all over the place. Haegr looked at him for a moment as if he could not quite understand what had happened. A look of confusion passed over his face as he reached for food that was no longer there. Then his piggy eyes narrowed and he let out an enormous roar.

A sweep of his arm cleared the berserker from the table. Haegr reared to his feet, like a mammoth rising from a mudhole. He had the same mass and power, but suddenly he was even larger and more threatening. He picked up the metal table. The bolts holding it to the floor snapped as he lifted it free and tossed it into the oncoming mass of drugged fanatics. It bowled them over and left them sprawling beneath its weight. Haegr reached forward and picked two up, one in each hand, and then used them as clubs to batter their companions senseless. He raced through them like an out-of-control behemoth, unstoppable as a charging rhino. Within seconds he had left a trail of maimed and battered foes behind him. Any that tried to get to their feet were stamped on. Their hands and legs shattered along with bionics and bones.

Ragnar threw himself back into the fray, lashing out at his opponents, careful to select only those who stank of combat drugs. He found himself face to face with Torin. He was smashing a couple of berserkers' heads together, until not even the drug could keep them awake. 'Best grab Haegr and get out of here,' he shouted.

'Why?'

'It might embarrass the Celestarch if we thrash any of the Arbites who come to investigate this.'

'Fair enough,' said Ragnar, glancing at Haegr. He had picked up a side of beef on a spit and was bludgeoning those around him with it. Occasionally, he paused to tear some meat from its flanks, and gnaw at it. 'But getting him out of here might be easier said than done.'

Torin nodded. 'He's enjoying himself, but this is for his own good. You get one arm. I'll take the other.'

Ragnar nodded and they rushed at Haegr. Ragnar grabbed his left arm, Torin the right, and together they began dragging him to the door.

Distracted as he was by the side of beef, it was like trying to tow a bull. It took several attempts. Occasionally, they were interrupted by Haegr's blows at the surviving berserkers. But they dragged him out into the night air and began to calm him down.

'Let me go,' said Haegr. 'There are still foes to thrash!'

'We'd best be going. Those sirens you hear are the Arbites.'

'So? We can take them all out. You know we can.'

'Aye, but it might cause the Lady Juliana some problems if we leave the streets of the merchants quarter filled with dead or dying judges.'

Haegr was not convinced. Ragnar could see the running lights of many flitters coming closer. Ground cars too. 'They are not our enemies,' he said. 'They are merely doing their duty as they see fit. Besides, we will have to come back here anyway. We have a mystery to solve.'

'And what would that be?' Haegr asked.

'Why those men attacked us and who sent them anyway. The Arbites won't help us do that if we put any of them in the healing tanks.'

'Very well. I can see that you and Torin have made up your minds. I will go with you and keep you out of trouble.'

Something moving on a nearby rooftop caught Ragnar's eye. He glanced up and caught sight of a shadowy figure receding from view. He could not be sure that it was not a trick of the light.

CHAPTER EIGHT

THE TOLL OF a distant bell dragged Ragnar from dreams of Fenris. He woke instantly and rose from his bed. As if summoned by his motion, servants appeared with bowls of elk stew and fish porridge – traditional Fenrisian food, or as close to it as he was going to get on Terra. He was more than a little startled by the way they had entered without being asked. 'Who sent you?' he asked the eldest looking, a lean aquiline man with cold calm features and fine silver hair. He wore the uniform of Belisarius more like a soldier than a thrall.

'No one, sir. We assumed you would want breakfast as soon as you rose. Have we erred?'

'No.' The servant waited politely to see if he had anything else to say. Ragnar did not. It seemed like servants were invisible here, coming and going about their duties unbidden, changing their routines only if asked. They seemed to have access to most places as well. He realised the servants were still waiting. 'Carry on,' he said, and they promptly resumed their duties.

Ragnar recalled the events of the previous evening. After they had dragged Haegr to the flitter, Torin had taken them over the nearest roofs. If there had been someone there, he had vanished in the few moments it had taken them to get aloft. Either that or he was camouflaged enough to baffle even the Space Wolves' keen night vision. Ragnar knew that was not impossible, but they would have to be using military issue wargear. That was not impossible either, he had decided.

'Master Ragnar, I have a message for you, from Master Valkoth.'

'Yes?' said Ragnar.

'When you have finished your breakfast, you should report to him to have your duties assigned to you. It is not urgent, but he would appreciate it if you could be there before the ninth bell. That is in forty-five minutes and twenty-two seconds, sir.'

'Thank you,' said Ragnar, snatching up his food. 'Plenty of time then.'

'Yes, sir.'

As he strode through the crowded section of the palace, Ragnar again pondered last night's events.

He was certain that it had been no mere tavern brawl. Not unless men went out drinking here with Fury in their pockets and a desire to do violence. He supposed that scenario was not impossible. From what he gathered, the merchants quarter had a reputation as a wild place, at least by Terra's standards. Many went there to blow off steam. Perhaps that was one way of doing it.

And perhaps Haegr would grow wings and learn to fly, Ragnar thought. He was surprised to find Torin had fallen into step beside him. He must have approached from a side corridor downwind.

'Morning,' he said. 'Looking forward to today's duties, are we?'

'I don't even know what they are.'

'Well, you'll find out soon enough. How did you enjoy last night's little adventure?'

'It was interesting. Although I still wonder why those men chose to attack us.'

'Doubtless the Arbites report will be on Valkoth's table by now. He'll tell us if anything important has shown up, though I rather doubt it will.'

'Why? Who do you think those men were?'

'Could have been any number of people: zealot bully boys who don't like off-worlders; agents of another House seeking to test us and embarrass the Belisarians; or young nobs trying to spice up a dull night.'

'Are they really stupid enough to attack three Space Wolves?'

'You'd be surprised what a man will do if he's drunk enough or high enough on Fury.'

'I would be very surprised if he chose to attack three of us.'

'To be honest, I would too. It felt more planned than that, didn't it?'

'Yes.' They passed a golden pleasure girl garbed only in diaphanous robes. She strode along as if she was not semi-naked. A whiff of pheromone attractants sailed on the air behind her and she was gone.

'What do you think?' Ragnar asked, as Torin's eyes followed the girl.

'She's very attractive.'

'I mean about the attackers.'

'Agents of some kind, although I am not sure whose. Or why, for that matter. You never can tell these things on Terra. Although things are getting a little tense at the moment.'

'In what way?'

'Politically. There is a lot of manoeuvring going on between the Houses.'

'I thought there always was.'

'More so even than usual.'

'Why?'

'Old Sarius, the Navigator representative to the High Lords of Terra, is dying.'

'Why should that affect anything?'

'Everybody wants to have a say in who elects his successor.'

'Is he that powerful?'

Torin laughed and smiled at a couple of serving girls who went past carrying bowls of some perfumed liquid. 'Quite the contrary. The Navigators' representative among the High Lords has always been little more than a figurehead.'

'Then why do people care who succeeds him?'

'Because potentially the Navigator's voice has power. All of the High Lords do. Sarius is powerless because he comes from a relatively minor House with very little support from the more powerful ones. None of the great Houses would allow any of their rivals to take that position. At least none of them has managed it in the past two thousand years. It would signal their pre-eminence among the Houses. The rest have tended to gang up on anyone who looks like they might swing it. A weak man from a weak House can be influenced by anyone. And he can be counted on not to do anything that would upset the balance of power.'

'It all sounds rather foolish to me. Leaders should be strong, not weak.'

'Spoken like a true Fenrisian warrior, Ragnar, old son. But no Navigator wants a strong leader for the Houses, unless it's them, of course.'

'But this time it's different?'

'Maybe. It's always a tense time. Every great House is scared that the others will try and steal a march on them. They watch each other like hawks. There's a lot of horse trading and influence peddling.'

'Fascinating,' said Ragnar. He did not want to seem overly interested. All of this seemed somehow beneath a Space Wolf. Torin chuckled.

'You remind me of me when I first came here,' he said. 'Study these things, Ragnar, learn them. They are important. They may determine who we fight tomorrow, or next month or next year – and how. It never hurts to understand the political situation.'

'A Space Wolf fights where he is told.'

'One day, Ragnar, you may be the one doing the telling.'

They had reached Valkoth's chamber. The older Marine was already enthroned behind his desk. It was almost as if he had never left it. A stack of papers was scattered around. Ragnar wondered whether he and Torin were mentioned in any of them.

'Good morning, brothers,' said Valkoth, as they entered. His manner was more melancholy than usual. 'You have a busy day ahead of you and an interesting one. You are going to see a place few Wolfblades have, at least not without heading a strike force.'

'Where is that?' said Ragnar. Torin grinned.

'The Feracci Palace. You are to escort the Lady Gabriella on a visit to her aunt. Do try and make sure she comes home in one piece, won't you? Go to her chambers now and await her pleasure.'

His words and manner were casual, but it was clear they were dismissed.

* * *

IF RAGNAR HAD thought his own rooms were opulent, he now felt like a pauper. The smallest room in Gabriella's suite was larger than his entire living space. Antique furniture filled it. Bookcases full of ancient musty tomes covered the walls. A massive desk dominated the chamber.

Looking out of the huge arched windows, Ragnar realised that even her balcony was larger than his chamber. Everything was monogrammed with the House emblem. Serving maids came and went at will. Ragnar waited. Torin studied the paintings on the wall. They were scenes of alien landscapes.

'Celebasio,' he said.

'What?' said Ragnar.

'The painter. Quite a famous one. He did the murals in the northern audience halls. The Belisarians were his last and richest patrons. Each of these paintings is worth a potentate's ransom.'

Ragnar thought they were beautiful, but hardly functional. 'On Fenris we would use them as kindling for the fire.'

'You are not on Fenris now, Ragnar, and stop trying to pretend you're Haegr. You would need to put on a hundred kilos and grow a moustache like a walrus before you could carry it off.'

Ragnar laughed in spite of himself. 'Who are the Feracci's?'

'One of the other great Navigator Houses – perhaps the greatest. They are the Belisarians' most deadly rivals.'

'I thought Gabriella was going to visit her aunt.'

'The thing about Navigators, old son, is that they are all related: they only marry other Navigators. They do this to preserve the bloodlines that give them their gift. But no Navigator can marry within their own House, for reasons you can well imagine – although I have heard it has happened anyway.'

'So they marry their enemies?'

'They marry who they are told. All marriages are arranged with a view to keeping the bloodlines strong. There are great books of genealogy detailing each bloodline's strengths and weaknesses. The Navigators procreate in the same way people breed dogs or horses.'

Ragnar reflected on this. He had known these things, of course, or at least the teaching machines had left the knowledge in his head. But having knowledge buried in the deep recesses of his mind was not the same as learning about it first hand. Before it had been simply a bit of lore – interesting but seemingly useless. Now that he was familiar with the people involved, it all seemed a little inhuman. Torin noticed his expression.

'It is their way,' he said. 'And the Navigator Houses predate even the Space Marine Chapters, so it must work.' He gestured at their lush surroundings. 'Some would say it has served them well.'

'I sometimes wonder why, when someone has all this wealth, they could want more,' Ragnar said.

'Ask Haegr. He can eat a hundred sweetmeats and still want more. Horus was the most powerful man in the Imperium after the Emperor. Something drove him to rebel.'

'Evil,' said Ragnar, shocked that Torin would use such an example.

'Ambition,' said Torin. 'At first, anyway.'

'I do not think the Rune Priests would like to hear you talk this way,' said Ragnar.

'I agree with you there, old son. But stay on this planet long enough and you will understand why I think the way I do.'

Ragnar considered Berek and Sigrid and the other Wolf Lords, with their thirst for glory, and their hearts all set on the Wolf Throne. You did not need to go all the way to Terra to find ambition.

'For some people, the more they have, the more they want. And the lords of the Navigator Houses are among the richest and most powerful people in the Imperium. Indeed, some claim they are the most powerful.'

Ragnar had heard that view before too. Without Navigators trade would be reduced to a mere trickle and Imperial fleets would only make short crawls between nearby stars. The Space Marine Chapters would be in a similar position. Huge expanses of the Imperium would fall out of contact and revert to barbarism or be conquered by alien powers. The Navigator Houses had an effective monopoly on long haul interstellar travel. If someone could

mould those fragmented Houses into a single combine, he would effectively control the Imperium, so
great would be his political leverage.

Perhaps that was why the Emperor had encouraged the creation of so many rival Houses, Ragnar
thought. Perhaps he had foreseen the consequences
of having one united guild of Navigators. Or perhaps he was letting his imagination take him too
far. He resolved to wait until he had a better grasp
of the facts before jumping to conclusions.

'What are the Feraccis like?' he asked.

'Ruthless, driven, manipulative, more so than
most Navigators. Their lord, Cezare, is thought by
many to be the most ambitious man in the
Imperium, and the most ruthless and cruel.'

'He has a lot of competition for those three titles,
or so it would seem.'

'The fact he has that reputation should tell you
something.'

'He can't be as bad as all that.'

'Playing the devil's advocate to draw me out, eh?
Very clever, old son.'

Ragnar felt a little embarrassed for being so transparent. Torin continued speaking regardless.

'Oh, he is a smooth devil, all right, and a great
patron of the arts – all the great lords are. I suppose
they have to do something with their money, but
beneath the facade, he's a plotter and weaver of
webs. Clever too. Obvious schemes conceal devious
ones, feints within feints within feints.'

'You sound as if you almost admire him.'

'I do have a certain respect for him.'

'You've studied him too, I can tell.'

'Ragnar, old son, he is the enemy. No matter what he says, no matter what you hear, no matter what anybody tells you, never lose sight of that fact. The Feraccis would love to see the Belisarians destroyed or at the very least humbled. There is a long-standing enmity between the two Houses. House Belisarius is a major obstacle in Cezare's way. He has a habit of removing such things.'

'And yet, the Lady Gabriella is about to pay him a social call.'

'Rivals, partners, relatives, that's the way it is here. Business must carry on regardless. Just because you are planning to slit a man's throat, it doesn't mean you can't both profit from a deal in the meantime.'

'It all sounds very complicated.'

'Keep it up, Ragnar. You play the simple Fenrisian very well. You'll fit in around here.'

'And what part are you playing, Torin?'

'Perhaps I am more of the simple Fenrisian than I look.' Ragnar found that very hard to believe.

At that moment the Lady Gabriella emerged from her chamber. She was garbed in the formal dress uniform of a Navigator once more with the badge of her House on her jacket and belt buckle. A sword in its scabbard and a holstered pistol hung from her belt.

'Shall we go?' she said. There was a slightly sour expression on her face. Ragnar wondered if she had been listening. He was starting to suspect that every chamber in these palaces contained hidden eavesdropping devices.

'TASTEFULLY UNDERSTATED, is it not?' murmured Torin as he brought the flitter into a holding pattern over the Feracci tower. Gabriella laughed loudly. Ragnar held back a smile. The Feracci tower looked as if its kilometre-high spire had been gilded. Statues and gargoyles occupied thousands of niches in its walls, flanking every arched stained glass window. It would have made an Imperial temple from the High Decadent period look tasteful. And yet there was no denying it was impressive. It was taller by far than the Belisarius Palace and was easily the highest structure visible to the furthest horizon.

Ragnar's keen eyes made out weapons emplacements concealed within the gilt work. He had no doubt that the walls were thick and heavily armoured. Even before they landed, they were intercepted and escorted by two very heavily armoured gunships each bearing the rampant golden lion insignia of the Feracci, the lion encased within an eye. It fluttered on the thousands of flags that adorned the building.

Armed men waited for them on the rooftop landing pad. They were accompanied by a tall, thin young Navigator. He was good looking in a gaunt way, his hair black as a raven's wing and flowing down to his shoulders.

Torin emerged from the craft on one side, Ragnar on the other. Only once they had both looked around to check for obvious threats did they signal for Gabriella to emerge.

'Greetings, cousin Gabriella,' said the young man, bowing formally. He smiled at her warmly as he rose. He treated the two Space Wolves as if they were not there. Ragnar was not used to being ignored. It spoke a lot of the youth's self possession that he was capable of it. Not many mortals were.

'Greetings, cousin Misha.' Gabriella returned the bow with one just as courtly. She smiled. Ragnar was surprised to note that this pair seemed to genuinely like each other. Either that or they were both impossibly good dissimulators. As they were Navigators, their scents were too alien for him to read.

'My father would be grateful if you would join him in his chambers,' said Misha. 'He will not take up much of your time. He knows you are keen to visit your aunt.'

'I would be honoured,' she responded.

'This was not on the agenda,' said Torin, so low that only a Space Wolf could have heard him. 'Let's see what we shall see.'

Moments later an elevator carried them into the bowels of the Feracci tower. The closing of the doors was like a trap snapping shut.

CHAPTER NINE

RAGNAR WAS SURPRISED by the setting where Cezare Feracci greeted them. It was a garden, a huge hothouse geodesic set atop one of the lower wings that thrust out of the tower's side. The air was hot and humid and smelled of all manner of exotic offworld blooms. They were led along a dozen twisting paths to the very centre of the place. It was all part of a pattern he told himself, along with the seemingly endless security and surveillance equipment they had passed through en route.

In the middle of a grove of beautiful orchid like plants stood a tall man. He resembled Misha, although run slightly to fat. He had a small double chin and slightly puffy cheeks. The flowing robe he wore concealed his slight paunch, but for all that

Cezare held himself well. It was obvious that there was hard muscle below the fat. His smile was pleasant, but his eyes were predatory. His face was very pale which contrasted with his very dark eyebrows and stubble. A circlet of pure platinum covered his pineal eye.

There was a definite family resemblance between him and Misha, more noticeable even than the one between Gabriella and the Lady Juliana. As the Wolves entered, Cezare looked up. He studied them with interest, and without fear. He was merely curious. There was a strange flatness in the man's scent that was different from any other Navigator's. If anything, he was even less readable than they. Ragnar felt as if he were in the presence of an alien being that happened to be wearing the flesh of a near-human. Reading Torin's scent, he could tell his fellow Wolfblade felt the same. There were other scents present that were partially concealed by those of the plants. They belonged to men – guards and observers within easy call.

Cezare smiled. There was a warmth and charm in his smile. His teeth were very white and square. 'Welcome, cousin. How do you like my garden?'

'It is very beautiful. It must take a considerable amount of work to keep it so.'

'All great and complex enterprises do,' said Cezare. 'Growing a garden is like running a House. You must know which plants to encourage and which weeds to prune out.'

Ragnar felt almost contemptuous of this man now, with his talk of gardens. Then he noticed what he was feeding the plants. He had extracted a small wriggling rodent from a sack and was pushing it still living and squirming into the bell of the orchid. After a few moments the animal's struggles ceased and its eyes took on a glazed and ecstatic look. Ragnar caught the whiff of narcotic perfume. His skin tingled faintly as his system analysed it and neutralised it. The plant had now swallowed the rat like a snake taking down its prey.

Seeing Ragnar's look, Cezare's smile widened. 'It's a prize this one, a Red Trapper Orchid, from Mako's World. Some of them can grow large enough to swallow a man.'

'I know,' said Torin. 'I have fought there.'

Ragnar realised there was a method to this madness. Thousands of subtle perfumes filled the air, and many of them were narcotic. The sheer profusion made it confusing, unless he concentrated. He felt like a man trying to hear a conversation in a room where very loud music was playing. Was Cezare aware of the Space Wolves' heightened senses? Almost certainly. Did he fear they might be able to read his emotions too, or was the meeting here for some other subtle purpose?

Cezare clapped his hands, and servants materialised from the forest of plants. Ragnar suspected there must be some concealed grav-tubes around here – so swift and smooth was their entrance. The sound of running water would easily cover the faint displacement of air. The men looked like servants, but Ragnar was sure they carried weapons.

He felt a little vulnerable. They were alone in the palace of one of Belisarius's greatest enemies, a man who had thousands of armed men on call. What would happen if they were to disappear here, he wondered? He dismissed the thought. If Cezare wanted them eliminated he would doubtless find a more subtle way to do it. He was simply off balance, confused by the unexpected surroundings and the scent.

Ragnar realised that it had been designed to make him feel that way. Without making an overt threat, Cezare had managed to make him uneasy and unbalanced. Torin was right. The man was subtle and dangerous. Still, even under these circumstances, Ragnar was sure he could snap his neck before a normal human could react. Cezare surely knew this and appeared completely at ease, even though Gabriella's bodyguards were far closer than his own.

He was brave then, and sure of himself. The servants produced a suspensor table and two floating chairs. Food and wine were swiftly placed on the cloth along with platinum cutlery. The food smelled highly spiced to Ragnar but that probably meant the Navigators found it a delicacy.

Ragnar moved around the clearing to cover one direction, while Torin moved in to cover the other.

The thick vegetation concealed almost all lines of approach. A hundred men could have been hidden there.

Suddenly, and so subtly that Ragnar almost doubted it, he felt a feather-light touch of a strange energy brush against his mind. Pysker, he thought. Immediately, he was on guard, automatic wards clanging into place in his subconscious. He began reciting protective litanies under his breath. He knew he should be safe – this was not a very bold or potent attack. Briefly he considered what he should do. Should he seek out the psyker? Should he accuse Cezare Feracci of employing sorcery against him? Considered reflection told him the answer was no. There was no proof, only his suspicion. Cezare would deny it easily enough and leave Ragnar looking like a fool. He held his tongue.

'You wanted to talk to me, Lord Feracci,' said Gabriella, smiling pleasantly. 'I am curious to know why the master of this House wishes to speak with me.'

'Two things,' he said. 'My son Misha likes you. He has done since the first ball you both attended. I am a shamelessly indulgent father. I would know how you feel about him.'

Ragnar almost felt Torin stiffen. He had not expected this. Gabriella too seemed flustered and a little off balance. Doubtless that had been Cezare's intention. Perhaps the subtle psychic probe had been aimed at him for a similar reason. 'I like him well. Are you talking of trothplight here?'

'Let us say I would find out what you and your family think of him as a potential match.'

'You must take it up with my family.'

'Indeed. We must open channels of consultation on this matter.'

Ragnar immediately saw that such channels could be used for other things. While negotiating a wedding, the two Houses could negotiate other things. Subtle indeed.

'I will take word of your… suggestion to my family.'

Cezare laughed heartily, reminding Ragnar of a tiger purring. He reached for his food and dug into it with gusto. 'Eat! Eat!' he said.

'You spoke of another matter,' said Gabriella, spearing some small silver fish that were swimming in the soup with her fork.

'Indeed. A most important matter,' said Cezare genially. 'Someone is assassinating Navigators. Just as they assassinated your late father. There have been attempts on my life. Two of my sons have disappeared. Several other Houses have taken casualties as well.'

'It would be in both our Houses' interests to find out who it is,' said Gabriella, obviously choosing her words carefully.

'I believe I already know,' said Cezare. 'What do you know of the Brotherhood?'

'They are a secretive society of zealots, popular among the underclasses. They preach in the ancient warrens below Terra. They call us mutants. They hate Navigators but no more so than other cults.'

'I believe they are the pawns of our enemies. Their fanatics slew your father. Two of them almost managed to kill me when I visited the Shrine of St. Solstice two days ago. Their intelligence is uncanny. Few were informed of my visit, and all of them were trustworthy. I confess at first I thought Alarik might be behind it but, taking into account the fate of your father, I am no longer convinced.'

Ragnar pondered the conversation. Why was Cezare confessing to weakness before a representative of his greatest enemies? There was more going on here than met the eye. Clearly Gabriella thought the same. Why had he mentioned the Belisarius chamberlain and then dismissed him? Such an accusation could have meant a declaration of war between Space Marine Chapters. Be careful, Ragnar told himself. You are not dealing with Space Marines here but something infinitely more devious.

'I can assure you that Alarik has nothing to do with this,' said Gabriella. Ragnar realised that was all she could say.

'I believe you,' said Cezare, his smile unwavering, but his tone full of contradictory meaning.

'What would you have us do about this?'

'We could pool resources, influence and information. To this extent I am willing to provide dossiers of our intelligence to you. I will have them delivered to your flitter before you depart.'

'That is most generous.'

'No. It is in my self-interest. These are troubled times. Our enemies multiply. The Navigator Houses must stand together or we shall all be swallowed separately.'

'You have given me much to think on. Be assured I will carry your words back to the Celestarch.'

'I can ask no more. Now if you will forgive me, I must go. The tides of commerce wait for no man. Prosper and be free,' he said, rising. Gabriella rose too. 'Please finish your food,' he said, stretching out his hand palm forward.

'Delicious as it is, I am not so very hungry, and my aunt waits.'

'Your loyalty to your family is worthy. The major domo will take you to her. Rest assured she is getting the finest care available on Terra. It is the least I can do for the first wife of my late brother.'

Cezare bowed to Gabriella, and nodded pleasantly to the two Wolves before striding off. Within seconds he was out of sight among the plants. There was a mere heartbeat in which the three of them were alone. Ragnar caught Torin's warning look. However, he was well aware that this was not the place to discuss anything.

'I trust you had a pleasant meal, milady,' said Torin.

'Delicious,' she replied. It was obvious they were exchanging a code phrase that Ragnar was not yet privy to. Perhaps Torin was simply letting her know they were not alone for a moment later, an immaculately clad man garbed in a long flowing top-coat of red and black emerged. His hair was cropped short and his spry walk suggested that he was a soldier, not a servant. He bowed, and said, 'My master has requested that you be shown to your aunt's chambers, milady. If you would be so kind as to follow me?'

Gabriella nodded and the man turned. The more Ragnar studied him, the more he was convinced that he was no simple servant. His movements and scent suggested a hard competence, as well as many sub-dermal implants. A cautious glance revealed that the man's hands were bionic, encased in synthi-flesh. One of his eyes seemed mechanical as well, although it looked so natural that most men would not have spotted it.

He was reminded of the men who had attacked them last night in the tavern. Was there some connection, he wondered? His mind drifted back to the psychic probe. There was a great deal more going on here than met the eye.

LADY ELANOR LAY in a huge suspensor divan that floated over the marble floor. Through her arched window Ragnar caught a view of the hundreds of lesser towers of the merchants quarter sprawling below. Enormous crowds of robed people flowed in endless tides along the roads. Ragnar had never seen so many, even on a hive world. But this was the navigators quarter of Terra, and a significant percentage of the trade of the entire Imperium probably passed through here.

Lady Elanor looked ill. One of her hands was cast in plaster. Her skin was sallow and jaundiced, the whites of her eyes were the colour of lemons. Her features were angular and gaunt, showing all the features of the Belisarius geneline. Gabriella set the small gift box she had brought on the table beside the bed and took her aunt's free hand.

'It is good to see you, child,' her aunt said, offering her cheek to be kissed. 'You have grown.'

'It is good to see you too, Lady Elanor. Although it pains me to see you so weak.'

'It will pass. It is the old ailment,' she said. 'So many of our clan have suffered.'

Gabriella paled a little. Ragnar heard her gasp sharply before she could suppress the reaction. 'How long do you have?'

'Months, perhaps weeks.'

'Have all the arrangements been taken care of?'

'Cezare is a very efficient man. He assures me I will be returned to the Belisarius Palace and the Vaults as soon as need be.'

Ragnar wondered if the woman was dying. Were the Vaults also some sort of necropolis? Perhaps that was why the Navigators were so secretive about them. Ragnar had seen many strange rites and rituals connected with death, and was aware of the tight security surrounding the protection of corpses.

The Lady Elanor certainly seemed ill enough. Her skin was so thin that it was translucent. A smell rose from the bed that was sickly sweet, like the corruption at the heart of an otherwise healthy plant.

'Anyway, I am glad you could visit. Come fill me in on all the details of your travels and the news of Belisarius. I understand you have been to Fenris.' She gave Ragnar and Torin an amused glance. There was a sly humour in it. Ragnar found himself warming to this frail, elderly-looking woman. 'Living among the Wolves.'

'Aye, that I have.' For the next few hours the two women exchanged seemingly inconsequential chatter, although, as Ragnar listened, he sensed concealed meanings beneath the surface like fish in a tidal pool. He wondered if he would ever understand the Navigators he had been sent to serve.

Two hours later, a man in the white and red uniform of a bonded physician entered the chamber. 'I am afraid that is all the talk I can allow for one day. The patient must conserve her strength.'

Gabriella nodded. The Lady Elanor clutched her hand once again. Ragnar could see that it was thin and all the veins were visible. 'Do come back and see me,' she said. There was a note of pleading in her voice.

'Of course, aunt,' said Gabriella, clasping the woman's hand with both of hers. 'But for now I had better go.'

Misha Feracci waited outside the chambers. A smile lit his handsome face. 'I thought I would escort you to your ship,' he said.

'I would like that,' said Gabriella.

RAGNAR WATCHED TORIN check out the flyer before they could climb in. A uniformed man presented them with a small folder before they departed. Gabriella placed it carefully within the internal storage compartment while Torin talked into the comm-net. Ragnar knew he was providing a record in case anything happened to them.

Misha stood on the ground below them and waved them off. The smile had not left his face during the whole trip back. The two of them walked along chatting amiably.

Ragnar did not like this development. It made him uneasy and he felt an instinctive dislike for the Feracci even as he found them impressive. Their tower was even more imposing than the Belisarius Palace and he had spent as much energy as he could memorising his way around it. It was unlikely he would be called upon to venture into the same places again, but you could never tell.

In any case, he had noticed incredibly dense surveillance. Televisor lenses and suspensor mounted floating eyes were everywhere, in far greater numbers than in Belisarius territory. But perhaps the Belisarians just kept them better hidden? Either way it spoke volumes about the nature of the House and its rulers.

No sooner had the bubble canopy slid into place than Torin said: 'Well, we're still alive.'

'That's hardly a surprise,' said Gabriella. 'Cezare Feracci would not have done anything to us while we were in his territory. It might provoke complaints to the Council of Navigators or draw unwelcome attention from the Inquisition.'

'We're not home yet,' said Ragnar. Torin had pulled the flitter into a steep climb and sent it arcing through the clouds towards the Belisarius Palace.

'What did you think of the place?' Gabriella asked.

'Security was very tight and very conspicuous,' said Ragnar.

'Don't be fooled,' said Torin. 'It was meant to be spotted. There are layers of more subtle sensors behind that.'

'How could you tell?'

'It's something of an area of expertise for me,' said Torin. 'I have studied it extensively since I came to Terra.'

'I believe my father spared no expense to see that you got a good education.'

'You believe correctly, milady.'

'Do you believe what he said about assassination attempts?' Ragnar asked.

'It's certainly possible. Religious zealots make no distinctions between the Navigator Houses. They want us all dead or at least off the sacred soil of Terra. "Suffer not a mutant to live", so they say.'

'Do you believe Cezare was serious about his offer of alliance?'

'It was not an offer of alliance, Ragnar. Far from it. He merely offered to share information. We shall see what his dossier contains. It might all be useless. Even if it contains useful information it might simply be a way of winning our trust or distracting us from Cezare's own plots.'

Wheels within wheels, plots within plots, thought Ragnar. 'No one here takes anything at face value, do they?'

'It would probably be a good idea for you to learn to do the same, Ragnar,' said Gabriella.

'He has already started, milady. Don't let Ragnar's barbarian act fool you. There is a mind at work there. I can almost see its wheels turning.' Ragnar did not know whether to be pleased or insulted by Torin's words, and he suspected that was his fellow Wolfblade's intention. 'A few years on Terra and Ragnar will be as smooth a plotter as old Cezare.'

That obviously was a joke, Ragnar thought. 'If he lives that long,' Torin added. Gabriella glanced over at Ragnar and smiled.

'What did you think of Misha?' she asked.

'I did not like him.'

'Why?'

'He reminded me too much of his father.'

'He seems pleasant enough.'

'Pleasant enough to marry?'

'I will never marry him unless I am ordered to.'

'Why?'

'I do not trust him either. And the Feracci bloodline has an odd, wild streak to it. It throws up many strange quirks – insanity and cruelty are common among them. They are brilliant but flawed, but then I suppose the same can be said of all the genelines.'

'Your aunt married into them.'

'Cezare's brother Lucio was one of the good Feraccis.'

'What happened to him?'

'He died mysteriously before Cezare came to the throne. Which is a pity since he would have made a better candidate.'

'How mysteriously?'

'A rare illness, or so it was said.'

'Like your aunt's?'

'No, that is something different.'

There was something in her tone that told Ragnar this was not a good subject to delve into. 'Some claim Cezare was behind Lucio's illness,' she said.

'And still he became lord,' said Ragnar disbelieving.

'They are strange ones, the Feraccis,' she said wistfully. 'It is said their Elders encourage the clan members to compete for the position of lord. They select the most ruthless and dangerous. If Cezare really was behind Lucio's death it would only serve in his favour.'

'That seems very wasteful,' said Ragnar. 'Killing a Navigator. You would think any House that did so would swiftly run out of members.'

'Only a very few are in the running to become Lord of Feracci and they know this from an early age. It would be wasteful and pointless to kill anyone who was not a rival. The Elders would not reward you for it.'

Ragnar considered this. It seemed that each House was as different from the others as the inhabitants of distant worlds were from each other. That was understandable. Over the millennia each House would have evolved its own culture and methods of survival. It was a big galaxy. There was room for numerous alternative and competing views. Indeed, he supposed it was better this way. If a weakness was revealed in one geneline's strategies, others would still survive. He guessed that any House that had managed to maintain its power and prestige since before the dawn of the Imperium must have evolved very efficient strategies indeed.

CEZARE LOUNGED BACKWARDS on the dais and considered the deadly man before him. He did not mind admitting that Xenothan made him nervous – more so than little Gabriella's precious bodyguards. The tall, slender, seemingly innocuous man was quite capable of killing everyone in this room – even Wanda, his pet psyker – and making it out of the Tower alive. Not for the first time, he found himself questioning the wisdom of the course he had charted. He smiled and shrugged. No great venture was ever undertaken without risks, and no great prize won without a gamble. His own career had proven this time and time again. The Elders had chosen him for his propensity for ruthlessness and cunning, and the fact he had eliminated all the other candidates including his own dear brother. He would not disappoint them.

'Well, what do you think?' he asked. His voice was clear, calm and commanding. It showed no trace of nervousness.

'The older of the two is a very dangerous man. The younger could become formidable given time. Both of them were aware of what was happening in the tavern.'

'We shall see he is not given time. You have them memorised?'

'Their look, their voices, their scents.'

'Can you kill them?'

'If you wish. When?'

'The time will be soon,' he said.

Xenothan smiled. There was no menace there, but it was chilling. Cezare told himself it was only because he knew what this man was – if 'man' was the term for a being so modified as he.

'You've decided, then?'

'Yes. Tell your master we will strike soon and eliminate our common enemies once and for all.'

A hint of menace entered Xenothan's manner. 'I have no master. Only patrons.'

'Then I should be obliged if you would inform your patron. We will move soon.'

He glanced over at Wanda. Soon she would need to send a message to her fellows in the Warrens below.

CHAPTER TEN

'WHAT DO YOU think?' asked Valkoth. 'What were your impressions? Tell me!'

Ragnar looked at the training area. The House guards of Belisarius were running the assault course under Valkoth's watchful eye. The soldiers were all Terrans. Many had long hair and drooping moustaches in the Fenrisian style.

They were trying hard but Ragnar knew that the youngest candidate for ascendancy on Fenris could have killed three of them easily. Then again, Fenris was a harder world than Terra. Men learned to survive there very early in the face of nightmarish elements, terrible monsters and even more terrible men. Those who did not learn quickly died.

He gathered his thoughts. It had been barely twenty minutes since the flitter had set down on the roof.

All three had been searched by a team of security retainers to ensure they had brought no long distance sensing devices into the palace. Gabriella handed the documents to the retainers for scanning and complete divination before heading off to present herself to the Celestarch. Torin had dispatched Ragnar to report to Valkoth, and had taken off on some mysterious mission.

'Cezare is a dangerous man.' Valkoth studied him carefully and Ragnar knew he was being measured and judged.

'In what way?'

'He is cunning, a schemer. He chose the location and the subject of the interview to throw us off balance. He conceals his emotions well. I find all Navigators difficult to read but he seemed even less human than normal.'

'I don't think you would find many people who would disagree with you, at least in private. People who speak out against the Lord Feracci in public tend to have short unpleasant lives.'

'That does not surprise me.'

'The Feracci are not sane in the way we define it, Ragnar. Most Navigators cannot be measured by any human standard, more so they. There is a streak of madness in them.'

'Why are they not put down like mad dogs?'

'Because that very streak of madness is what makes them superb Navigators. Feracci ships can travel further and faster than almost any others thanks to their Navigators' prowess. Only Belisarius, Helmsburg and True produce Navigators as good. The Imperium needs them. It needs all the Navigator Houses. It tolerates them as long as it goes on behind closed doors.'

On the training area, the men were engaged in mock skirmishes now. They had been divided into two sides and were armed with guns that fired pellets of dye. The dye contained an astringent which would cause pain but no permanent harm. They moved around obstacles that had been apparently set at random, towards goals at either end of the field.

'Anything else?'

'I have no doubt that we were observed with deep penetration scanners from the moment we entered the place. There was all manner of surveillance – from servants who followed us, to suspensor mounted televisors. I am equally sure our route was chosen so that we passed through sensor arches. I also believe there was some sort of psyker nearby.'

'It is rumoured that Cezare has a tame witch. A very powerful one. Perhaps several.'

'Bonded, of course.'

'Not even he would be mad enough to keep a potential heretic in his palace. Anything else?'

'The man intends harm to us all.'

'Of course he does. The two Houses are hereditary enemies. But they are also heads of the two largest and most powerful rival factions among the Navigators.'

'You do not think his offer of mutual aid was serious then?'

'Perhaps, but only if in the long run there is more advantage in it for him than us. We should be asking what he expects to gain from this.'

'All I know is he wants something,' said Ragnar. 'And I suspect he has planned something nasty for the very near future.'

'What makes you think that?'

'Instinct.'

'You would do very well to trust that instinct, Ragnar. I am certain that Cezare is setting a trap. We just need to make sure we do not set our heads in the noose.'

'What about the betrothal?'

'It might be serious. Gabriella is a superb Navigator which is why we got her. If her children receive her talent, they too will be great. Such children are a House's greatest resource.'

'So Cezare wants Gabriella then?'

'Maybe, or perhaps he wants to place his son within Belisarius. Who is taken in by whom would depend on the marriage contract.'

'Isn't that dangerous? It would be like having a spy within the House.'

'Perhaps. Adopted sons and daughters become members of their new House. They are supposed to be loyal to it. And they are closely monitored.'

'It sounds like madness.'

'It is their way. Some might consider them hostages. It depends on relations between parent and child.'

'From what I saw of Cezare I doubt he would hesitate to sacrifice a son.'

'He might surprise you, but I doubt it. Still, don't you think he must know that the Lady Juliana would be aware this?'

'I know that thinking about it is making my head spin.'

'Then I have something for you that will be more to your taste.'

'What?'

'We have a lead on the zealots who killed Adrian Belisarius.'

'How?'

'From the Lady Elanor.'

'What?'

'She passed her message on while you were with her.' Ragnar reflected on this. He had seen nothing change hands, but he knew there were ways. Dermal patches, microspores. The two women had probably been talking in a complex code as he had considered earlier. Alternatively, there could be a subtle psychic bond between kindred Navigators.

'How was that done?'

'They have their ways, and they choose not to share them with us. Nonetheless, the information was exchanged.'

'Under the very nose of Cezare! That seems rather too fortuitous.'

'Quite,' said Valkoth. 'Nonetheless, it corroborates information from Alarik's other sources.'

'How did she find this information? Why would she risk communicating it to us? I would take it all with a pinch of salt. It could easily be a false lead.'

'Indeed. The fact that she told us anything at all, means she is quite desperate. She appears to think that the survival of House Belisarius itself is at risk.'

'Could she not have waited for two weeks?'

'It's good to see that you use your brain more than Haegr. However, even if it were the case, the fact itself tells us something.'

Ragnar was intrigued now. 'Like what?'

'Like if the information is false we will have a chance to go over it in more depth when the Lady Elanor is returned to the Vaults in the next two weeks. Like the fact that she does not think we have two weeks.'

Ragnar turned this over in his mind briefly before saying, 'It sets a deadline. It tells us that if this is all part of some greater scheme, Cezare is expecting it to be done within the next couple of weeks.'

'Torin is right: you do have a brain. Also consider the fact that the information may be useful and true.'

'A sprat to catch a sea-dragon.'

'Precisely. The Feracci might be trying to suck us in to something bigger with useful information.'

'Is it really likely that Cezare would allow her to return to the Vaults when the time comes?'

'Yes.' There was absolute certainty in his voice.

'You seem very definite.'

'Ragnar, there are certain things that are sacred to the Navigators and limits that even Cezare will not transgress. The return of someone like Elanor is one of those things.'

'Why?'

'When you need to know, I will tell you.'

Ragnar was shocked. Valkoth appeared to be siding with Belisarius over his own Wolf brothers. What was the secret? What was so important about returning a sick woman to her family for burial? It seemed obvious that Valkoth was not going to share this with him, so he decided to try a different tack.

'What is this information?'

'There is a merchant, Pantheus, who fronts money for the various zealot Brotherhoods. There is a connection between him and House Feracci.'

'Which is?'

'Money. Power. Influence. We have had our eye on him for sometime. We believe he is the link between Feracci and certain zealot Brotherhoods.'

'If you have had your eye on him all this time, then Cezare must know he is compromised. He loses nothing by handing him to us.'

'Again, you are thinking, Ragnar. Pantheus disappeared some time ago. He went to ground just
before the assassination of Adrian Belisarius. We
believe we know where he is now. Elanor gave us
the last piece of the puzzle.'

'Or some fine bait for a trap.'

'Once you close your jaws on something, you
don't let go, do you, Ragnar? It's an admirable trait
in a Space Wolf.'

'Where can we find this merchant?'

'He has what he believes to be a secure mansion
in the asteroid belt. We are going to prove that it's
not secure. We will take off this evening. You will be
there.'

Ragnar nodded. Trap or no trap, this was more
like it. He was suddenly excited. The prospect of
combat was appealing. At least now the enemy was
clear and the goals straightforward.

THE BRIEFING ROOM was small, which was hardly surprising, since it was located in a small, sleek courier
ship belonging to the Belisarians. Present were
Valkoth, Torin, Haegr and Ragnar along with a
group of guards. Alarik, the House's Chief Intelli-
gencer and chamberlain was also there. At the
moment, he stood stage centre at the holo-pit,
dressed the same as he had been when Ragnar had
first seen him in the Celestarch's throne room.

'Pantheus is a rich man, because he fronts for various religious Brotherhoods on Earth. We have

gained access to certain Inquisition reports that suggest some of these Brotherhoods are recruiting grounds for our enemies. All of them have access to clandestine funding networks that they use to buy arms and equipment for their missions. Some run a nice sideline in extortion.

'Pantheus also has a lot of dealings with the Feracci. He started out with them in Gellan system fifty years ago, before branching out on his own. We believe his initial seed money came from Feracci. Interestingly, he worked directly with Cezare when the Lord Feracci was senior House representative in the sector.'

'There is a direct connection between Cezare Feracci and the Brotherhoods?' Valkoth asked.

'Almost certainly he has infiltrated agents into them. Most of the Houses have.' By implication, Ragnar thought, so have the Belisarians. Power, money, religion, and politics. They made a strange mix.

'In any case, Pantheus is not a nice man. He also deals in a number of illicit substances: narcotics, combat alchemics, as well as weapons. Every man is entitled to make a living, but this is going too far. We are going to pay Pantheus a little visit and administer suitable chastisement. I will be responsible for the interrogation.' Ragnar sensed there was a real personal animosity between the chamberlain and this merchant. He appeared to be looking forward to the questioning.

'We shall forcibly board his asteroid mansion. We shall kill his guards, and then seize him and his records. On departure we shall destroy the asteroid and any evidence of our visit. The main security datacore must be seized before we go. Jammers will prevent any comm-net transmissions so, unless Pantheus has an astropath with him, no one will ever know what happened.'

'You are certain he is there?' said Valkoth.

'The Lady Elanor has confirmed our suspicions. We have had a shielded monitor at the asteroid itself for some time. His ship arrived a day after Adrian Belisarius's assassination. It appears logical to assume that Pantheus himself was on board. The Lady Elanor seems to indicate that we must find out what he knows quickly if it is to be useful to us.'

'Guards?' asked Torin.

'He has a security detail recruited from Brotherhood thugs. They are tough and well armed. Some have bionic enhancements. All have access to military weapons and a supply of proscribed alchemics. They are all fanatical. It may be hypno-conditioning but I doubt it. I believe they are the genuine article.'

'How many guards?' asked Ragnar.

'One hundred and five.'

'That's a lot of security.'

'This assignment is a reward for loyalty. Many pleasures are available on the asteroid. Not all of the men will be on duty, although all will be capable of fighting at a moment's notice.'

'Defensive systems?'

'The asteroid has the usual anti-piracy defences. They will be neutralised before you go in. This ship has the capability.'

Ragnar did not ask why they were so sure. Normally in a battle between a ship and a fortified asteroid there could be only one winner. It was possible to mount more firepower on a hollowed out rock than in most small ships. The others seemed certain though. Presumably Belisarius's sources must be reliable. Or this ship must be a lot better armed than it looked.

'Gravity?' asked Torin. It could be important.

'No artificial sources. It comes from spin.'

Ragnar considered this. It meant the deeper they went into the core of the asteroid the less centripetal force there would be. This could create sudden fluctuations in apparent weight. Such things could be important in zero G combat.

'What about survivors?' Ragnar asked.

'There will be none. When you leave it will look like there has been an unfortunate but catastrophic collision with a stray meteor. Such things happen.'

The other Wolves grinned. Ragnar considered the odds. There were just the four of them but, as the plan was outlined, he considered that it would most likely work. They would fly in from the shielded ship using jump packs. Once down, they would use thermal charges to blow out a large section of the wall and let themselves into the tunnels. There was no point in being subtle. Any opening of an airlock would be noticed, and airlocks could easily become deathtraps if you were sealed in one.

Explosive decompression would cause the mansion's safety systems to kick in. Under the circumstances there would be confusion inside as the cause of the system failure was tracked. The enemy would waste time suiting up and going through standard decompression drills. The closing of bulkheads would divide their foes and isolate them in portioned sections, so it would be easier to dispose of them. The Wolves would move inwards towards the central datacore killing anything that got in their way. They would secure the record core, acquire the data and depart.

It was a simple enough plan, which was good. But Ragnar had enough experience to know that no matter how simple, no plan ever went smoothly even when executed by Space Wolves.

RAGNAR GRASPED THE controls of the jump pack and applied power. A jet of compressed gas from the attachment pushed it away from the side of the shielded ship. He was on the long slow trajectory towards the distant asteroid. He could hear nothing but felt a slight tremor in the pack as he moved.

The gas jet would give out no heat signature. And no power was being used so it should not be traceable by sensor divination. They were carrying too little metal to show up on magnetics. A human being would be too small to set off a standard proximity detector designed to warn of collisions with ships and large asteroids.

There was a slight chance that if someone was looking closely, they would notice the occlusion of the stars but here in the asteroid belt that would happen often enough with tumbling rocks and space debris. The chances that objects of their size could be spotted were infinitesimal, but the chance remained. It was enough of a possibility to send little shivers of controlled fear through Ragnar. It was one thing to die in battle in the fury of hand to hand combat. It was another to be blasted into non-existence by a defence laser in the cold, silent void of space.

His helmet was down and in position. His recyclers were working perfectly. If need be he could live for weeks out here in the void. Like all of his battle-brothers he was virtually a small, self-contained spaceship. Not that it would make much difference if they got this wrong. There was no way to drift anywhere close to civilisation if they could not make it back to the ship. If anything went badly wrong he would become just another piece of tumbling debris in endless orbit around the sun.

He wondered how many others were out there already. When he considered all the battles that had been fought in this system since long before the Imperium and the Horus Heresy, he was sure it was not a few.

The asteroid grew larger in his field of vision. He could see lights winking on its side. He could make out the huge crystal geodesic dome of the gardens that provided the mansion with some of its atmosphere. At one end of the asteroid was a forest of antennae and dishes that connected the asteroid to the comm-net. In a few minutes they would be jammed and shot out by the Belisarius courier. He wondered if there was anyone down there looking at him now, unaware of how little time he had left to live.

It is amazing how old ideas stay with you, he thought. In the immense void of space, down was a meaningless concept. The asteroid's gravity was insufficient to draw him in. From the outside a man could leap into space, its escape velocity was so low. Any direction could just as easily be up or down. Yet his brain insisted on imposing a framework on it. The asteroid was down. The ship was up. He told himself such preconceptions could be dangerous because in space combat you had to be able to think in three dimensions. Limiting yourself with concepts like down and up could be fatal.

The asteroid swelled, becoming first the size of an apple, then a boulder, then a house. It was as large as the icebergs in the Sea of Dragons in winter. Tunnels extended below its surface. He had the plans the Belisarian spies had managed to provide him with locked in his suit's systems.

He wondered how accurate they were. Presumably they were good for the Navigators to be risking so much on this raid, but you could not always be certain. All it would take would be for the informant to have missed one section or one hidden defence and the outcome could be terrible. Still, these were the risks you took. Ragnar was confident that he could overcome anything thrown in his path. He was one of the Chosen of Russ, after all. Be careful, he told himself. Overconfidence has killed more men than bolter shells. This was a hellishly inhospitable environment, and any mistake could easily be your last.

He glanced over and saw his comrades making the long drop. Somehow each looked exactly as Ragnar had imagined they would. Torin had his arms folded across his chest, holding the demolition charges, and a heavy bolter dangled in a sling at stomach level. He suggested relaxed confidence.

Haegr looked odd with his helmet on and his custom armour. His bulky silhouette was nothing like that of a normal Space Wolf. A huge hammer was strapped to his chest. Valkoth looked stern and forbidding even in freefall. His back was straight, his hands firm on the controls.

Ragnar turned back to the asteroid. He knew that perfect timing would be called for. It would take a five second burst of gas to kill his velocity before he impacted. A hard landing might result in injury, armour breach or even death. It would not be a glorious way to go. Ragnar did not want to be inscribed in the annals of the Chapter as the man who lost the Spear of Russ and then killed himself by banging into a rock.

The proximity detector attached to his armour gave its alert. Ragnar piked and twisted the throttles on the flight pack. In his peripheral vision he could see his comrades do the same. A moment later he braced his knees for impact. His boots grated on the hard surface of the asteroid. They were down.

The easy part was over.

CHAPTER ELEVEN

THE ASTEROID ROTATED below him. Its motion threatened to throw Ragnar off. He lifted his feet as the surface moved smoothly underneath him. He used the jet pack to move with slow controlled bursts. The others did the same. They resembled fish cruising along the bottom of an ocean.

In seconds they reached the point they intended to breach – a large window above the observation deck. From inside it would probably look more like a glass floor. The asteroid's rotation would push people down towards the outside walls as it simulated gravity.

Torin slapped the thermal charge into place. They scooted away from the blast area, taking cover in the crevasses covering the asteroid's rocky side. A moment later, a brilliant flash lit the shadows of the small canyon. Ragnar looked up and saw a glittering trail of crystal debris erupt. Air crystallised as it streamed into space. Plants and paintings and small pieces of furniture followed it.

They headed in. Ragnar increased the power of the jets to compensate for the outward rush of the gas. They could have waited for the decompression to be complete but time was precious now. Glittering contrails and earthshaking explosions told him that the courier had struck, taking out the comm-dishes and external defences.

Disorientation struck Ragnar as he piked through the blast hole. Suddenly up seemed down and down seemed up. He had gone from being on the outside to the inside of this hollow world and the two directions were now reversed. He somersaulted through the air and landed on his feet, hitting the restraint release button on the pack's harness with one hand while drawing his bolt pistol with the other. Before it hit the ground, his chainsword was in his hand and he was moving along the corridor.

Men lay on the ground with blood pumping from their noses, ears and mouths. They writhed in agony as decompression ruptured lungs and eardrums. He swung his chainsword, not wanting to waste bolter shells to put enemies out of their misery. The temperature dropped rapidly. Warning runes flashed on the walls proclaiming danger to any survivors within.

Ragnar did not like this. The helmet constrained his senses. He had to rely on his eyes now. Hearing and scent, the Space Wolves' primary sources of information, were useless when they were suited up. All he could catch was the sound of his breathing and the recycled stink of his own body. He glanced around and saw his companions moving into position, weapons drawn. Torin slung his heavy bolter over his shoulder as he fingered his utility belt for tools. Haegr brandished his enormous hammer.

For now, they were comparatively safe. Any foes would not yet have had time to suit up. Doubtless they were confused, unsure of what had hit them. Torin had moved to one of the internal airlocks. This was the risky part. If they wanted to take Pantheus alive they needed to get into the air-filled interior of the mansion. This meant using an airlock. Hopefully the confusion would help them, but things were still tricky.

Torin knelt by the door. He had a tool-kit in his hand and was swiftly stripping the lock's external covering. At the point of decompression, all the doors had sealed automatically but they could still be manually over-ridden. In seconds there was another cloud of freezing air as the door slid open. Moments later they were inside and letting air cycle out. Now things were getting dangerous.

If anyone was monitoring the airlock system at that moment, their position would be given away.

Hopefully, anybody at the control altars had other things on their mind. They might construe one airlock opening as some sort of system failure, but even if they did so, it would still attract their attention. An airlock malfunction in any sealed environment always would.

At least he could hear now, as air rushed in to fill the lock. There was little space for four huge Marines along with their weapons in this small space. Once again it was made graphically clear to him why airlocks had such a well-deserved reputation for being death traps in boarding actions. All it would take would be one well-placed grenade and the four of them would be sent to Russ's Iron Halls to await the Last Battle.

Ragnar found himself holding his breath, his eyes focused on the internal door. His weapon was at the ready. If someone was waiting to attack, he was certain he could snap off a shot before they could. His reflexes were far, far swifter than a normal human's, except if they were on combat drugs. This thought niggled at his mind.

Air filled the chamber now. Green indicator lights showed that pressure had equalised. Torin opened the internal door. They were in. There was air here too, and sound carried well enough. Ragnar could hear the warning klaxon's blare. Ahead of them lay a corridor and an elevator shaft leading upwards. Elevators were another death trap to be avoided. Ragnar unsealed his helmet and tasted the air. It was pure and breathable. His helmet would not have unlocked if it had not been.

A rush of unfamiliar scents hit him: purification essences, body odours, the never-quite extinguishable sewage smells of humans in a sealed environment. He greeted them all like old friends, taking in deep breaths, and orientating himself. He felt immediately more confident and capable, the master of his environment. He clipped his helmet to his belt. His comrades had done the same.

'Avoid the elevator. There should be a maintenance ramp around the corner,' said Valkoth. His dark lean face looked grim and more pensive than usual. He held his bolter steadily though, and there was no sign of tension in either his stance or scent.

They moved off past the elevator, Ragnar in front, Torin at the rear, and the other two in the middle. Ragnar felt adrenalin flood through him, bringing a peculiar sense of joy. He might die here, but he felt fully alive, knowing each minute could be his last. A wave of scent warned him before he turned the corner that he would find humans there.

There was a group of confused men, running to their emergency positions. One of them shouted into an intercom, demanding to know what had happened. They all carried sidearms. Ragnar did not wait for them to see him. He pumped bolter shells into the leader, and watched the man's head explode as if hit with a mallet. A second later Haegr stepped forward and reduced the rest of him to bloody shreds of red meat.

'What's going on? Report!' demanded a voice from the other end of the intercom. Torin strode past and bellowed, 'Hull breach, decompression, what the hell!' then he smashed the device with his gauntleted fist.

They raced up the ramp and entered a large open hallway. The wall hangings were luxurious. The lighting was dim and off centre. A great deal of religious imagery covered the walls: icons depicting the golden throne and the Emperor's Slaughter of the Mutants. One could almost have mistaken this place for the monastery of a particularly sybaritic religious sect. Perhaps that was what it was. Ragnar was not impressed by this outward show of piety. He had seen the followers of darkness wear the cloak of holiness far too often in the past.

Ragnar noticed that he felt lighter as they rose. More and more scents filled the air, criss-crossing and fading as the fans mingled the odour trails. There certainly were plenty of men in this mansion, he thought. One of them appeared in the arched doorway at the opposite end of the hall.

'Who the hell are you?' he asked. Ragnar shot him.

They proceeded towards another ramp. More men appeared behind the first and a volley of fire from the Wolves took them down. Ragnar heard footsteps receding. Obviously someone was trying to get away. He must not be allowed to sound the alarm.

Ragnar sprinted forward, and rolled through the archway, coming up in a crouch, hoping he would be below the line of fire of any enemy. A man dressed in brown stood at the far end of the corridor. He was shouting something into another intercom. Ragnar took aim and fired. The man went down with a huge sucking wound in his chest. Another shot smashed the intercom. Too late. The sound of the klaxon had become a jagged, rising wail. Ragnar surmised that this was a security alert.

'Looks like we've been spotted,' said Haegr from behind him.

'Really?' said Torin. 'I would never have guessed.'

'Good,' said Haegr. 'I never liked killing people who couldn't fight back.'

'You'll kill anybody necessary to get this job done,' said Valkoth. 'Don't you forget it!'

Haegr grunted. They moved onwards. All around them, Ragnar could sense the enemy mustering. The Wolves increased their pace. The faster they got away from the site where they had been spotted, the harder it would be for the enemy to use their superior numbers and their control of the facility against them.

As THEY ROSE towards the asteroid's core, the displays of piety grew more luxuriant and profuse. Glass cabinets in the walls held relics marked by golden placards. In swift succession they passed the finger bones of saints, prophets and scholars, the death masks of Imperial heroes, a bolter that had been borne by Commissar Richter. All the relics shared one thing in common: they were connected with famous men who had hated deviants with a passion.

It was not something of which Ragnar would normally have disapproved. His entire upbringing and all his training had drilled into him the idea that the mutant was mankind's greatest enemy. Strange, he thought, that now he was fighting in defence of those who many considered to be mutants. He pushed these thoughts to one side. He was coming dangerously close to the Sin of Relativism.

A wave of scent told him that doors had opened down the corridor. He whirled in time to see a group of armed and armoured men. Some had donned full-body armour, others were wearing military flak, and all carried lasrifles. Before any of them could fire, Ragnar opened up. His battle-brothers joined in. More men were cut down. Las beams splashed off the walls behind Ragnar, and blistered his armour. He ducked and weaved, trying to make himself a difficult target. In this narrow space, with a sufficient concentration of firepower, the enemy could not avoid hitting them.

A small egg-shaped object flew overhead from behind Ragnar. It bounced and rolled down the corridor into the chamber where the cultists lurked. A moment later an explosion smashed through the men. Screams and the scent of blood told Ragnar that it had even got those out of sight. They moved on.

A crackle of static in Ragnar's earbead told him that the courier had managed to patch itself into the asteroid's internal comm-net. He could hear a dozen voices gabbling away now.

'There are dozens of them!'

'Hull breached in three places.'

'Enemy sighted in quadrant four.'

'Have found bodies. Signs of mutilation.'

'I swear I saw Space Marines.'

'What?'

'What is going on?'

'Wolves.'

'Belisarius. It must be Belisarius.'

'The Emperor watch over you!'

Ragnar muted the volume in the earbead so that it did not interfere with his concentration. It sounded like the defenders were reeling in shock and confusion. Hardly surprising: the runes on his chronometer told him that they were barely minutes into the mission. Until now, many of the survivors would still be busy suiting up and trying to deal with the hull breach.

So far, so good, he thought, wondering exactly when things would start to come unstuck.

* * *

THEY FOUND THE door of Pantheus's chamber sealed and locked down. He had obviously decided to barricade himself in until the source of the emergency was clear.

Ragnar looked at the portal. It was a heavy blast door with some sort of complex security lock. It would take heavy cutting gear to get through it. They did not have the gear. He patched into the comm-net. Voices told him that the enemy was starting to regroup and sweep the place for their foes. They obviously had not yet realised their comm-links had been breached so their progress could be monitored.

Valkoth looked at Torin. 'How long?' he said.

'It's an old design. Responds to digital code or eye-scan.'

'I did not ask what it was. I asked you how long to get through it.'

'Thirty seconds,' said Torin. He knelt with his tools and began to prod at the interior of the lock. Ragnar wondered where he had learned these skills. They had certainly not been taught during his training as a Wolf.

'Ragnar stop gawping at Torin and cover the corridor. Haegr you take the other direction. Maybe you could stow the hammer and use a ranged weapon for a change.'

'That's hardly sporting,' said Haegr, clipping the hammer onto straps on his back harness, and drawing a pair of bolt pistols. Ragnar swung his attention to the corridor, keeping his bolt pistol ready for any foe that should appear. An enormous belch told him that Haegr was bored.

Ragnar tuned back into the comm-net. Their foes were closing in. Some of them had broken out heavy weapons. The fight looked like it was going to be a lot more difficult now. The real problem would be taking Pantheus out through a firefight. That was where they were going to need all their skill.

A whoosh of air told him the lock had given way. 'That was forty-five seconds,' said Valkoth.

'The mechanism had a booby trap attached and activated. I thought it better to take the extra time than to have the lock melt and take my hand off.'

'He couldn't comb his moustache if he lost a hand,' said Haegr. 'A tragedy.'

Torin was already in the chamber and covering it with his bolter. The furnishings were fit for a Navigator Prince. A massive mirror dominated one wall.

'He must be as vain as you, Torin,' said Haegr.

'But not as handsome,' said Torin, admiring his reflection.

'Less jokes, more speed,' said Valkoth. 'Where is the bastard?'

He moved deeper into the chamber. A moment later he was reaching into a massive wardrobe and pushing aside a mass of heavy furred robes. Quickly he pulled out an enormously fat man. Ragnar recognised Pantheus from the intelligence briefings. He floated lightly in the low gravity of the core. Doubtless that was why he had chosen this place for his apartment.

'Not as handsome as me, but almost as fat as you,' said Torin.

'He lacks my rugged Fenrisian nobility,' said Haegr.

'Haegr cover the door,' said Valkoth.

'Good choice,' said Haegr. 'Torin would spend too much time admiring himself in the mirror.'

Valkoth pinned Pantheus to the wall and inserted the muzzle of his bolter into one nostril. It was a tight fit. 'Where do you keep your records?'

The man's fear was palpable but he controlled himself well. 'This is an outrage. I will lodge a complaint with…'

'You are exactly one heartbeat away from death,' said Valkoth. His cold smile revealed his fangs. There was nothing remotely human about his expression at that moment. Pantheus might well have been looking at some hideous legendary ogre. Valkoth's scent told Ragnar that he was not going to kill Pantheus, but there was no way the merchant could know that.

He reached down towards his chest. Valkoth's free hand caught his wrist. The merchant winced. 'I keep my records in a memory crystal locket. I am not reaching for a gun.'

'It would be the last thing you would ever do,' said Valkoth.

'Don't you think I know that?' Pantheus produced a glittering gem on a platinum necklace. Ragnar could sense the tension in his comrades ease slightly. They had been prepared to respond if the merchant had drawn a protective device. There was nothing threatening about him, particularly.

Valkoth took the gem and inspected it, dropping the crystal into a small scanner he produced from his utility belt. Runes showed it was safe and a data-source.

'And the rest,' said Valkoth. Pantheus nodded to the wall. It was a portrait of himself looking considerably younger and thinner. The apparition was so different it could have been another person.

'Open it,' said Valkoth. 'No tricks or you die.'

The fear smell intensified. Here was someone who obviously believed the worst about the Space Wolves.

Pantheus walked over to the portrait and passed his hand over a series of runes. He muttered an incantation of opening under his breath. The picture slid aside. Treasure glittered within. Not just memory crystals but jewels of all sorts. The merchant kept a small hoard here for emergencies. Judging from the way Torin was sweeping it into a rolled up pillowcase it would soon be swelling the coffers of the Belisarians.

Valkoth passed his scanner over the pillowcase. It bleeped, and runes told of datacrystals there. It looked like they had got what they came for. Now all they had to do was make their way to an escape pod and rendezvous with the courier. Easy, thought Ragnar sardonically. He knew better. Things had gone too smoothly. They were bound to take a turn for the worse soon.

The sound of Haegr's pistols blasting away told him he was right. Trouble had already found them.

CHAPTER TWELVE

'Take it, take it all,' said Pantheus. 'Just let me go.'

Valkoth smiled grimly. His drooping moustaches and long fangs made it look more like a snarl. 'You're coming with us.'

'What? Where?' The merchant looked ready to burst into tears. He hardly seemed like a deadly conspirator. Maybe he was just in shock. It was not every day four Space Wolves broke into your secure asteroid and abducted you from your sleeping chamber. It would be enough to unsettle most people.

'You're coming with us. That's all you need to know.'

'But my collection. I can't leave all my precious icons.'

'They will be leaving you soon enough.'

'What do you mean by that?'

Valkoth raised his bolter and aimed it directly at Pantheus's head. 'No more chatter. You're coming with us. Ragnar, watch his back.'

Valkoth turned on his heel and moved with Torin towards the door. Ragnar put his bolt pistol to Pantheus's spine. 'Move,' he said. 'Or you'll have a hole in your stomach big enough to put your head into.'

Pantheus moved.

HAEGR HAD ADVANCED down the corridor. Ragnar could tell by the sound of bolter blast. Las fire splattered the walls. The surface had fused and run, and paintwork was blistering off to reveal the hard rock beneath. Torin and Valkoth moved out. Torin turned to cover behind them, while Valkoth bounced forward in the lowered gravity, adding his bolter fire to the blaze of Haegr's pistols. Nothing much remained alive in the corridor now. A pile of corpses smouldered slowly. Haegr and Valkoth moved through them.

Ragnar prodded Pantheus with his bolt pistol again. The merchant moved forward effortlessly, well adapted to the low-gravity. For the moment he did not appear to be having much difficulty in keeping up with the Wolves. They would see what happened soon when he felt the increased weight of his bulk on the lower levels.

* * *

COMM-NET communications told Ragnar that the crew of the asteroid had worked out what was happening. They knew Pantheus's chamber had been breached and that he was taken. It should be fairly easy for them to work out what would happen next, although so far no one had. If he had been in charge, he would have had all the external airlocks and escape pods covered.

Perhaps he was being unfair to the enemy commanders. They had other things on their minds and normal men simply were not capable of thinking and responding as fast as Space Marines. The walls of their asteroid had been breached and unless they were resealed, they would be dead. He doubted there were enough reserves of air to replace what was being lost. And then there was the courier, a formidable enemy craft that had sliced through their long range comm dishes and defensive emplacements. It looked like the element of surprise had been overwhelmingly successful. His chronometer told him that less than ten minutes had passed since the operation had begun.

As they progressed down the levels, resistance stiffened. Everyone was aware that there were enemies on board. They were watchful, and armed, mostly garbed in light space armour. Such was the speed of the Marines' advance that they swiftly overwhelmed anyone they encountered. They always fired the first shot, and often that was the last.

* * *

PANTHEUS'S BREATH CAME in gasps and he seemed in danger of foundering. Ragnar guessed he was feeling every extra kilo, although the gravity here was still far less than Earth's. He wondered what the man did when he was on the surface of Terra. Doubtless he used suspensors to lighten his weight.

Ahead of them lay the escape pod they had marked for their escape. Just as they entered the corridor a group of men in brown uniforms appeared at the other end. Haegr opened fire cutting them down. Ragnar bundled Pantheus into the escape pod.

'Go with him, Ragnar,' said Valkoth. Despite feeling the urge to stay and fight, Ragnar did not. They could not take the chance that the merchant might activate the pod without them. Without their locator beacon, the pod would be destroyed by the courier. The Belisarians were not about to risk anyone escaping to tell the tale. Ragnar threw himself in beside the merchant, weapon at the ready.

Outside, the others continued to blast away. Ragnar understood why. Like elevators, escape pods could be death traps if attacked at the wrong moment. If someone tossed a grenade while the door was open, the blast could be catastrophic in a contained area. Las fire bristled all around the Wolves now. Some of it hit. Ceramite armour blistered in several places. One by one, the others jumped in through the pod's doorway, until only Haegr was left.

'Come away now!' said Valkoth when it looked like he might want to blast away all day. Haegr growled. His beard bristled, and his piggy eyes squinted. It looked for a moment as if he might disobey. Valkoth growled and there was no mistaking the menace and command in his voice. It was like a wolf pack leader calling down a young and inexperienced challenger. Somewhat abashed, Haegr snapped off a couple more shots and then threw himself in.

'Strap yourself in,' Valkoth barked at the merchant. The rest of them were already fastening the restrainers, and slamming their helmets back into place.

Torin hit the quick release rune, and the escape pod blasted free of its restrainer bolts and headed down the launch slip into space. On the comm-net the Wolves finally broke silence as their beacons began to toll out. Acceleration pushed them flat into the padded couches. Pantheus's fat rippled like waves. The effect was particularly noticeable on his double chins.

'Well, we made it,' said Torin.

'Only if the Belisarians manage not to blow us to bits,' said Haegr.

Ragnar looked through the porthole and saw the asteroid recede behind them. Moments later an inferno of explosions bristled on its surface as the courier began to reduce it to rubble.

'So much for an asteroid impact,' said Torin.

'I don't think anyone will be coming to look soon. And once they finish with the devastator charges, there will be little enough to find.'

Pantheus gulped air. He was very pale. Ragnar was hardly surprised. He was watching billions of ducats worth of mansion being reduced to rubble. And he was in the grip of men who would not shrink from doing him serious personal harm. The merchant had doubtlessly known better times.

It was almost an hour before the courier picked them up, and waiting was uncomfortable for Ragnar. As always, there was the possibility of something going wrong. A stray rock or munition might hit them. The systems might fail and kill Pantheus. Such things had been known to happen. He was glad when the huge form of the courier appeared in the porthole and scooped them into its maw, like a whale gulping down krill.

Alarik awaited them in the landing bay. Sailors on the courier covered the escape pod with lasrifles, doubtless in case they had made a mistake and taken the wrong pod. Valkoth stepped out first, bolter pointed at the ceiling. Under the circumstances, when armed men were nervous, it was best to take no chances of there being any misunderstanding.

'I see that you got him,' said Alarik.

'Did you doubt it?' asked Haegr.

'Things sometimes go wrong,' said Alarik. 'No matter how good the troops are and how good the plan.'

'Well they didn't,' said Haegr. He sounded almost huffy. 'They never do when mighty Haegr is involved.'

'Haegr fights like two men,' said Torin. 'Which is easy for him since he has the bulk of four.'

'I see I have neglected your customary beating too long, Torin,' said Haegr. 'All here know that I have the valour of five men.'

'And vanity enough for ten.'

'I see you are determined to deny the truth and get the last word,' said Haegr. 'Fortunately I am not so base as you.'

Alarik's men took Pantheus off into custody. He looked defeated and shrunken, like an inflated bladder that has had the air let out of it. Ragnar noticed he was limping. He was obviously not used to bearing his own weight, and was well aware of what was waiting for him in the interrogation chambers.

'I would not feel too sorry for him, my friend,' said Torin. 'Pantheus has been responsible for the deaths of many good men.'

'I'm hungry,' said Haegr. 'Killing always works up my appetite.'

'Sleeping usually does that as well,' said Torin.

'Go, get something to eat. Take a rest,' said Valkoth beginning to stride away, adding, 'Well done.'

* * *

AFTER THE VIOLENCE of the attack on the asteroid, Ragnar felt unsettled. The moments of battle lived in his memory with peculiar intensity, and everything else seemed dull and colourless compared to it. He had heard it said that Space Wolves were made that way. Parts of their brains had been altered to respond precisely that way, so they were keen for combat. Ragnar was not sure this was the case. Perhaps it was simply a product of the process that had awakened the beast within him. Perhaps the heightened memories were simply a product of his heightened senses working to keep him alive.

He prowled around the ship, like a wolf coursing for the trail of deer. He did not want to sleep. He had no desire for wine or ale. He was not hungry. He was uneasy. It was partly due to the unfamiliar scents around him. Normally when he came back from a battle there would be the scent of many brothers around him. If they were on a ship, the air would be filled with the familiar scents of Fenris and the flesh of those who had served in the Chapter's fleets.

Now he was somewhere else. The incense in the recyclers, the icons on the duralloy walls, the uniforms of those around him were not what he was used to. All that reminded him of home were the faint scent trails of his fellow Wolfblades. But even these were different: they carried the effects of many years of living on Terra, consuming different food, being surrounded by different things.

He was a long way from home now. Get used to it, he told himself. It is your duty to serve the Emperor and the Chapter no matter where they send you. If you live long enough you will doubtless be sent to stranger and less hospitable places than this.

It was one thing to possess knowledge of the complex mix of Imperial politics. It was another thing to live through it, and learn it first hand, just as there was a world of difference between reading a tale of a battle in a scroll, and actually meeting a foe breast to breast, and sinew to sinew.

His footsteps had taken him to part of the ship he had avoided. He noticed there was an immediately recognisable taint to the air. Blood, he thought. And sweat, and pain all mingled with faint traces of ozone. He moved closer and his ears, keener than an ordinary man's, picked up what could only be screams from what was meant to be a sound-proof door. As he rounded a corner, two men in the uniforms of Belisarius's guard raised their weapons. Their movements seemed absurdly slow to Ragnar. Before they had brought their weapons to bear, he could have drawn his own, or sprung forward and snapped both their necks.

They recognised him and lowered their weapons once more. He could not help noticing that they both looked pale and there was a faint sheen of sweat on their brows. Clearly they knew what was going on beyond the sealed door. Ragnar did too.

Pantheus was being questioned. He shook his head in disgust as he strode past. This was something he did not like.

It was one thing to kill your foes in clean combat, it was another to torture them for information. He shook his head again as he considered his softness. He knew that torture was one of the instruments of Imperial rule. The Inquisition used it. Planetary Governors used it when information was needed. He knew all the arguments in its favour. Better a dozen heretics should know agony than a single innocent suffer. Did heretics not deserve whatever punishment was heaped on them?

Maybe, he thought. He understood the logic of it, but once again, it was one of those things where knowledge and reality were two separate things. And he knew that no matter how long he lived, he could never approve of it.

The idea that Pantheus might not even be a heretic but a devout follower of the Emperor gnawed at him. What was going on here was nothing to do with the protection of the Imperium or the preservation of humanity. It was about one faction seeking political advantage over another. It was just another skirmish in the long struggle in which one immensely rich and powerful group within the Imperium sought to gain the upper hand.

The beast within him stirred. It understood cruelty and darkness and the compulsion to triumph over your rivals. It whispered that his life might depend on the knowledge gained here, along with his honour and the security of House Belisarius that his Chapter had pledged to uphold. And it might not, came the response. The man whimpering beyond that mass of sealed metal might know nothing. Only time would tell.

He strode down the corridor, wishing that he could leave his evil thoughts behind, but knowing that he could not.

'WHAT'S THE MATTER with you, Ragnar?' Valkoth asked as he strode into the chamber where the others meditated. 'You look like orks pissed in your ale.'

'There are some ales on Terra that would improve,' said Haegr knowledgeably.

'I passed the place where Pantheus is being questioned.'

'And?' Valkoth sounded genuinely interested, and his scent confirmed this. The others were giving him their full attention.

'It sounds like they were carving the blood eagle on his back.'

'I doubt the Navigators would do anything so unsophisticated,' said Torin. 'They are using machines. Neural induction coils, electrodes. Drugs as well, I would imagine.'

He sounded a little too knowledgeable for Ragnar's liking.

'The old ways are the best,' said Haegr. 'Though I doubt any of those effete Terrans would have the stomach for the eagle. They might get some blood on their nice uniforms.'

'Maybe you should go and show them how it's done,' said Valkoth sourly.

'Don't suggest it,' said Torin. 'Haegr would only forget what he was supposed to ask and try and learn where he kept all his food.'

Ragnar did not find the joke funny. He was shocked by their attitude. They obviously shared none of his qualms or queasiness about what was being done. He could tell from their manner, their voices and their scents. Was it possible that he was the only one who saw anything wrong here? If so, was it possible that he was the one who was wrong, who was out of step with his comrades and his world? Was all this just the sign of some weakness in himself?

He shook his head and stared bleakly out of the porthole. The steel clad mass of Terra was visible once more. He was not glad to be back.

CHAPTER THIRTEEN

RAGNAR LAY IN his chamber in the palace and stared at the ceiling. He could not help but notice the elaborate plaster patterns there, complex swirls of leaves and coins forming what he thought was the star pattern over Fenris. He would have much preferred the actual stars himself, but it seemed no one was consulting him.

Gravity tugged at him again, and the air held the distinctive tang of Old Earth. He considered it. This was air that had been breathed a billion, billion, billion times. It was tainted with the dust of ages. The weight of the buildings around him appeared incredible and oppressive. He realised that this palace was older even than the Fang. Yet the Fang was a solitary miracle, a huge base hidden in a gigantic mountain that was one of the wonders of the galaxy. This palace was surrounded by buildings just as old and situated atop layers of buildings even more ancient. He had heard it said that all the ancient civilisations of Earth could be found here still, buried in layers. And if you dug deep enough you would find the remains of even such legendary ancient places as Atalantys and Nova Yoruk. It certainly seemed possible.

A strange languor filled him. The events of the previous day could have happened to someone else in a different lifetime. The thick pile carpet, the heavy wooden furniture, and the ancient works of art conspired to make his memory of the battle dream-like. Such things could not happen here, they whispered. Everything was too ancient, too civilised, too comfortable.

He forced himself upright. That was an illusion, he knew. Many many times, the streets and warrens of old Terra had run with blood. No doubt battles had been fought within the walls of this very palace. Certainly there must have been killings, and stealthy murders a plenty.

Someone knocked on the door. The scent told him who it was before he said: 'Enter.'

'Greetings, Ragnar of Fenris.'

'Greetings, Gabriella of Belisarius. What brings you here?'

She paused for a moment. 'I wanted to see how you were finding things here.' Ragnar rose from the pallet and moved across the room towards the food on the table. It was simple Fenrisian fare.

'Strange,' he answered truthfully. 'Not what I expected.'

'What did you expect?'

'Holiness. Sanctity. The radiant presence of the Emperor.'

'You will find all of those on Terra, though not in the Houses of the Navigators. Our religion is commerce. For us gold has a sanctity all of its own.'

Ragnar knew he should have been shocked to hear such words spoken but he was not. They echoed only too well what he thought himself. 'You sound as if you do not approve.'

It was her turn to smile. 'I fear I have spent too much time among the stalwart warriors of Fenris. It may take me a little time to get used to being back here.'

'You'd better not take too long,' said Ragnar. 'It might prove fatal.'

'Yes,' she said. 'That is the hard part. In all my time among the Wolves I have seen a great deal of action and faced no small amount of danger, and yet I was never threatened by those around me. I had no need to guard my words or thoughts. I knew who my enemies were. They did not smile or offer me wine or feign interest in my conversation. They fired weapons at me across the gulfs of space. I miss such simplicity. And I fear I shall miss it more in the days to come.'

He studied her closely, wondering if he should take her at face value. He thought about it from all angles, as he always did. It was a mark of how his few days on the holy soil of Terra had changed him, he thought. If he took them at face value, he could sympathise with her. He too felt out of place amid the murky waters of Navigator politics. But there were other things to be considered. If she was not speaking generally, and he doubted she was – for he had learned that Navigators rarely did anything without purpose – then she had talked with those she felt were her enemies. It was possible she did fear for her life.

'Why are you telling me this?'

'Because you are a familiar face from the time before I came back. You are a link to that simpler time.'

It could be, Ragnar thought. It made a certain emotional sense although he was hardly what she could call a close friend. And he had saved her life, so maybe she felt secure with him. Furthermore, she had every right to feel threatened: her father had just been assassinated and her clan was surrounded by potent enemies.

'Has someone threatened you?' he asked.

'Not specifically.'

'What do you mean by that?'

'I mean that I feel uneasy, and I sometimes see hidden meanings in the simplest things.'

'That I can understand,' said Ragnar.

'Perhaps, but I doubt you can understand precisely how complicated my life is.'

'Explain it to me.'

'Things are very simple for you, aren't they?'

'Are they?'

'I see you have not spent your time here without profit.'

'You have not explained your situation to me. Do you not wish to?'

She paused for a while and then spoke calmly and clearly. 'There are factions within Belisarius, just as there are among the other Navigator Houses. You know what they say: when two Navigators meet you get three conspiracies. Since I have been away I have not been part of any political camp. Now, several of them have approached me, to see if I will support them.'

'Is that such a bad thing?'

'No, it is to be expected. But there are the usual hints and veiled threats.'

'From whom?'

'From various people, Skorpeus included.'

'Do you take them seriously?'

'After what happened to my father and what happened on the ship? I take everything seriously. Things are in a state of flux now. The whole family teeters on the edge. There are those who would take advantage of this and they are not scrupulous.'

Ragnar thought perhaps things were exactly as she said. Perhaps she was merely talking to him because he was outside the family power structure and so was no threat to her. Perhaps. Then again she might have some ulterior motive. Was she trying to recruit him? He had saved her once. It might be convenient to have him do it again. He considered this and could see nothing wrong in it. He was here to protect the Belisarians, even from each other. Still, he wanted to be sure that he understood exactly what was going on.

'Do you want me to be your bodyguard?'

'No. That is not your decision to make anyway. You must perform the duties the Lady Belisarius gives you.'

'True, but there is nothing to stop me from keeping my eyes and ears open. You of all people should know how keen they are.'

'Would you?' There was hope and gratitude in her voice, and a few days ago it would have stirred his heart. It did so now but it also excited his suspicions. He felt as if he was being drawn more tightly into a web. He knew that there would come a time when his personal loyalties and duties might come into conflict if he allowed this to continue. He drew back his fangs in a snarl. He would cross that bridge when he came to it.

'I am meeting with my cousin Skorpeus in an hour. I would be pleased if you would accompany me.'

'I doubt your cousin would talk freely with me present.'

'Perhaps that is my purpose.'

Ragnar shrugged. 'It would be my pleasure to accompany you.'

THE VIEW FROM the top of the Belisarius Palace was stunning. Ragnar could see as far as the horizon, through the polluted haze. Pollution diffused and refracted the sunlight creating a rainbow effect across the entire sky. He had a view of all the craggy old starscrapers and massive temples and palaces of the navigators quarter. Gabriella pointed out the various abodes of different Navigator families, and their own personal space fields.

She seemed happier now, and more pleasant to be with. Her cares had fallen from her. She seemed almost playful, although that was perhaps too strong a word given her Navigator's self-control. Behind the playful mask he sensed steely self-control.

All around them servants came and went constantly. She seemed no more aware of them than she was of the furniture. Ragnar was; he had to be. Every person who came within striking distance was a potential threat and had to be treated as such. There had been one attempt on Gabriella's life already, and her father had died even though he was surrounded by his own guards. He wondered how easy it would be to get another assassin into the palace. Easy enough, he supposed, with the right contacts.

It was as wearing as spending nights on patrol, constantly having to be on guard and concentrating on the conversation at the same time. He knew that he needed to pay attention. Navigators did not waste words. Indeed they believed in making one sentence carry as many meanings as possible, most of them ambiguous. Was it part of their mutation he wondered? Did their minds think in this mazy fashion because of the way they were born, or because of the society they were born into? Perhaps a little of both, he decided.

A servant came too close and Ragnar glared at him. The man backed away, startled. Ragnar could smell his fear and the sense of panic he inspired. It was a little galling, he thought. Here he was standing beside a known mutant, and he, one of the Emperor's chosen, was the person that normal people were afraid of. It did not make a whole lot of sense.

'What are you thinking about?' The Navigator asked.

'Why are the people here so afraid of me? Some of them hate me, and they do not even know me.'

'You are a Space Marine,' she said, as if that explained everything.

'So?'

'The people of Terra have bad memories of Space Marines.'

'Bad memories? The Chapters have defended humanity for ten thousand years. They should be grateful to us.' Ragnar was surprised by the strength of his avowal. Something had touched a nerve.

'The Warmaster tore this planet apart. He reduced areas with populations of hive worlds to molten slag. His people offered up millions to his dark gods.'

'Horus was not a Space Marine,' retorted Ragnar immediately, but even as the words left his mouth he regretted them.

'No. He was a primarch. His followers were Space Marines.'

'That is perilously close to being an insult.'

'It also happens to be the truth.'

Much as he would have liked to deny it, Ragnar could not. 'Surely the folk here know that the Wolves had no part in Horus's rebellion? We came here and fought against it.'

'Aye, and your forebears were not gentle either. They killed many people.'

'Many heretics.'

'That may be, but the people here remember them as their neighbours and friends and kin. They remember you as off-worlders who brought fire and death to the soil of Terra.'

Ragnar was silent. His training and indoctrination had not prepared him for this. He had always thought of his Chapter as heroes. He had imagined that those who knew them would at least respect them, while others would admire them. He had not expected to be hated. And this woman was telling him that the folk of the most sacred world of the Imperium feared and hated them.

'Fire and death are the shield maidens of war.'

'And you think that good. But people whose trade is not battle do not.'

'They are weak.'

'Such contempt will win you a great deal of friendship, I am sure.'

Ragnar could see that this was not an argument he was going to win, particularly as he suspected that Gabriella was telling an unpalatable truth. Did it change anything? Ragnar supposed not. The Wolves would do their duty regardless of whether the people they protected loved or hated them. In reality what they felt was irrelevant.

The Navigator smiled as if she could read his thoughts.

'You can see why my people and yours are natural allies,' she said. 'We are both powerful groups that the Lords of the Imperium have no reason to love.'

Perhaps it was true, but it was not the reason they were allies. 'The Wolves are bound to you by the word of Russ. That is why we are allies.'

'And do you think Russ did not see the reasons why such an alliance would be necessary? He too was a primarch and far sighted.'

Ragnar was not sure that was entirely correct. Most of the tales of Russ portrayed him as a bold warrior, a little reckless and heedless of the needs of politics when honour was involved. Still, he was a primarch, and who could say what visions such a mind could encompass? These thoughts brought him back to the Spear of Russ that he had so thoughtlessly lost. Was it possible that Russ had foreseen this, or was Ragnar thinking this because he wanted to believe it?

A faint whiff of perfume and the pheromone trace of the Navigator gene told Ragnar that someone approached. He turned his head and saw it was Skorpeus and his ever-present henchman. If the would-be inheritor of the throne of Belisarius was disconcerted to see him there, he gave no sign of it. He smiled smoothly and bowed to his cousin and then to Ragnar. Ragnar nodded back.

'Sweetest cousin, it is a pleasure to see you once again. Shall we walk?' He offered her his arm, and they linked arms and strode across the roof. Ragnar and Beltharys fell in behind. They were far enough behind that they could not hear anything but close enough so that Ragnar was aware of every word being said.

'I hear talk of marriage in the air, lovely Gabriella,' said Skorpeus.

'Whose?'

'Why, your own! There is no need to be coy. It is the talk of the palace. We all know the purpose of your visit to that old monster Cezare.'

'I visited the Feracci tower to see our aunt. She is sick.'

'Of course,' said Skorpeus, giving a sardonic little cough. 'But other things were talked about. They always are.'

'Other things were talked about, but why is this of interest to you?'

'A Feracci married to a Belisarius, a strengthening of the ties between our two Houses just as old Gorki lies on his death bed. Do you think this is a coincidence?'

'There have been many marriages between our Houses before. Two hundred and twelve to be precise.'

'I see you have been studying the Books of the Blood, sweet cousin, to know the figure so exactly.'

'Obviously I have an interest.'

'Obviously. Do you not think it… interesting that old Cezare has offered his son as a prize to our House while all the time he is twisting the arms of the lesser Houses right and left to get that same son elected to the High Council of the Administratum?'

Gabriella stopped short. She turned and looked directly into her cousin's face for the first time, laying her hand on top of his. He seemed to flinch from the contact for some reason. 'That is news to me.'

'It is news to most folk but nevertheless I assure you it is true. The Lady Juliana knows it as well as I.'

'How do you know? Was it written in the stars?'

'I have other sources than my charts. You have been away too long if you do not remember that.'

'The other Houses would never stand for it. To see a Feracci on the Navigators' throne. It would break the old compact and give Cezare too much power.'

'Nonetheless, Cezare obviously believes it possible, or he would not even make the attempt. He is too cunning to try and fail.'

'It is not possible. Every time one of the great Houses tries, it runs into the massed opposition of the others. That is why the likes of old Gorki are always picked – a non-entity from a lesser House, who could not do anything if he tried.'

Skorpeus gave a cruel little laugh. 'I fear it is a little crude of you to speak so ill of the dying, true though your words might be.'

'Crude or no, we both know it to be the truth. If Cezare Feracci intends to change that then he will be upsetting a pattern that has kept the peace among the Houses these past two millennia.'

'And you think that would trouble our dear kinsman by marriage? Do not be so naïve, sweet cousin. He is the most ruthless and ambitious man in this galaxy and he has friends in very high places. I tell you, Cezare means to put one of his brood on the throne and become *primus inter pares*.'

'No one has claimed that title since Jormela the Mad.'

'Just because no one has done so does not mean that many have not thought about it.'

'Perhaps including yourself.'

'How could I covet such a thing? I do not even occupy the throne of my own House.'

'No, but neither does Misha Feracci.'

'I am gratified that you take what I say so seriously.'

'Do you really believe it is possible?'

'Look around you. Cezare is spending his coin like water. The leaders of three of the great Houses are conveniently dead. New, inexperienced lords rule. Now he proposes a marriage alliance with us: between you and his young inexperienced and malleable son. Such a thing might be construed as an offer of power sharing.'

'But you do not believe it to be so.'

'Cezare will share power with no one. You must understand this as well as I.'

'Are you seriously suggesting he had a hand in the killing of three lords – in the death of my father?'

'I am merely saying it is a strange coincidence that they should all happen just as the Lord Feracci plans the greatest coup in two millennia.'

'Surely he knows he could not get away with it?'

'Dearest heart, you are repeating yourself. Cezare *is* getting away with it.'

'Surely he must know there will be reprisals?'

'Will there? If his chief rivals are dead and his son is seated on the Navigator throne, he will have shown himself to be the greatest power to arise among the Navigators since Tareno. The minor Houses will line up to do homage to him.

The Lords of the Administratum will court him. The great Houses will do their best not to offend him.'

'It is not possible.'

'Sweet cousin, the great Houses have become fat, complacent and sure of their success. At such times, the predators always emerge from the undergrowth. Cezare Feracci is a predator.'

'Why are you telling me this?'

'It seems to me that we must either accommodate ourselves to a new order or we must strike before Cezare becomes too mighty to be brought down.'

'This is a conversation that should be had with the Lady Juliana.'

'It has, but she needs time to consider the matter.' The sneer was faint but audible.

'Then why tell me?'

'You are the one who may be married into the Feracci family.'

He did not need to say the rest. Even Ragnar could follow the chain of implications. Gabriella might be married into the Feracci family. Her father had been killed by Cezare, if what this subtle man said was true. Was he really hinting that she might consider the assassination of the lord of the Feraccis?

'I will think on what you have said, cousin,' said Gabriella, unhooking her arm from his and bowing formally with hand on heart.

'Do not take too long,' said Skorpeus, bowing to her and then to Ragnar before retiring. It seemed to Ragnar that the Navigator looked knowingly at him before departing.

CHAPTER FOURTEEN

TORIN SWEPT THE eavesdropping augur over the room once more, then relaxed and smiled. Ragnar was glad that he had come straight here after his meeting with Skorpeus and Gabriella. Torin seemed exactly the man to turn to for advice under these circumstances.

'Ah, Ragnar, old son,' he said. 'Here less than a week and already knee deep in conspiracies. That's the spirit.'

Ragnar heard the mockery in his voice, and felt the hackles on the back of his neck rise. Torin's smile widened as if he knew what Ragnar was feeling, and then just as suddenly it vanished.

'A subtle man, Skorpeus,' he said. There was disdain in his voice. Ragnar was not sure whether this was because Skorpeus imputed subtlety or because Torin thought the Navigator was not subtle enough.

He glanced at his battle-brother's chamber. It was the opposite of his own. There was a four poster suspensor bed and ancient paintings of distant landscapes. One showed a one-armed warrior mounted on a horse, shouting commands as he rode dramatically through the snow. Doubtless he had been a great warrior in his time.

'Is he correct?' Ragnar asked.

'Almost certainly. There has been talk about this for months among the Navigators. They are very good at avoiding eavesdroppers, but they some-times forget how keen our ears are.'

'What would it mean for us if Cezare got his catspaw on the throne?'

'By "us" do you mean the Wolves?'

'What else could I mean?'

'You are a bondsman to Belisarius now, Ragnar.'

'Our interests in this matter are the same.'

'You are more subtle than you seem, young Wolf,' said Torin. He poured himself a glass of narcotic wine and sipped it delicately. The crystal glass and ornamental decanter looked incongruous in his gauntleted hand, and his expression was one that would not have been out of place on the face of a Navigator.

'You think he means to use Gabriella to assassi-nate Cezare?'

'Do you really think she could?'

'At the cost of her own life perhaps. Everyone is vulnerable if you get close enough.'

'The Lord Feracci will be extraordinarily well protected.'

'So you are saying no, then.'

'She could not do it, but there is one present who could.'

'You mean either Beltharys or myself?'

'Now you simulate obtuseness, Ragnar. What need would Skorpeus have of discussing this matter with her if he intended to use Beltharys?'

'He would not have known I was listening.'

'Men like Skorpeus never forget such things, old son.'

'Then why not approach me directly?'

'Because he could not deny doing that. But if a certain hot-headed young Space Wolf were to take it into his own head to do Skorpeus's killing for him he could honestly say, even under truth machines, that he had never talked about it with you.'

'It seems a subtle distinction.'

'You need to start thinking like a Navigator.'

'How could he have known that I would be accompanying her?'

'Perhaps they cooked it up between them.'

'What?'

'You heard me.'

'Are you saying the two of them are in league?'

'I am suggesting it is possible. A gallant, naïve young Space Wolf, fearing a threat to a young woman whose life he has already saved once, acts to save her from potential harm. It has a certain tragic romantic ring to it.'

'It seems very unlikely.'

'Ragnar, when you have been on Terra as long as I have, you will learn when it comes to Navigators' plots nothing is too far-fetched to escape consideration. If Skorpeus wants Cezare dead, and there is a slight chance that you would do it, why would he not take the opportunity? He has nothing to lose, and everything to gain.'

Ragnar could see a certain logic to this. The question was did he really believe Ragnar was stupid enough to fall for it? He supposed that was also possible. 'It seems to me that you are suggesting the Navigators think too highly of their own intelligence and too little of ours.'

'We are barbarians to them, Ragnar. Useful barbarians, but barbarians nonetheless. But do not underestimate them. The Navigators are, for the most part, as clever as they think they are. They would not survive otherwise. They are born and trained to conspiracy as we are born and trained to war.'

'That's an interesting thought.' Ragnar could see that it was true too. Wild dangerous worlds like Fenris bred hardy warriors. Rich ancient ones would shape something else. A new idea lodged itself in his mind. It occurred to him that if the Navigators saw only what they expected to see when they looked at him, they were likely to continue to underestimate him. Very few foes were ever likely to do so on the field of battle but this was another arena entirely, and he needed to seize any advantage he could.

'You are looking duplicitous, old son.'

'Am I so transparent?'

'Only to a brother Wolf.'

'I was thinking that it would be well for them to continue looking at me and seeing a barbarian.'

'Indeed. And there is another thing you should never forget.'

'What is that?'

'You *are* a barbarian.'

'As are you.'

'I make no claims to be otherwise.' Ragnar doubted this, but was not about to say so.

'We come from the same place, Ragnar. We passed the same tests. We serve the same Chapter. I have not lost sight of that.'

He sounded as if he were trying to convince himself. Perhaps he had been on Terra too long and it had seeped into his veins. It seemed unlikely to Ragnar but you could never tell. For all his cleverness and confidence, Torin did not seem entirely at ease in either of his two worlds.

'You really think Gabriella and Skorpeus might be in league?' he asked.

Torin's smile flashed again, as if someone had hit a switch, but there was a hard malicious edge to it.

'Perhaps. Or perhaps he wants to get rid of a rival.'

Ragnar met his gaze and felt the hair on the back of his neck begin to rise again. 'Kill her?'

'Kill her.'

'Then why go out of his way to recruit her?'

'Schemes within schemes, Ragnar. Perhaps he really does want to convince her to try and kill Cezare. Perhaps he wants to get her guard down. If one thing does not work, perhaps another one will. Also, the Navigators believe in keeping their friends close at hand and their enemies closer still.'

'A few minutes ago you were saying that she was in league with him. Now you are suggesting he might kill her.'

'One does not preclude either, Ragnar. Also, I did not say they were in league, I merely pointed out the possibility that they could be.'

'What do you suggest I do?'

'Is any of this really your business, brother?' His gaze was suddenly probing, and Ragnar sensed that all of Torin's attention was focused on him. He could see what the older Wolf was getting at. His loyalties should be to his Chapter and to the Celestarch. He had no business letting them stray. He considered his feelings and thoughts carefully. He had saved Gabriella's life, and he liked her. He was not about to stand by and let her be killed, if she was in any danger.

'I am making it my business,' he said eventually. Torin nodded as if he had expected nothing less.

'Well spoken,' he said. 'But all you can do is keep your eyes and ears open. Don't get too involved in any of this. Look at it like the Navigators do. Treat it as a game.'

Ragnar knew he was not capable of that. He was surprised that any Wolf could even suggest it. 'It's a game where the stakes are life and death.'

'Possibly,' said Torin, 'but that's the way it's played here, and no one would have it any other way. And here's one last piece of advice…'

'What's that?'

'Remember that on Terra, you never have the whole picture.'

Ragnar was still thinking of a reply when the comm-net summoned them to the presence of Valkoth.

'WE HAVE ANOTHER mission,' Valkoth said. His face was even more grim than usual, the lines on it even more pronounced.

'Pantheus talked?' Ragnar asked.

'They always talk eventually,' Valkoth said.

'What did he have to say?' Torin's voice drawled almost like a Navigator's.

'A lot of things. He says that money is being filtered from the Feraccis to the Brotherhood.'

'What?' asked Ragnar. 'That makes no sense. The cult would have Cezare's head on a spit if they could.'

'It does not make them any less useful to him, if they are killing his enemies,' said Torin. His words came out very quietly but they were perfectly audible.

'What else did he say? Was there any proof?' Torin asked.

'Nothing the Celestarch could take to a Tribunal of the Houses. Cezare could simply say the man would say anything under torture and he would be right.'

Ragnar thought of the inquisitors he had known. 'An inquisitor could find out the truth – one with psychic powers.'

'True, but the Houses would never let the Inquisition look at their business. There is no love lost between them and the Navigators. It would give the Inquisition too much leverage over them, and they still sniff the taint of heresy on the Navigators even after ten millennia.' There was something odd in Valkoth's scent, Ragnar realised. It was as if the man was concealing something.

'You did not bring us here just because the fat man squawked about Cezare,' said Haegr. It was a surprisingly intelligent statement coming from him. Then he spoiled the effect by gnawing on a whole shank of beef. Seconds later he was crunching the bones with his fangs.

'You are correct,' said Valkoth. 'I brought you here because the Celestarch has need of your services.'

'Good,' said Torin. 'I could use a little excitement.'

'I thought you got that trimming your moustache,' said Haegr from around a mouthful of beef. 'And admiring yourself in the mirror.'

'By Russ, a talking whale has snuck into your chamber while we were listening to you, Valkoth,' said Torin.

'A talking whale probably could creep in, given your level of alertness,' said Haegr. 'I am surprised you can smell anything over the scent of your pomade.'

'Enough,' said Valkoth. His voice was soft but the command carried weight. Torin snapped shut his mouth almost involuntarily, and the retort on the tip of his tongue vanished forever. 'There is work to be done.'

'What would you have us do?' Ragnar broke the sudden silence.

'Pantheus gave us the location of another nest of vipers,' said Valkoth. 'You will go there and clean it out.'

'Where is it?' said Torin.

'The under city,' said Valkoth. 'Deep down in the under city.'

The very tone of his voice made it sound ominous.

'You have scouted this out?' Torin asked. 'It could be a trap.'

Valkoth's lips twisted in what might have been a smile. 'I am not a Blood Claw, Torin. Our agents have already been through the area. The Brotherhood has been building up its forces there for weeks. We were going to have to do something about it eventually. They are too close now. They have a munitions dump and base camp right here beneath the navigators quarter.'

'I don't like this. Things are moving too fast,' said Torin. 'We are constantly reacting, not acting. It's like we are following a path set out for us by someone else, and I think we can all guess who that someone else is. This is a huge distraction coming conveniently as the Houses jockey for the Navigator throne.'

Valkoth nodded almost imperceptibly. Ragnar could tell from his scent that he agreed with Torin but there was not much he could do. 'Yes. But the threat is still there.'

'You two are being overcunning,' said Haegr. 'It ill befits two true sons of Fenris. How can this be some huge plot? How could Cezare know that old Gorki was about to shuffle off to hell?'

Even Ragnar could answer that. 'Perhaps he arranged that too.'

'There are many poisons that can simulate illness. If anyone can find a way of having them administered it is Cezare.'

'It's a huge risk though, isn't it?' said Ragnar.

'No one ever said Cezare lacked nerve,' said Torin.

'Whether you are right or wrong, Torin, you still have a mission to perform,' said Valkoth. 'Let's get to it.'

THE CORRIDOR WAS dark and gloomy. The crumbling walls looked like they had been here since the first cities were built on the ancient soil of Terra. The air was filled with the scent of fungus, rot, polluted water and rust. Huge rats scurried away from them into the dark.

'I've been in more cheerful places,' said Ragnar. 'This is a side of Terra the pilgrims never see.'

'I could have cheerfully lived out my life without seeing it myself,' said Torin fastidiously wiping a spot of muck from his shoulder-pad. He had been meticulously cleaning it ever since the water started to drip from the ceiling. Behind them a full company of House guards moved through the gloom. They were the best troops the House could muster. They would spearhead the attack. Valkoth remained above, guarding the Celestarch. Torin was their acting commander.

'This is not what I expected,' said Ragnar quietly as they moved along. The tainted water was ankle deep now. He wondered if anybody down here really drank it. Without the digestive system of a Space Marine they would most likely be poisoned or mutated within weeks. 'This is more like a hive world. A run down hive world in a sector that has suffered a hundred-year industrial decline.'

Torin moved along, bolter held casually at the ready. He had taken the lead ever since they had been dropped off at the entrance shaft that led down into the depths of the Earth. 'This is like no hive world you ever visited, Ragnar. There are hundreds of layers of buildings above us. Each of them represents a century of history or more. This part of Terra was built and overbuilt and then built on again. Parts of it were cannibalised to build the layers above, and what was left was slowly crushed down by the new stuff above. We're walking through history. Some of these walls around us were built before the Emperor entered his golden throne. Much of these corridors were the same when Russ walked this earth, ten thousand years ago.'

'You sound like one of those guides who show pilgrims round old temples,' said Haegr, belching thunderously. 'The ones who are always praising the wonders of Old Terra and trying to sell locks of the Emperor's hair.'

'If they tried to sell you a sausage made from the flesh of Horus you would buy it,' said Torin. 'Most likely eat it, too.'

'Hush,' said Haegr, raising his hand. At first Ragnar expected another joke, but the expression on Haegr's face told him differently. He strained his ears to catch whatever it was the huge Marine was listening for.

Ragnar thought he heard something up ahead. Voices. They were nearing the inhabited area of this eerily empty zone. Good, he thought. He did not like the feeling of those tens of thousands of tons of plascrete pressing down above his head. They should do what they had been sent to do and get out. They were to cleanse this nest of cultists and seize their leaders for questioning if they could. Mostly they were to make an example of them, and make them think twice about striking at the Navigator Houses.

Ragnar questioned the wisdom of this course of action. These were men driven by relentless hate. Killing a few of them would only give them more reason to hate, and deepen their sense of grievance. Still, it was not his job to question the strategy of the Celestarch. It was his job to see that it was carried out.

Once again the numbers would be against them. The thought did not trouble Ragnar very much. Ten or a hundred to one, the odds did not matter. They would be much better armed and armoured and far faster and stronger than those they attacked. And they had the element of surprise. That was why they were sending in such a small force.

Torin signalled for the House troops to remain where they were. He gestured for the other Wolfblades to advance and scout out their goal.

Ragnar's nostrils flared as he caught another scent. There were definitely people up ahead. His keen eyes picked out a disturbance in the surface of the water just ahead of Torin. His brother Wolfblade had already spotted it. He stepped over. There was something hidden just below the surface.

'Tripwire, Haegr,' he said. 'Just in case you were too busy thinking about food to notice it.'

'Since even you could notice it, there is no reason why the ever-vigilant Haegr could not,' replied Haegr.

'No reason other than not having a brain to notice things with,' murmured Torin – so low that only the ears of a Wolf could have caught it. His caution had increased considerably now that they were near their objective.

Slowly but surely they by-passed and disarmed the tripwires. Other men would have failed to notice them in the dark, but Space Wolves were not like other men. Ahead of them more lights were visible. There was a smell of recycled methane, which was hardly surprising. An area like this could not be connected to the great electrical furnaces that fed power to the surface.

So much the better, Ragnar thought. Normal human sight would be far less efficient in the gloom than the ears and noses of the Marines. He felt a tension in his stomach as he prepared for combat. He knew that the folk they would soon encounter would be desperate, hard-bitten men. From what Valkoth had said, they had fled the surface of the world, and the ancient privileges of job and caste to come here. He knew too that they would be armed with the best weapons that could be stolen from the well-stocked armouries of Terra.

They emerged above a wide open space. Water dripped from the access tunnel in a slow turgid waterfall down into a polluted pool below.

Flickering gaslights lit the whole shady area. Ragnar took it all in with one long appalled glance. The ancient, crumbling caverns teemed with life. Here and there dozens of other tunnels entered the chamber. In their entrances were lean-tos made from salvaged steel and hardboard. A motley assortment of jerry built huts barnacled the walls and floor. Hundreds of armed men moved around. All of them wore cowled robes and the red and black armbands of the Brotherhood.

High atop a makeshift altar of welded pipes and plates of metal, a masked man bellowed a sermon of hatred to his avid listeners. He spoke of the evil mutants that lurked on the surface and sullied the sacred soil of Terra. He talked of the whore of commerce that was corrupting the values their ancestors had held dear. He talked of the evil that the Navigators concealed beneath the mask of loyalty and the robes of righteousness.

It was a fiery speech and passionate. Ragnar could see that it fanned the flames of hatred in the heart of every listener. The man was plainly telling his audience what they wanted to hear, he was playing on their fears and hatred and their resentment of the wealth and luxury enjoyed by the Navigators. It was easy to see that this was a spark that had found dry tinder. The men down here were exiles living the lives of rats in the walls of the world. They had nothing to lose. Their lives held little meaning even for themselves.

'Quite a little rat's nest down here,' murmured Torin. 'You'd think they were getting ready for a war.'

'Maybe they are,' said Ragnar. He'd seen enough rebellions and uprisings on other worlds to know that this was how they started. Heretics and fanatics had to have a hard core of warriors around which to build their insurgencies. They had to have weapons to provide to the dupes they conned into fighting with them, and to train the pitiful fools too. He had seen variants on the likes of this camp on a dozen worlds. It was a seed of disruption and heresy and it was his task to see that it never sprouted.

The little group down there might not look like much when you compared it to the massed forces that guarded this world, but there would be others like it. Even if there were not, such groups could so often be like the small pebbles that started avalanches. A world as densely populated as this one contained hordes of the poor, dispossessed and angry. Sometimes, it did not take much to turn that anger to rage, and then focus that rage on war. He had seen it happen many times before.

Even as the thought passed through his mind, the sheer audacity of the people below appalled him. This was Terra, the father world, the hub of the Imperium, the most sacred soil in the galaxy, and these men intended to profane it.

And why not? Most of them probably felt that they were doing nothing but cleansing the sacred soil of the unrighteous. He had heard that rhetoric countless times too. Without ever having heard his particular words, he could probably reconstruct the speech of the fanatical preacher down there. The alarming thing was that they were so close to the things he himself had been taught. It was one of the weaknesses of Imperial dogma, he thought, that the same words that could strengthen a community could also be used to undermine it. The robe of religion could conceal the form of the fanatic revolutionary just as easily as that of the loyal and devout citizen.

Now was not the time for philosophy. It was the time for action. He looked at Haegr and Torin. He knew they were thinking the same thing. It was time to summon the rest of the troops.

Just as the thought occurred to Ragnar, the preacher suddenly touched his ear and glanced up. It was not possible he could have seen them, Ragnar thought. But somehow he had detected them. He gestured with his right hand, and pointed an accusing finger towards the shadows in which the Wolves lurked.

Torin's finger tightened on the trigger of his heavy bolter. A hail of fire tore the preacher in two. It took his appalled followers a moment or two to realise what was happening. 'We're going to have to do this the hard way,' said Torin. 'Looks like the munitions are over there! Frag them!'

'Good, I like these odds,' said Haegr. In that moment, with surprising agility, he vaulted over the makeshift banister and landed on the corrugated roof of a hut below. Ragnar glanced at Torin, then shrugged and followed him. Doubtless the big man would need someone to watch his back as he carried out his insane assault.

Moments later, they advanced into the tight mass of fanatics. Ragnar's bolter kicked in his hand as he took out first one man and then another. His chainsword sliced through skin, muscle and bone, splattering those around him with blood. Haegr's monstrous hammer did even more damage as it pulped the flesh of anyone who got in his way. The big man raced through the crowd like a runaway mastodon. It was all Ragnar could do to keep up.

The fanatics had not realised how few attacked them. Many broke and ran for cover. Others snatched up weapons and let fly into the gloom. Muzzles flashed and lasbeams lit up the gloom, adding to the confusion. Before they knew it, groups were engaged in combat, each believing the other to be some deadly enemy. Others had fled unthinking into the darkness.

Ragnar proceeded forward, first giving cover to Haegr, then being covered in turn by Torin, as he advanced towards their goal. He rested for a moment in the shadow of one of the huts, when he heard a mighty voice bellowing orders. 'Stand firm! There are but three of them. Ready yourself for battle. The righteous shall prevail.'

Ragnar was astonished. How could this newcomer know the exact number of attackers? There was only one way. They had been betrayed.

CHAPTER FIFTEEN

'Bones of Russ,' Ragnar cursed. He glanced around. He could see enemies entering from all sides. They were heavily armed and obviously prepared. They must have been waiting outside the Wolves' line of approach. In their need for speed and surprise, they had not done a complete reconnaissance of the area. They were going to pay for that now.

'They knew there was going to be only three of us,' said Haegr.

Ragnar's keen hearing could make out his voice despite the background roar of heavy weapons. At that moment their foes were concentrating their fire on the balcony where Torin stood. A glance showed Ragnar that the Wolfblade had already dropped out of sight.

'They knew when we were going to attack. That means someone informed them – and recently.' Ragnar could see Haegr nod as he checked their foes' weapons. Those heavy flamers and bolters out there were capable of penetrating even their armour. This was not going to be easy. There was one consolation: in the maelstrom of conflict the enemy could not get an exact fix on them. They might still get away.

'They are over there, amid the bubble-water shanties,' bellowed the same commanding voice.

'He has good eyesight,' said Haegr.

'Or some other means of knowing we are here,' said Ragnar.

'The holy light of the Emperor's sanctity will smite the mutant lovers!' As the deep ranting voice spoke, a wave of white light flashed overhead. Ragnar's hiding place began to glow. 'Hear me, I, your prophet, the Prophet of Light, call upon you, blessed Lord, to smite these sons of Darkness.'

'Look out!' Ragnar shouted, throwing himself forward. Haegr moved, not a heartbeat too soon. Moments later their flimsy shelter exploded in a shower of shrapnel. It was like nothing Ragnar had ever seen, but that did not surprise him. He already had a good idea of what had caused it. A glance confirmed it – a halo of light surrounded a figure of glowing whiteness. It would have dazzled Ragnar had his protective second lid not dropped into place to protect his sight.

'Psyker!' he shouted, snapping off a shot as he continued to roll. The bolter shell flew true but was repelled by the aura around the cultist. It ricocheted off at right angles. *Things are going from bad to worse*, Ragnar thought.

'See how the light of the Emperor's holy brilliance smites his foes,' the psyker shouted. There was a thrilling undertone to his voice that Ragnar recognised as one of compulsion. No need to ask why these mutant haters helped the person they avowed to despise. Ragnar had seen and heard of a hundred instances like this. Doubtless the psyker claimed that his powers came directly from the Emperor, and they were proof of his holiness for his credulous followers. An aura of compulsion would aid their weak-willed credulity. Knowing how the trick was done would not help him survive it. They needed to find a way out of here, and fast.

Whips of blazing light smashed through the flimsy structures in which the Space Wolves had taken cover. Tendrils of whitish golden ectoplasm sought them like probing limbs of some giant beast. It was only a matter of time before they made contact.

As the tendrils moved like great oily serpents of brilliance through the wreckage, hundreds of bolter shells, bullets and lasbeams criss-crossed the air above his head. Ragnar hunkered low, knowing that their enemies believed them to be pinned in place by the crossfire. He glanced at Haegr, who nodded to show he understood. There was only one thing for them to do: attack.

Ragnar threw himself onto his belly and writhed forward towards the psyker. Ghastly, ghostly limbs passed overhead, seeking him out. They looped around, apparently knowing where he was.

Ragnar tapped his belt dispenser and caught the grenade that dropped into his gauntleted palm. A quick touch set the fuse, and he lobbed it at the psyker. A moment later the explosion smashed into the man.

Not even his powers could fully shield him. He was tossed backwards off his feet and the glow around him flickered. The ectoplasmic tentacles momentarily became misty. Acting on the instinct that allowed them to coordinate without even speaking, Haegr charged.

The enormous power hammer connected before his glowing shield could spring back entirely to full luminescence. The psyker let out a groan of pain but gained control once more. Ragnar smelled blood. The glow sprang into place once again although its brilliance varied and strange veinous seams of red ran through it. The tendrils returned and continued to loop down, fumbling for Haegr. It was as if their owner were no longer able to concentrate on two targets at once. So, thought Ragnar, they had managed to do some damage.

A second later the sorcerous limbs found their target, wrapping themselves around the giant

Wolfblade. There was a strange sputtering sound as the ceramite of his armoured carapace began to bubble and melt. Haegr grunted and attempted to break free but even his massive strength was ineffective against the psyker's power. Snarling, he was pushed inexorably away from his foe. Ragnar wondered how he could help, but realised all he would do was get caught like a fish on a hook. However, if the psyker was killed, then his ectoplasmic tentacles would no longer be a problem.

Ragnar moved closer to study his target. He was in no doubt that the man was badly wounded. Another grenade would most likely do the trick. He lobbed it forward and it flew true to its target before detonating. This time, however, its effects were less than Ragnar had expected. The blast made the shield dim momentarily, but it had somehow adapted to protect its owner against this form of attack. The psyker did not even flinch this time.

So much for that idea, thought Ragnar. This heretic was powerful. 'There's more than one way to skin a dragon,' he said, and continued forward, springing from a crouch and launching himself directly at the psyker.

The man had bodyguards but they were all standing back from him as he used his unholy powers. They were concentrating their fire on the balcony where Torin had been. Ragnar suspected that the Wolfblade had most likely already slipped away.

Ragnar offered up his thanks to Russ for the distraction, as it enabled him to get a clear leap at his prey and to keep out of the line of fire. His chainsword was in one hand, his bolter in the other. As he flew forward, he fired, pumping shell after shell into the false prophet of the Brotherhood. The glowing shield repelled them all except one. They impacted where the glow was at its faintest, and where the red veins of light were at their thickest.

One of his shells passed into the glow. He heard a faint, muffled scream. It appeared that the Prophet of the Light was not used to pain. Ragnar intended to show him a lot more of it. He aimed his chainsword at the darkest blotch on the shield and thrust. For a moment he thought it would pass right through, but it met resistance and the glow brightened once more. No matter, Ragnar thought, bringing his bolter to bear on the area of the glow where a human head should be. Even if the shield repelled the shells, he hoped the effect would be like a blow to the helmet. Perhaps the shock would stun and disorientate his target.

Once more he was rewarded with a groan. The tentacles snaking over him to hold Haegr began to pulse and flex. Ragnar sensed their approach behind him. He sprang to one side as a tendril of ectoplasm passed through the space where he had been. As an experiment he lashed out at the thing with his chainsword. The whirling blades passed through it, severing it, but moments later the thing had congealed together again. Ragnar abandoned this ploy and returned to smiting his original target. He smashed blow after blow into his prey.

Although their reflexes were mortal, the Prophet's bodyguards finally reacted. Some of them opened fire. Ragnar writhed. Even the most glancing impacts felt as though his armour had been struck with a heavy hammer. He had hoped the cultists would have withheld their fire for fear of hitting their leader, but he realised that they believed him to be protected by the glow. He sprang to one side, putting the body of the Prophet between himself and the rabble, and was rewarded with the impact of a dozen weapons on the glowing screen.

'Cease and desist, brethren!' said the Prophet, his voice like thunder. 'The power of the Emperor's light is all that is needed to slay this mutant loving degenerate. See to it that his companions are cleansed from this area. I will deal with this one myself.' Ragnar could tell from the tone of the man's voice that he intended to make him pay for the pain he had inflicted. At that moment, the Prophet's followers swept past him, intent on reaching Haegr. The huge Wolfblade had slumped to the ground as the tentacles withdrew. Was this psyker really so confident of overcoming him, Ragnar wondered?

The glow around the man flickered, dimmed then intensified. This time the tendrils came straight at Ragnar with unbelievable speed. Not even Ragnar's superhuman reflexes could carry him out of the

way. His armour sizzled where they hit him, and
worse than that waves of pure agony passed
through him from the points of contact. The pain
was not the product of the heat, rather of the touch.
He was amazed that Haegr had been able to endure
it without shrieking. Ragnar resolved to do the
same.

He clamped his lips shut and offered up a prayer
to Russ. He sensed a far off, distant supernatural
presence. Perhaps it was only a figment of his pain-
wracked imagination but instantly his agony
diminished. Furthermore he noticed that the glow
surrounding the Prophet had dimmed and that a
bright red area had appeared over his heart.

With his chainsword free he stabbed forward. The
angle was awkward and he could not get much
leverage, but this time his blade successfully passed
right through the glow. He could feel it rip through
flesh and grate on bone. A snarl of triumph twisted
his lips as the glow faded to reveal a man in blood-
spattered white robes. A sweep of Ragnar's blade
separated the Prophet's cowled head from his
shoulders and sent it bouncing and rolling into the
nearest open sewer. Another sweep of the blade
carved the carcass in two.

A heartbeat later he was amid the bodyguards,
attacking them from behind as he came to Haegr's
aid. His blade flickered with electric speed, killing
and maiming with every blow. His bolter could
not help but find targets amid the closely packed

bodies. Step by step he carved a bloody path to his companion. Haegr looked bad. His armour was fused and rent in a dozen places, the ceramite cracked and blistered by the power of the Prophet's psychic onslaught. Worse still, he appeared tired and drained by the pain he had endured. Even so, he reared to his feet and began lashing about with his hammer. His speed and power were greatly reduced, but at least he was fighting.

Ragnar hewed his way forward, chainsword carving flesh from bone and severing tendons and veins. He felt a surge of glorious berserker rage begin to take hold of him. A fierce unholy joy in blood and battle surged through his veins. He fought it back. Now was not the time to give in to bloodlust. He needed to keep a clear mind to get out of this desperate situation. It was difficult, but he fought the beast within him, until it was under control.

He risked another glance up at where he thought Torin was. No sign. He hoped his battle-brother was not on the balcony awash in a pool of his own blood.

With a savage kick sideways, he collapsed one man's ribs like rotten twigs, sending him tumbling back into his friends, with blood pouring from his mouth. He drowned in his own blood. A vicious swipe of the butt of his bolt pistol smashed the skull of a man who was clinging to his legs into jelly. He lowered the gun and fired point-blank into the face of another, decorating the surrounding area with a splatter of blood and brain. He found himself back to back with the reeling Haegr, defending him from the onrushing horde.

All discipline seemed to have been lost by the mob now, which was to the Wolves' advantage. Had the heretics held their ground and maintained a steady stream of fire, they would have won, thanks to their sheer weight of firepower. However, their desperate desire to rescue their Prophet had undone them. They were engaging in a melee with two men who were physically superior and their casualties were immense. Still, thought Ragnar, it was only a matter of time before their greater numbers told, or someone realised that they should fall back into a firefight again. Meanwhile, before they had the chance to do so, he needed to think of a plan to extricate himself and Haegr from this trap.

A heavy built man slammed into his chest. He had barrelled through the fanatics and launched himself forward in a mighty bound. He was huge – at least as big as Ragnar and he was obviously used to overbearing his foes through sheer bulk. But it was a mistake this time.

Ragnar absorbed the impact with a flex of his knees, his armour's internal gyros compensating for the force of the impact. The warrior reached for Ragnar's throat, but failed to find the windpipe and so he gripped his neck with both hands. He made a twisting motion obviously intending to snap the

Marine's neck. Idiot, thought Ragnar, as he brought his bolt pistol up to the man's belly and pulled the trigger. The reinforced vertebrae of his neck could withstand far more stress than any mere mortal man could bear. Ragnar realised there was no way the man could have known about this, just as he would not know that Ragnar's altered lungs could keep him alive far longer than a normal man, even with the air to his lungs cut off.

In a blinding flash of inspiration Ragnar knew how they could escape. It was obvious. 'Haegr,' he shouted. 'Head for the water.'

The giant Wolfblade nodded groggily, seeming to understand. Immediately he began to smash his way towards the smell of the polluted stream. Ragnar watched his back, all the while whirling and striking to left and right, constantly on the move to prevent anyone drawing a bead on him. Within seconds Haegr was at the bank. He paused, looked back and swung a blow that took down the men closest to Ragnar. Then he tumbled backwards like a man shot into the water. The waves closed over his head and he disappeared from sight. So far, so good, Ragnar thought.

He angled towards the bank himself. A hail of lasfire was flashing out of the darkness now. Hundreds of tracer bullets seared across his line of sight. Overhead were men obviously intent on killing him at range. They no longer seemed to care whether they hit their fellows, because the fire pouring into the area took a terrible toll on the men around Ragnar. Lasfire splashed his armour. A heavy bolter shell smacked into his chestplate and he felt it crack. It was time to go.

Just then, two more men flung themselves forward, oblivious to the sleet of death about them. They grabbed Ragnar and attempted to restrain him, all the while howling curses and death threats at the man who had slain their prophet. Vengeance was the only thing on their minds.

Ragnar did not care. He continued to dive forward carrying them with him by sheer force of momentum. Instinctively, he took a huge lungful of air. Moments later wetness engulfed him and the horrid clammy waters closed above his head. He kept a grip on his weapons as he began to sink towards the bottom. The weight of his armour was pulling him down, while the force of the flow carried him away. His skin tingled from the pollutants and poisons. A trail of bubbles overhead guided his eye to where the two men he had grabbed were making their way towards the surface.

The membrane protecting his eye from chemical irritants allowed him to see fairly well in the murk and gloom. Unless they were using filters, the men above had lowered their life expectancy by drinking the foul water. Ragnar doubted that these death-seeking fanatics worried about such things.

He looked around for Haegr. There was no sign of him, but Ragnar was not concerned. Unless his armour was damaged to the utmost extremity, its locator beacon would enable Ragnar to find him if need be. It looked as if they had avoided the ambush after all.

Just as the thought swirled through his mind, there was an enormous tremor, and a wave of incredible force and violence drove him through the water. It took him a heartbeat to realise what was going on. The fanatics were lobbing grenades into the water. Unless he did something quickly, they would kill him.

CHAPTER SIXTEEN

ONCE MORE, ENORMOUS quakes set the water roiling. Contrails indicated where more munitions were going to fall. They had all been aimed at points from which he had disappeared. None had thought to blast towards where he might be going. But that would soon change. The concussions caused Ragnar a great deal of pain, as changes in pressure smashed into his sensitive eardrums. It affected a Space Wolf a great deal more than it would a normal man.

He fumbled his sword and bolt pistol back into their holsters. They were Space Marine weapons; continued immersion should do them no harm. He had to grit his teeth and keep swimming, and get as far away from the explosions as he could.

Charges were starting to fall near to him now. Ragnar considered making for the bank, but realised that would only make him more visible and more vulnerable. He needed to keep going and try to win his way free.

He swam on, glad that he had learned to do so in the turbulent waters of Fenris as a boy. Even so, this was bad, like trying to negotiate the maelstrom at the centre of a storm while all around giant monsters bellowed and sought your life.

Another tremor smashed through the water close by and sent Ragnar tumbling end over end. He became completely disorientated, unsure of which way was up and which way down. His head felt as if it was going to split. For some reason, the water tugged at him more strongly. The invisible fingers of the current were like those of the hag maidens of Fenrisian legend who were said to lie in wait for drowning mariners. Ragnar kicked out with the current, letting the flow carry him towards the far end of the chamber. As he did so, the impact of the quakes lessened as they travelled further through the water.

All around the water bubbled and boiled. Another blast boomed through the water, and he felt himself suddenly hurled forward and out into space. All around him the water thundered and yet he felt clear patches of air around his flailing limbs.

He knew now what had happened. The underground river had carried him all the way through the chamber and out of the other side. He was tumbling down some sort of exit sump, and falling towards incalculable depths below. As the water smashed against him Ragnar strove to straighten his body into a diving position.

Vague terrors filled his mind. He had no idea how far he was going to fall, or what awaited him at the bottom. There might be jagged rocks or piles of broken metal waiting to impale him. There might be a swampy morass that would suck him down forever.

Horror and doubt threatened to overwhelm him. Every moment stretched until it felt like an hour. It was not his predicament that scared him as much as the sheer impossibility of knowing what was going to happen. He almost wished he had emerged from the water and sold his life dearly in the slaughter that would have followed. That would have been a man's death. Now he might fall far from where his comrades could find him and recover his gene-seed. It was possible that his remains might never be found.

In those brief moments, Ragnar came closer to despair than he ever had in his whole life. The beast within him howled in rage and fear. His monkey mind gibbered and rattled the cage of sanity. But suddenly his long tumble ended and he smashed into blackened waters. The force of the fall drove him still further down.

With powerful strokes, Ragnar swam out of the range of the current, and headed in the direction that his armour told him was up. It was possible that his sensors had been damaged and that they were malfunctioning but they were the only guide he had. Moments later his head broke the surface. He saw a beam of light spearing towards him and sensed splashing in the water near by. Haegr's pain-filled voice called out: 'I see you made it as well, Ragnar.'

Relief filled him. He was still alive and had found his comrade. Or, more correctly, his comrade had found him. They had escaped from the deadly trap above and were alive. 'Aye, Haegr it is me.'

'I see Torin managed to avoid a bath once more.'

'Let us hope that he got away with his hide intact.'

'Do not worry about him. It will take more than a few hundred angry cultists and their pet wizard to put him down. If they wanted to lure him into a trap, they would have had to set up a corridor full of mirrors.'

'This is hardly the time to be talking like this,' said Ragnar, swimming closer. 'We need to find a way out of here ourselves.'

'That should not be too difficult. Just keep heading upwards and we will get there eventually.'

Ragnar did not bother to ask him why he had not suggested activating their beacons. Any enemy that knew they were coming would be able to locate them by it. It was only a matter of tuning in to the correct comm-net frequency and knowing the scrambled codes. A few hours earlier he would have said that was impossible. Now he was not so sure.

'I think we were betrayed,' he said. Judging by the echoes around them, they were within a large cave or tunnel. The walls could not be too far. The only question was whether there would be dry ground there. There was only one way to find out.

'Maybe,' said Haegr. 'The self-proclaimed prophet was a psyker. Maybe he foresaw our arrival.'

Ragnar considered this. It was possible, but he did not want to abandon his own theory. There was too much else that pointed to the presence of a traitor within the ranks of House Belisarius. 'Maybe.'

'You don't think so, do you?'

It must be written all over his scent, Ragnar thought. He began swimming towards the shore, with his head above water so they could talk. He did not fear the possibility of being followed down here. The Brotherhood members would have to be suicidal to cast themselves into the waterfall.

'It is possible.'

'But?'

'There's the assassination of Adrian Belisarius, and the attempt on Gabriella. Too much points to there being an insider.'

'There always are insiders among the Navigator Houses, Ragnar. You are not on Fenris any more. Every House is filled with spies. Every one of them is compromised.'

'But back there, you thought we had been betrayed.'

'It was my first thought until I saw that blasted sorcerer at work.'

There was something to what Haegr was saying. A psyker could predict their arrival and perhaps tell their number. Such feats were not beyond some of the Rune Priests of his Chapter. It beggared belief that other psykers would not also be capable of them. He did not know which idea he liked less: traitors in their midst or their enemies having recruited powerful psykers to fight for them.

'A rogue psyker, right here on the holy soil of Terra,' said Ragnar.

'Who says he is a rogue, Ragnar? There are many factions who might be pulling the strings of the Brotherhood. Some of them employ psykers.'

Ragnar could only think of two off the top of his head. It seemed ludicrous that the Astropaths would want to get rid of all the Navigators except one. 'Are you suggesting the Inquisition might be behind this?'

'No. This is not their way. But Ragnar you forget many of the High Lords of Terra, and the organisations they represent have access to psykers as well.'

The bank was ahead of them now. Ragnar could hear water lapping against rock. A moment later a sheer wall was picked out by the pen-beam on his shoulder-mounted light. He sensed a disturbance in the depths below him. Was there something living down there? Some mutated creature of the depths surfacing from below? Were hungry eyes watching him from the cold depths?

He swam to the edge of the water and studied the wall of plascrete ahead. It rose sheer about three metres and above it there appeared to be a ledge. He unhooked a grapnel from his belt and tossed it upwards. It caught the first time and he tested its hold with a few sharp tugs. Moments later he had swarmed up the wall and lay on the edge, Haegr right behind him. He flopped onto the bank like a beached walrus. And not a moment too soon. Something large and luminous was rising from the depths, but it did not quite reach the surface. Sensing its prey had gone, it slowly receded into the deep dark waters.

Ragnar listened carefully. All around he could hear the sound of falling water. Not just from the nearby falls, but from a great distance as well. It seemed as if there were other sources feeding this vast reservoir, or whatever it was. He could not see the far side of the lake – for that was how he was beginning to think of it.

He watched Haegr as the older Marine flopped down beside him. He was badly beaten up. His armour was cracked in many places and had been broken through completely around his left shoulder and forearm. His whole face was horribly burned. His beard and whiskers had been singed on one side of his face. It was nothing that competent healers could not repair, but they were far away from medical help. Perhaps Haegr had internal injuries as well, he appeared to be moving slowly and favouring his right side. Things were not looking good. Any time a Space Wolf did that, it spoke of an enormous amount of pain.

'You think one of the High Lords might be behind all of this? To what end?'

'Don't ask me, Ragnar. I am only a humble Space Wolf. Torin could doubtless tell you.'

'There is nothing humble about you, and I am sure you have some ideas.'

Haegr grinned wryly. 'Who can tell anyone's motives in the tangled weave of Imperial politics? A lord might be trying to curry favour with the Inquisition, or ride the wave of a jihad to supreme power. It's been tried before, even here on Terra, and it has succeeded too.'

Ragnar stood upright and almost offered to help his battle-brother to his feet, but a warning glance told him it would be unwise. A Space Wolf would have to be in his last throes before he would accept help of that sort.

He took in their damp and unwholesome surroundings. How old was this place, he wondered? So old that even the gargoyles had crumbled and even the so-called 'ever-burning' lights of the ancients had faded.

The air smelled damp and fusty. There were currents in it that spoke of a recycler in action somewhere far off. If he concentrated he could hear the distant hum of machinery muted by the sound of falling water.

They strode forward towards the direction of the air-currents. A few hundred strides brought them to a massive archway. A canal ran out through it, flanked on either side by a path. Hundreds of corroded metal pipes lined the walls. Water leaked from them and had discoloured the stone and brickwork. A gigantic mosaic depicting what might have been the Primarch Sanguinius, or one of the angels of the ancient's religion, decorated the wall above the arch. The figure stood so that his legs bestrode the entranceway. Ragnar could make out one huge wing, but more became visible as he traced them with his shoulder light. Did Sanguinius ever carry a huge horn? Ragnar did not think so. Or a flaming sword with which he smote daemons? There was much here the artist had got wrong, Ragnar thought, as he followed the limping Haegr along the canal bank.

'I sometimes wish I was back on Fenris. Life seemed much simpler there.'

'Perhaps, but if you went back now I doubt you would still think the same way.'

'What do you mean?'

'Terra changes men, Ragnar. Once you get used to seeing scheming behind everyone's actions it is very difficult to stop. You will take new eyes back to Fenris when you return.' There was a strange note in his voice and an odd glint in his eye. It was said that the closeness of death brought on the skill of foretelling in some men.

'You seem very certain that I will.'

'I am a good judge of men, Ragnar. I know you will. You have that look about you. You have been marked out for great things. That is your fate.'

Ragnar considered Haegr's words. 'I have been marked out for great calamity. I lost the Spear of Russ.'

'No, Ragnar. You used the Spear of Russ. You smote a primarch with it. It responded to you. Do you think that any man could cast such a weapon? Even a mighty hero such as I?'

Ragnar did not consider himself blessed, rather accursed. But there was something akin to envy in Haegr's voice. Ragnar wondered if there was any truth in his words. He couldn't think of a response. Instead, another thought struck him. He should try and contact his companions. He patched himself into the comm-net, but caught only static, which was unusual. Haegr gave him a knowing smile.

'The local relay must be down on this level.'

'They need relays down here?' Ragnar was astonished. He had never encountered such a thing before.

'Yes. Some of the levels were built with seals, or materials that somehow resist the net. You need to be near a relay to use the net and this one must be down.'

'Down! That is criminal incompetence.'

'But it happens. Maybe by accident, maybe by design. We'll need to find another level, or a relay station.'

'Come on then, we need to get back to the surface and see if we can smoke any conspirators out.'

AHEAD OF THEM were lights. Ragnar moved forward cautiously. He gestured for Haegr to stay where he was. He was worried about his companion – he appeared slow. His wounds were bad. Normally a Marine would have begun self-healing by now, if he were capable. His system must be overloaded trying to keep him alive. Judging by his pallor it might even fail. Despite this, Haegr managed to grumble about the lack of food.

All through the long weary trudge up from the reservoir, he had been uncharacteristically silent, moving slowly as if conserving his strength. The only time he had become animated was when some huge rats had scurried away from their lights. He had even made a half-hearted attempt to catch some.

Ahead of them lay a large empty chamber. It looked as if it had once been an open square surrounded by high buildings. There were still walls and windows and doorways enough to give the illusion an air of reality. If this place had once been open to the sky, now it was roofed over with plascrete. Doubtless that was where the next level began.

Ragnar could see many people. Some dwelled in what looked like huge over-turned metal barrels. Others were in translucent blisters that seemed stuck to the walls above. Some clambered up to the higher windows on towering metal ladders. A few seemed to have got into a vast metal pipe through holes in its side and had made their home there.

In the centre of the square was a small building. On the roof towered an armoured figure representing the Emperor from before the time he was entombed in the golden throne. It was an early archaic symbol of the Imperial cult. Perhaps it was the sign of some branch of the Adeptus Ministorum he did not know. Perhaps it actually dated from a time when the Emperor walked the streets of this world.

Ragnar wondered whether it would be best to skirt this community. After all, it might be allied with the Brotherhood. But if it were not, they might be able to find a healer. Haegr was in a very bad way. Any medical help, no matter how primitive, was critical now. Ragnar decided to risk it.

Many robed and cowled figures moved through the underways. Methane gas recycled from sewage was used to light the whole area. Ragnar could smell both both the gas and the processing works; neither was a treat to his sensitive nose.

Doorways lined the tunnel walls; some were blocked by pieces of corrugated metal, others were hung with drapes. The smell of roasting meat mingled with the methane burners over which it was cooked.

The people up ahead moved slowly. Every now and again, a skinny emaciated hand or face was visible. Whoever these people were, they were not thriving. Most of them were not armed either. This reassured Ragnar. This place had neither the look nor the smell of the Brotherhood camp.

He moved forward through the gloom, certain that no one would detect him until he was really close, unless he wished it. Ahead of him he could see a small skinny man, moving along. His walk was a crooked waddle, as if his legs were bowed. He was helped by a long staff carved from bone. Ragnar tapped him on the shoulder, and was surprised when the man leapt into the air and shrieked. He would have bolted had Ragnar not restrained him.

'Peace, stranger,' he said. 'I mean you no harm unless you try to harm me.'

The little man turned round to look at Ragnar. The light reflected on his round spectacles, turning his eyes briefly into circles of fire. 'In the Emperor's name, I doubt that is possible for the likes of me, sir.'

His voice was high-pitched and quivering, his manner shy and tentative. He sounded more like a scholar or a clerk than a member of the Brotherhood. 'And who are you?' Ragnar asked.

'I am Linus Serpico the third, junior clerk third class at the Imperial sprocket works number six, like my father, and his father before him.'

He paused for a moment and considered his words. 'At least I was. Until the sprocket works blew up.'

'Blew up?'

'An unfortunate industrial accident, sir. It does not reflect on the management in any way. Although I have heard it say that it would never have occurred if they hadn't spent the entire safety budget on a gold-plated statuette of Saint Theresius for the high foreman's retirement.'

Ragnar cocked his head to one side, baffled as much by the speed of the man's garbled speech as by his words.

Linus took Ragnar's silence the wrong way. 'Not that I place any credence in such scurrilous rumours, sir. You can always find people who will read the worst into anything. Just because the high foreman, his wife and the under-foremen retired to their own private gallery on sub-level 5, it does not mean that they were illegally appropriating funds for their own use.'

'If you say so,' said Ragnar. The little man let out a long sigh.

'I do not say so, unfortunately. As junior clerk third class it was my misfortune to have to scribe and blot the great account books, and if I may say so I suspect – although I do not firmly accuse anyone – I suspect that there were certain irregularities.'

'Do you indeed?' said Ragnar.

'I do. And in time, once the evidence was suitably corroborated I would have been in a position to put the evidence before the auditor general of sprockets. It would have been my duty to do so, sir, and it was a duty from which I would not have shirked. Unfortunately, the whole factory was reduced to rubble by the unfortunate aforementioned blast. Had I not been abroad on an errand for Supervisor Faktus, sir, I would most likely have been blown to high heavens with it.'

'Indeed. You are a resident here?'

'I am sir. At least I am temporary, although I pride myself on being a better class of person, sir, than most you will find here. I am not indigent, but alas there are few openings for a scribe of the third level these days.'

'You could always consider other work,' said Ragnar a little taken aback.

'Other work, sir! Impossible! Why the very thought of it! My forefathers would turn in their graves if I accepted a position of lesser merit. I am a scribe of third class like my father before me, and his father before him.'

Ragnar was a little astonished by the ferocious intensity of the man's speech. He sounded almost as if he had been insulted by the Space Wolf's words.

Fascinated as he was by this encounter with a Terran, he had his plans and he needed to move closer to fulfilling them.

'Be that as it may, I need a healer.'

'If you don't mind me saying so, sir, you look the picture of health, although your canine teeth could use a little work by the look of them.'

Ragnar let out a long growl that made the little man cringe backward. 'It is not me that needs help. My companion is hurt.'

Linus seemed to notice Ragnar for the first time. He took in his size, his weapons, his dented armour and his threatening appearance. Then he shrugged. 'Why did you not say so immediately, sir? I am sure Brother Malburius will be able to help. Come let us seek him.'

'First I must bring my comrade.'

'Of course, sir, of course.' He acquiesced so quickly that Ragnar's suspicions were aroused. Was the little man preparing to lead them into a trap? With Haegr wounded and himself at less than one hundred per cent things might go ill if that were the case.

Slowly, partially supporting Haegr now, they made their way towards the temple in the middle of the square. By the time they reached the doorway, Haegr had all but collapsed.

CHAPTER SEVENTEEN

Brother Malburius was a tall lean man with a grey, well kept goatee beard. His hair too was grey and his face was lined. He had a slight stoop. He wore the robes of the Adeptus Ministorum with a weary pride. He looked tired and not at all happy to see two battered Space Marines cluttering up the inside of his ministry.

'Space Wolves, eh?' he said. 'Attached to House Belisarius, no doubt.'

'How do you know that?' Ragnar asked. His suspicions were fully aroused. He glanced around the converted tunnel that was the temple. He noted nothing threatening – only some salvaged pews, worn Imperial saints that looked as if they had been scavenged from a dump and a massive Imperial

271

eagle embossed altar. The temple looked as run down as its artefacts, but at least it was tidy.

Brother Malburius looked closely at Haegr and beckoned them to follow him into the depths of the temple. Behind the altar was an antechamber packed with run-down looking medical equipment. It smelled of blood, pain and antiseptic incense. As he walked, the priest talked. 'It was hardly difficult. One look at you tells me your Chapter, Brother Ragnar. The Wolfblades are the only Space Marines on Terra. Your kind has not been popular here since the Heresy.'

'Is that so?' said Haegr, grimacing. 'I would never have guessed from the reception we got.'

Malburius gestured for Haegr to lie down on an examination table. Much to Ragnar's surprise the big man obeyed, slumping down on top of it. The bronze and metal table, a mass of universal joints and moulded gargoyle heads, flexed under Haegr's weight, but held firm.

Malburius screwed a magnopticle into one eye, and bent to examine the Space Marine's wounds. He adjusted some dials on the control altar and invoked the Machine God. Two globes of light flickered to life on either end of the table. Malburius attached dermal divination sensors and lit two sticks of medical incense.

Ragnar was not sure what good those would do given the armour that covered Haegr and the changes that had been made to his physique when he became a Space Marine, but he did not say anything.

No sooner was the connection made than the sensors began to pulse wildly. Malburius banged the machinery with his fist and uttered an invocation to the tech-spirits but it made no difference. He thrust a thermal sensor into Haegr's mouth. Linus Serpico watched, eyes wide, saying nothing.

'Don't eat it,' said Ragnar. Haegr grimaced. The fact he did not speak indicated to Ragnar that the situation did not look promising. After a few moments, Malburius removed the sensor and shook his head.

'It does not look good,' he said. 'I have to assume there is internal damage. I will need to remove the carapace and take a look inside.'

'Are you sure you are qualified for this?' asked Haegr with a fixed grin. Brother Malburius looked at him.

'If truth be told, no. I received basic medical training in the seminary. I can perform basic battlefield work and anything necessary to treat my flock. I was never taught to deal with the likes of you. Judging by the readings of my old instruments, I expect to find all manner of alterations to the basic human bio-form. Will that not be so?'

There was disapproval in his voice. Ragnar was not used to this and resented it. Haegr nodded. Malburius had an aura of competence that commanded respect.

'I expect that your battle-brother here...' A gesture indicated Ragnar. 'Could most likely perform any surgery as competently as I.'

'This is not what I wanted to hear,' said Haegr. He looked at Ragnar as if expecting confirmation. Ragnar knew the basics of field medicine but he was not a trained chirurgeon. 'You have probably had more experience than me,' he said.

'I've had plenty of practice down here. There are always accidents and fights and there is no one else to patch people up.'

Haegr looked as if he was weakening rapidly. He concealed his pain from the priest but Ragnar could sense it. He also sensed that Malburius was nervous and was trying to delay the operation for as long as he could. Ragnar came to a swift decision. 'Do what you need to. I will assist you in any way I can.'

Malburius nodded and moved to the nearest cabinet. He spoke directly to Haegr. 'I have painkillers, somnabulium and surgical tools here. I can render you unconscious and…'

'That will not be necessary,' said Haegr. 'Begin at once. A hero as mighty as myself need not fear a little pain.'

'Ah, the famous Space Marine hardihood,' said Malburius. He glanced at Linus. 'Friend Serpico bring me boiled, purified water and lots of it.' He looked at Ragnar. 'There may well be a loss of blood. I doubt your blood type is common among people here. I may need to transfuse yours.'

Ragnar knew what he was talking about. Many types of blood were incompatible. Fortunately all Space Wolves shared the same type. It was part of the process that turned them into Wolves. 'You can use mine,' he said. Malburius nodded and headed over to a strange contraption of translucent tubes and accordion fan pumps. He wheeled it over to the long table. 'I don't get much call for this sort of thing usually. Normally it's appendectomies, or childbirths or amputations after roof-falls. You two have been in battle.' It was not a question, although he made it sound like one.

'We fought with some of the Brotherhood of Light and their prophet.' Ragnar wanted this out in the open. If Malburius had any sympathy for the heretics he wanted to know before the man stood over Haegr with a las-scalpel in his hand. Malburius only nodded.

'I wondered how long it would be before someone took action against them,' said the missionary. 'They have been building up their numbers in the area for a while. It was only a matter of time before someone did something.'

The man was sharp and fishing for information. Ragnar could see nothing to be gained either by contradicting him, or agreeing with him, so he kept his mouth shut.

Malburius slapped the table and looked at Haegr. 'We'll need to remove your chestplate,' he said.

Haegr muttered a curse and bit his lip as they did so. His massive tusks must have made it painful. Ragnar could see that the black filament layer was badly damaged. There were gaping holes in it through which pink flesh, clean white bone and glistening internal organs could be seen.

Linus entered bearing a bucket of steaming water and Malburius washed his hands and sprayed them with a chemical designed to kill disease spores. It came from a standard military dispenser marked with the Imperial eagle. Swiftly and competently he hooked Ragnar and Haegr up to the blood machine. 'There is no power grid near here, Brother Ragnar,' he said, 'so you must power the machine. If there is a need, you must work this pump with your foot. If the pain becomes too intense, say so, and friend Linus will take up the task.'

Linus did not look at all happy to be here.

'I am a scribe third class, not a medical auxiliary,' he said.

'Nonetheless,' said Malburius, 'you will help. This man's life may depend on it. And believe me, the Imperium places considerably more value on his life than it does on yours. Is that not so, Space Wolf?'

Ragnar growled. Linus swallowed deeply in a manner that did not inspire confidence, but he nodded. Malburius kneeled and offered up a prayer to the Emperor and then took up his las-scalpel. Ragnar leaned forward watching closely, ready for any contingency, and prepared to deal with any threat. If Malburius attempted treachery, he would die for it. This maze of thin pipework would not even slow Ragnar down.

Malburius gave no sign that he was aware of how close he was to violent death. He unscrewed the magnopticle and donned a pair of goggles of thick smoked glass. Ragnar could see that they contained some sort of optical magnification system. He lifted the las-scalpel and touched the activation rune. A beam of pure intense light sprang into being. It was about a hand-width long.

Malburius twisted the body of the scalpel and the beam shortened. He leaned forward and began slowly and carefully cutting away the carapace. Then he sliced the flesh to expose the internal organs beneath. Haegr flinched. The smell of seared flesh filled the air.

Malburius moved very carefully. The priest was obviously used to dealing with normal humans, and there was much about a Space Marine's anatomy and skeleton that apparently confused him. The bones were thicker and reinforced to be strong as steel. The ribs were much wider and flatter than a mortal's, designed to provide an extra layer of armour over the vital internal organs. Most of these were in different places, intermingled with grafts that had no place within a human's body.

'Are you sure you know what you're doing, priest?' asked Haegr, through gritted teeth. Sweat beaded his brow. 'I am very fond of my belly. It has taken a long time to bring it to the peak of perfection that it enjoys today. I would not have you reducing my manly girth.'

'Perhaps you would like to do this yourself,' said Brother Malburius. He shook his head and tutted. 'This is what comes from letting your patients remain conscious,' he added.

'Perhaps you could give me a sermon, priest. They usually put me to sleep quickly enough.'

'And blasphemy as well,' said Malburius. 'Little wonder the Emperor has seen fit to withdraw his favour from you.'

As he spoke, the missionary leaned forward and pushed aside the oolitic kidney. Ragnar could see that it was inflamed. Blood was flowing from several places. The wounds did not look good. He pointed this out to Malburius.

Swiftly the priest moved the las-scalpel over the perforations and with practiced skill, cauterised them closed. Haegr gritted his teeth. He was becoming paler, but emitted no gasp. Malburius looked at him, but the Wolf gestured for him to continue.

Sweat was dripping from Haegr's brow. Ragnar studied him closely, wondering whether his friend would remain conscious.

Haegr had lapsed into complete silence, as if he were concentrating on conserving all his strength for a superhuman effort to come. His breathing sounded strange until Ragnar realised it was the faint flexion of the lungs themselves. Malburius moved to them and attached suction cables. Blood pumped into the translucent plasmite as it drained away. Ragnar felt a faint sting as his own blood was drawn forth. Haegr was obviously losing the precious red stuff quickly. Still he gave no sign of complaint.

A faint dry retching indicated that Linus Serpico was finding it difficult to remain sanguine. He was obviously not used to dealing with situations like this.

Brother Malburius sucked in air, and leaned forward. It was obvious that he had found something amiss. He reached down and wafted some antiseptic incense onto an area. Haegr let out a stifled moan. Malburius again leaned forward and began making practiced careful movements with the scalpel. 'Artery sealed,' he muttered. 'Let's see what else we can find.'

He continued to explore the wound gently, probing with his fingers. Ragnar maintained his silence until the priest seemed satisfied. 'That is the best I can do,' he said eventually and began to close up, carefully cauterising the wounds and sealing them with synthi-flesh. 'I would recommend to most people that they spend the next few days abed, but you are Space Marines. I have heard much of your miraculous healing powers. I now begin to believe it. Much of the internal damage was healing itself even as I operated. Only the major perforations needed work although they needed it desperately. It is astonishing, and a testimony to the greatness and mercy of the Emperor.'

'If you say so,' said Haegr opening his eyes and belching. 'I rather think it a testimony to my heroic powers of recuperation.'

Ragnar shook his head. Weak as he was, Haegr was incorrigible.

'It's time to begin closing you up,' said Malburius. Only now did he permit himself to look nervous. Ragnar saw him swallow. Swiftly and precisely he began to set about the task.

'What do you know of the Brotherhood?' he asked Malburius as the man worked.

'They call themselves "The Righteous", and they are certainly filled with righteous hatred.'

'You agree with them?'

'They choose to interpret the Emperor's words in a way that suits their prejudices.'

'Suffer not a mutant to live?' asked Ragnar.

'Aye, but they spread their nets too widely.'

'What do you mean?'

'They hate those to whom the Emperor gave shelter, and to whom he extended the cloak of his protection.'

'The Navigators?'

'Aye, the Navigators.'

'You think they are wrong?'

'If the Emperor himself chose to spare the Navigators, who are they to contradict him? It seems to

me that they combine the sins of wrath and pride.
They are arrogant.'

'Yet they do not seem to lack supporters.'

'The layfolk are ever easy to lead into error. That is
why my brothers and I must continue the great
work here on the sacred soil of Terra. Even in this
holding, despite all my efforts, they have sympathisers.' There was an obvious sincerity in the man's
voice when he spoke of the holy nature of the home
world. It commanded respect, even though Ragnar
disagreed with him. As Ragnar listened he constantly watched the doors, as well as the priest who
sutured and repaired his colleague's flesh. He would
give any sympathisers of the Brotherhood of Light a
warm welcome if they intruded.

'WE THANK YOU for your help, brother,' said Ragnar.
He glanced at Haegr. The big man had regained
some colour. 'Now we must find our way to the surface.'

'That will not be easy,' said Malburius. 'It is many
days' march to the great access conduit and a long
climb from there. I should know. I made the journey myself coming down.'

'It is something we must do,' said Ragnar. 'We
have work to do up there.'

'I would show you myself, but I have duties here.
Linus will show you, I am sure.'

'I am not a guide,' Linus retorted. 'My family
would never stoop to such a function.'

'It seems to me that you no longer have employment as a scribe,' replied the priest. 'And it seems to me that these men are engaged in the Emperor's work. You must help them.'

Ragnar added. 'I am sure House Belisarius could find work for a reliable third class scribe,' he said. 'If you would help us.'

'I am not sure,' said Linus. 'My grade applied only to Imperial sprocket works number six. I do not know whether it is transferable to the upper levels.'

'Perhaps it might be worth finding out,' said Ragnar. 'You have nothing to lose and everything to gain.'

Linus appeared undecided. Ragnar was about to ask Brother Malburius for a less timorous guide when the bird-like little man spoke up. 'Very well, I shall do it.' He seemed to be addressing his proud ancestors as much as the Wolves. 'I will do all that needs must in order to regain my accustomed station in life.'

'And maybe improve it,' said Haegr, rising from the table. He had begun to apply repair cement to his chestplate, temporarily patching the holes until they could find an armourer. Linus looked a little shocked.

'Maybe even that,' he said eventually, in a tone that suggested he was appalled by his own daring.

'Rest here for a few hours,' said Brother Malburius. 'I will provide you with provisions for your journey.'

'We have no need of provisions,' said Ragnar.

'No, but Brother Linus has.'

'As have I,' reprimanded Haegr. 'After all, Ragnar, it has been hours since I have eaten, and I need to regain my mighty strength.'

'Please wait here,' said the priest. He seemed astonished that Haegr could even speak of food so soon after surgery. 'The fewer people who see you, the fewer tales will be told. No doubt, word of the strangers' arrival has gone round the whole holding by now.' He strode out.

Ragnar watched him go, uncertain of what to do. Doubts flickered into his mind. What if the priest were in league with the brothers? What if he had gone to summon them? He dismissed the thoughts immediately. Malburius did not seem that sort of man. His scent marked him as one who was trustworthy. He had shown no hint of duplicity. Even if he was treacherous, it did not matter. Ragnar felt sure that they could deal with any threat. He settled down to wait patiently, keeping watch on his companions.

Haegr complained about how hungry he was then he boasted about how many of the Brotherhood he had slain in hand to hand combat. Linus Serpico looked progressively more worried as the huge Marine rambled on. He was obviously having second thoughts about travelling in their company. To distract the little man, Ragnar asked, 'How long do you think it will take us to get to the conduit?'

'Two sleeps at most,' said Linus. 'If we walk fast and avoid the lurkers in the dark.'

'The lurkers in the dark?'

'There are many different sorts. Huge spiders. Giant rats. Cannibal men who are outside the Emperor's law.'

'Who would have thought it on Holy Terra?' said Haegr sardonically.

'We are deep beneath Holy Terra now, and far from those who enforce the Emperor's law.'

'We enforce it,' said Ragnar. 'And we shall protect you?'

'But how will I get back?' asked Linus.

'I thought you were coming to the surface with us, to seek employment with House Belisarius.'

Linus looked unsure once more. He seemed to be having profound misgivings. How could my destiny find itself entwined with a mouse like this, Ragnar thought, but dismissed the question. Linus Serpico was not a son of Fenris, he had not been bred for battle and war. It looked as if even a short march from this shabby holding was a major adventure.

Suddenly Ragnar realised that for Linus it would be. In his scheme of things, this was a mighty journey. It had been once for Ragnar too. There was a time, not that long ago, when he had never left the island of the Thunderfists. Then the very concept of an interstellar journey would have been incomprehensible. He smiled to himself, and oddly that seemed to reassure the little man.

'Of course, I will come with you,' he said. 'Of course, you will protect me.'

He sounded as if he needed reassurance, so Ragnar nodded. Perhaps he was right to be worried, despite the relatively short distance. Doubtless this vast underground world was packed with dangers. Perhaps Ragnar was wrong to be overconfident. After all, the Brotherhood of Light was looking for them. And there may be others. He shrugged. All he could do was be prepared for the worst and, as a Space Marine, he always was.

CHAPTER EIGHTEEN

BROTHER MALBURIUS returned with food. There was a thoughtful expression on his lean bearded face. Ragnar could tell from his scent that he was uneasy. He could sense Haegr responding to that as well. In the brief time the priest had been away, he had already started to recover. Malburius inspected Haegr. 'Astonishing,' he muttered, 'you are up and about already.'

'You should expect no less from a great hero of Fenris,' said Haegr. 'Do you have anything to eat?'

'What is going on, Brother Malburius?' Ragnar asked. 'You seem a little nervous.'

'Some of the men have disappeared. It may be nothing. They may have just gone spider hunting.'

'But they may not…'

'The ones who are missing – Burke, Smits, Tobin and the others are all the ones who listened most closely to Brotherhood doctrines.'

'You think they may have gone to contact the zealots?'

'Let us say I don't rule out the possibility.'

'Will you be safe if you stay here?'

'It will not do the Brotherhood's reputation for piety much good if they start killing priests, will it?' His voice was steady but Ragnar could tell that he was not quite as certain as he appeared. Nevertheless, he was determined to stay with his charges. Malburius was certainly a brave man. 'You had best get going! It is a long way to the surface.'

'Are you sure you will not come with us?'

'My work is here. My folk are here. I must continue to deliver the Emperor's word to them.'

'Then may the Emperor watch over you,' said Ragnar.

'And you too, Space Wolf.'

'What about food?' demanded Haegr? 'A man could starve around here.'

'I am not sure you should be eating,' said Malburius with humour.

'So the torture is to continue,' said Haegr.

But the priest produced loaves and a bunch of mysterious meat that smelled like giant rat. Haegr did not care. He dug in with gusto. 'You should save some for your journey,' said Malburius. 'This was all I could collect from the holding.'

Ragnar nodded and began to check his weapons. It never hurt to know they were in perfect working order before entering potentially hostile territory. Haegr continued to eat while Linus Serpico watched appalled. At least, Haegr was less troubled by his wounds.

'What do you think has happened to Torin?' Ragnar asked.

'He probably found a mirror somewhere and is busy admiring himself,' said Haegr. 'The man's vanity is overwhelming.'

Ragnar could tell from his scent that Haegr was more worried about his friend than he let on. 'Unlike your own,' he said.

'My pride in my manly prowess is entirely justified,' said Haegr as he let out a thunderous belch. He paused for a moment for a reply, but when none came he carried on eating.

'We'd best get going,' said Ragnar.

THE NARROW CORRIDORS of the holding were empty and very quiet. Ragnar could hear furtive movements all around him. He knew people were trying to watch them unobserved. There was nothing menacing about the noises or the scents. The people were merely nervous around strangers, and Ragnar could understand why. They were poor, ill fed and unarmed. And two massive Space Wolves must be very intimidating. He and Haegr would be like legendary daemons of the Horus Heresy to them. It was an odd thought that rankled deep within him.

'Look at the rats hiding in their holes,' jeered Haegr with his customary sensitivity. 'Don't worry, we won't hurt you!'

Your manner will certainly do nothing to improve their impression of us, thought Ragnar. Haegr sensed his disapproval and quietened down. He contented himself with rambling about what he would do if they encountered any of the Brotherhood of Light. He showed considerable imagination in his descriptions of mutilation. Linus Serpico began to look queasy. And the sicker he looked, the louder Haegr boomed. The huge Wolf was enjoying the little man's discomfort.

Despite his bombast, Ragnar remained concerned. It was still only a few hours since his surgery, and the big man was not at his fighting peak. He moved slowly although his long strides still matched Linus Serpico's,

Ragnar turned to their surroundings. They were down deep, and the air smelled dank and musty. Somewhere far off ancient systems must still be working to keep it in motion, but everything had a stale smell.

All around were ancient buried buildings, and fragments of defaced murals that spoke of a time when these streets might have been exposed to wind and sun. Judging by their depth that would have been when Terra had seas of open water and not toxic sludge. Some depicted a sort of sailing vessel that would not have been out of place on the waters of Fenris. It was hard to imagine that there was once such a time. It was all so incredibly ancient. Ragnar wondered how many feet had trodden these stones before him, wearing those smooth indentations into the very surface. Too many to count. The weight of history pressed down on him as much as the weight of the ground above his head. He felt trapped and claustrophobic, not for the first time in his life.

He noticed his unease had communicated itself to Haegr for he had raised his head and was glancing around. As they left the inhabited warren behind, Ragnar became aware that the place had begun to stir once more. The people seemed shy and timorous, so that even Linus Serpico looked bold. Ragnar wondered if they were hiding something, a stigma of mutation. But he caught none of the giveaway scent traces and he was sure Malburius would never have stood for it, despite his tolerance of the Navigators.

He pushed all thoughts of the people they were leaving from his head. It was better to concentrate on their surroundings, and their destination.

The corridors were becoming narrower and more oppressive. In some places they were merely tunnels, excavated and propped up with bits of broken girder and salvaged plasteel. These were traces of old roof-falls. It was testimony to the skill of the ancient builders that there were so few. Common sense indicated that no architect of Terra would have built anything that could not support the new structure. The real question was why they had done so. Why had all these layers accreted over the centuries? What had compelled them to build atop what must have been perfectly good houses and palaces and warehouses? He cursed. Curiosity was an affliction of his, just as hunger was Haegr's. He asked Linus Serpico.

The little man glanced at him, like a sparrow looking at a hawk. 'I know not,' he said. 'Most likely it was either population or economic pressure. Tales tell of how the structures beneath were still occupied even as new ones were built.'

'Economic pressure?' Ragnar asked. He understood population pressure. He had seen the worlds of the Imperium where billions were crammed into massive hive cities, but the concept of economic pressure was more difficult for him to grasp.

'Land is very valuable here,' said Linus, not without pride. 'The most expensive in the galaxy. Every square metre is titled and deeded to someone – a Navigator House, a great noble of the Adeptus, a religious order. Selling is rare. Rents are high. When you can't build outwards, you build upwards. New layers are constantly being added.'

Ragnar's grasp of economics was good enough to tell him one thing. 'Surely that would reduce the value of all the land beneath.'

'You would think! But no – it means they simply charge more for the new space above. Eventually, after millennia of this you end up with places like we have. The rent rolls must be fascinating. Some of them date back more than ten millennia.'

Ragnar had assumed that the area of warrens was abandoned and the people there were squatters who lived free. Linus soon corrected him.

'No, we pay rent. Not much by modern standards, but we pay according to the agreed schedule. The toll collectors still come and enter our payments in the book of records. Interesting work for a scribe – you get to see a bit of the world.'

'Not the most appealing bit,' said Haegr. 'Judging by this place.'

'I suppose not,' said Linus. 'But then you have lived on the surface.'

He made it sound as if he were talking about some distant and luxurious planet, not that which lay directly above his head. Another heavy impression imprinted itself on Ragnar's mind – there were countless generations that lived and died here without seeing the sun or the sky. He began to get a sense of how blessed he had been to be born on Fenris, despite its dangers.

'You will see the surface soon,' said Ragnar.

'Indeed,' said Linus. He sounded both hopeful and astonished at his own temerity.

They moved on through the gloom, the shoulder lights of the Wolves flickering on automatically as they entered pockets of darkness. Ragnar did not bother to suppress them by over-riding the automatic controls. He wanted some light to see by, and he was sure that his own eyes gained more advantage from the lights than a normal man's. Besides, in these twisting winding corridors, he would catch wind of anyone approaching in time to dowse the lamps if the need arose.

In some places the ceilings grew so low that Ragnar had to crouch and Haegr had to bend almost double to work their way through. Linus had no such problems. Ragnar wondered if his small size was some sort of adaptation to his surroundings rather than a product of a poor diet.

He smiled. There was a time when he would not have considered such things, but the strange knowledge the teaching engines of Fenris had placed in his brain chose the oddest moments to surface.

There were faint animal smells around them now, and he began to notice small holes in the walls; places where long feral things that looked more like weasels than rats emerged, with a baleful glitter in their eyes. They glanced at the three companions as if to see whether they were edible. Linus flinched, but the creatures recognised the threat the Wolves represented and did not attack. They probably sensed Haegr's hunger. The big man was more likely to eat them than they were to get a bite out of him. Ceramite probably did not smell particularly appetising to them either. A tasty bite of Linus Serpico would be different, though.

Ordinary men like Linus lived in a different world, where even these rodents might prove a threat. In his own diffident way the scribe was showing more courage by making this journey than either of the two Wolves. Linus was risking his life. It was not just the rats – it was the diseases they might carry, the poisons in the tainted water, things to which he was not immune. By making him come with them, they were putting their needs before his life. Ragnar wondered if Linus realised that, and how great his courage really was.

Everything is relative, thought Ragnar. He realised he was coming dangerously close to heresy. The Imperium was built on absolutes: the absolute truth of the Emperor's revealed word, the absolute supremacy of man in the universe, the absolute evil of Chaos and mutation that must be opposed by the defenders of order. These formed the bedrock of Imperial faith.

He did not need to start thinking in terms of relativity – that way leads to weakness and worse. The truth of it was that every man, woman and child had a place in the great scheme of things. It was up to Ragnar to stand between mankind and its enemies. It was Linus's place to write down facts and figures. They had simply been given gifts of strength and courage proportionate to their responsibilities. There was no need to look further than that.

The great edifice of the Imperium had lasted ten thousand years, and would last ten thousand more as long as men adhered to their sound beliefs. Anything worth settling had been done by the Emperor and the primarchs at the dawn of their history. That was the end to it. There was no need to start attributing more courage to Linus than he had, or to belittling himself and Haegr because of it. He and Haegr were worth more to the Imperium than Linus and a hundred like him.

And yet… part of him did think that way. It was a flaw in him that he must wrestle with ideas. Not all heresies were obvious; the most dangerous were the subtlest. Pride was the greatest of all sins, the one that had led the Warmaster astray. Pride in intellect was the worst of all, and Ragnar suffered from precisely that. He needed to talk it over with a Wolf Priest when he saw one. And he realised there would be penances.

Haegr possessed a simple acceptance of what went on around him, and a simple faith in the rightness of the old ways. But Ragnar was being hypocritical. He was not like Haegr, and would not be happy to be like him. Pride again, he thought. There is no escaping it.

His feelings were partly a reaction to being on holy Terra itself. He had been expecting something special, a glow of sanctity, the touch of the divine, such as he had experienced in the shrine of Russ on Garm. Instead he had found politics and corruption and crumbling corridors. A deep sense of disappointment had settled in.

'I think we should head left now,' said Linus. They had come to a fork. One path led up and to the left, the other down and to the right. From both emitted fusty air, dank and redolent of rust and the smell of ancient machines blew.

'You think,' said Haegr. 'That's reassuring.'

'It's been a long time since I came this way, and I was headed in the other direction.'

'You are an excellent guide,' said Haegr. He sounded peevish. Ragnar put it down to the pain.

'I am sure you are correct,' said Ragnar, striding confidently up the crumbling stairwell, much to Haegr's astonishment.

It became obvious that there were people all around them. These crumbling corridors were as full of them as rotting cheese was riddled with maggots. They were squeezed into nooks and crannies, shyly trying to avoid the sight of the Marines, but unaware of how great their failure was. There were women and children and old men. They sat beside traps that they inspected for rats and large insects to eat. They pumped dirty water from standpipes. They moved silent as shadows and ghostly as wraiths. They were the dispossessed poor of this ancient planet.

Now and then, Ragnar smelled alcohol in a raw state. It was always accompanied by the sounds of muted laughter and quiet discourse. There were taverns down here of the most basic sort, where brewers fermented drinks from sugary waste and mixed it with tainted water. Everything echoed with the brighter world of the surface. These people might as well have been ghosts of ancient days, he thought, for all the life that was in them. The trip had taken on a strange quality. It was like a journey through some mythical afterlife, or a primitive civilisation on which the shades of the departed fed on dust and performed odd parodies of the tasks they had done in life.

They moved on through the spectral gloom and Ragnar was filled with a growing sense of unease. He wished he had more brothers with him. Where was Torin, he wondered? The shadows gave no reply.

CHAPTER NINETEEN

THE CORRIDORS GREW wider, more like avenues. Ancient statues, dull and dusty and crumbled with age lined what had once been a street. Ragnar's unease grew and he could smell that, despite his cheery demeanour, Haegr was growing tense too. The huge Wolf had started to favour his right side again. Not even the fabled healing powers of a Space Marine could make him entirely immune to the effects of his injuries. Ragnar raised his head and sniffed the air. Something was making him wary.

He padded forward cautiously and studied a statue. It was robed like a member of the Administratum, and doubtless represented some forgotten hero of an ancient struggle. It held a book in one hand and a bolter in its outstretched right arm. Who were you, Ragnar wondered? Did the citizens erect a statue in your honour, or did you erect it as a monument to your vanity? The whole place seemed like a storehouse of monuments to forgotten struggles and peoples.

'What is it?' asked Linus Serpico, in the tone of a man who has just been told he has a fatal disease by a chirurgeon.

'I don't know,' said Ragnar, 'but something's not right.'

'It's my stomach,' said Haegr. 'It thinks my throat's been cut.'

'It just might be, if you don't shut up.'

'I am not sure I like your tone, little man. I may have to give you a sound beating.'

Haegr was scanning their surroundings intently. Perhaps, thought Ragnar, a brain did lurk behind that ox-like façade after all.

'What is it?' repeated Linus. There was an increasing note of desperation in his voice. Ragnar noticed that he had produced a small clasp knife. It would have been as useful against a Space Wolf's armour as a child's toy. But maybe it could do some damage to an ordinary man if he got close enough. Ragnar could not picture the little scribe being able to use it. He had not liked the sight or the smell of blood.

'Gunmetal,' said Haegr. His nose was fantastically keen. It must be useful for sniffing out food. 'What do we do now?'

Ragnar was surprised to be asked. He shrugged and waited. He needed more information before he came to a decision. He could sense people in the distance, but there was a scuttling furtive quality to their movements. It was as if they were trying to move rapidly but with caution. It was the sound of troops on patrol in enemy territory.

Ragnar sniffed again. Faint and far away he caught something.

'Must be twenty or thirty of them,' said Haegr. Ragnar was surprised again. Whatever he thought of Haegr's brains there was nothing wrong with his senses. Few men were as keen as Ragnar and, if anything, Haegr was his superior in this area. He could hear Linus Serpico gulp. The stink of fear clung to the little man. 'Stand or fight?' Haegr asked.

Ragnar considered. There was nothing to be gained from standing and waiting. There was nothing to be gained from fighting. They might get wounded, or lose Linus and be back where they started. He did not consider the possibility that they might be killed. 'Neither,' said Ragnar. 'We run!'

'Run?' said Haegr. He sounded outraged.

'There's no time to argue,' said Ragnar. 'Let's go.'

He did not wait to see how Haegr responded. He had found it best when giving a command to behave as if it would be obeyed implicitly. He broke into a run, doing his best to keep ahead of his pursuers. He hoped they could reach their goal before they were overtaken. Linus needed no encouragement. A few seconds later he heard a curse, a grunt and heavy footfalls as Haegr did his best to sprint.

As the statues blurred past Ragnar wondered if he was doing the right thing. Any moment, he expected to feel a las-blast in his back. He half expected to hear Haegr stop running and turn to face their attackers. If that happened it would be bad. He would have no option but to do the same. A Space Wolf did not desert his battle-brothers.

'They know where we are going,' said Linus. His breath was coming in gasps but he was just managing to keep up with the Marines.

'What?'

'They know we are heading for the access conduit.'

'How?' asked Haegr, who did not sound much better than Linus.

'Where else would we go? It's the shortest route to the surface from here.'

Ragnar considered the possibilities. If he were the enemy leader he would have posted a force ahead of them to cut them off. There was no sense in assuming their enemy would do anything different. In which case the force behind them were not just pursuers, they were like beaters in a hunt, driving the prey into a deadly net. 'You're right,' said Ragnar. 'Is there any other way up?'

'None so easily accessible.'

'I say we fight our way through,' said Haegr. He was panting loudly. 'It beats all this running about.'

Ragnar glanced over his shoulder to see if anyone was following. He detected no one close. They had temporarily outdistanced those behind them. He ducked through an opening in the wall and found himself in an abandoned chamber. The others followed. Both looked at him as if he were mad.

'First it's run, now it's hide,' said Haegr. 'Make up your mind.'

Ragnar shook his head and smiled bleakly. There was no point in running blindly forward. They were foolishly doing what their enemies wanted.

'You said there were other ways, although not so easily accessible,' said Ragnar to Linus Serpico.

'There is a place traders come down by. I have only been there once for supplies.'

'Can you get us there now?'

'Maybe.'

Ragnar assumed the main escape route would be covered by their foes. Was he willing to take a chance that Linus could find this other one? Or would it be best to proceed? There were too many variables here, and he did not have enough information. He supposed they could spring an ambush on their pursuers, who were closing in fast.

'Think you can take them?' Ragnar asked Haegr.

'You jest? A couple of dozen of these earthlings against the mighty Haegr – perhaps I should tie one hand behind my back.'

'I don't think that will be necessary.'

Ragnar could hear their pursuers coming closer. They were moving fast, confident that their prey was in full flight ahead of them. That was a very dangerous assumption. 'We stay,' said Ragnar.

'But of course,' said Haegr. He was outraged that Ragnar might think anything different.

'I want a prisoner.'

'Why?'

'Information. We need intelligence.'

'Speak for yourself,' said Haegr, and then added, 'that sounds like something Torin always says about me.'

Ragnar knew the big man was wondering where his battle-brother was. 'We wait here. We let them pass. I will take a prisoner. You will guard Linus.'

'Why do you get to take the prisoner?'

'I am the stealthiest.'

'My heroic form is not best suited to skulking,' said Haegr. ''Tis true.'

'And they might hear your wheezing kilometres away.'

'I do not wheeze,' said Haegr. 'I merely take bigger breaths than you midgets. My mighty frame needs more oxygen.'

'Your boasting certainly does,' said Ragnar. 'Now be quiet and let them pass.'

Haegr quietened. His stentorian breathing quietened too, after a while.

They did not have long to wait. The sound of jogging feet echoed outside the doorway. Both Ragnar and Haegr waited with weapons ready in case they had been spotted and needed to fight. Ragnar would not have minded. The beast within him was keen to start bloodletting. He was almost disappointed the pursuers went by.

'How long to the access conduit we originally headed for?'

'Perhaps twenty minutes,' said Linus.

'It will not be long before they realise they have missed us and double back,' said Haegr exhibiting a certain amount of thought. Ragnar nodded. He needed to be swift and sure. He made a sign to tell Haegr to wait and be silent, and moved to the doorway. He concentrated but could sense nothing close. He ducked out and loped swiftly but silently in the direction of their pursuers' scent.

He did not have far to go until he overtook them. They were the same sort of warriors they had fought earlier in the presence of the prophet. They were armed with lasrifles with bayonets attached. There was no sign of any psyker for which Ragnar was profoundly grateful. He held back in the gloom trusting that his eyes were better than the men's and his senses keener. Now all he needed was a little luck.

He got some immediately – but it was bad luck. As if warned by some sixth sense, one of the men glanced over his shoulder. Ragnar barely had time to duck into a narrow doorway. He held his breath and counted silently to ten but could detect no sign he had been noticed. He risked a quick sidelong glance and saw that the man was standing waiting. In fact the telltale smell and a faint glowing point showed that the man had lit some form of narcotic bac-stick. Were they really so confident, Ragnar wondered, or was this man very addicted? If so, he was going to regret it. Ragnar stalked closer, bolter held lightly in his hand. He could hear the man's companions recede and as he came closer he could smell sweat and stale bac-stick fumes. He could hear the man's gasping breath. He was obviously tired and resting. He did not seem to be in such good condition as his fellow zealots, perhaps because of the drug he smoked.

Ragnar walked right up to him from behind, looped a hand over the man's mouth and placed the muzzle of his bolter against the man's spine. The man began to sputter and gasp and Ragnar realised that he had swallowed the bac-stick. Doubtless the flame was burning his tongue. It could not be helped.

Lifting the man effortlessly, hand clamped over his mouth, Ragnar turned and loped back in the direction of their shelter.

By the time they had arrived, the man's face had turned an interesting shade of purple. He had given up trying to free his sidearm from its holster.

'What have we here?' said Haegr as he entered. 'A new toy?'

Ragnar let the man go. He opened his mouth to shout and Haegr buffeted him to his knees with what for him was a gentle love-tap. 'I don't like zealots,' said Haegr. 'I think I am going to pull this one's arms off.'

He was very convincing. Even Ragnar wondered whether he meant it. Perhaps he did. He advanced on the man and jerked him to his feet as if he were a puppet. He held an arm in each massive fist. The zealot tried to scream but nothing came out. His face looked even paler. It was framed by long dark hair.

'What's your name?'

'Crawl back to your hellworld, offworld scum,' said the man. Haegr imprisoned the man's wrists in one hand and casually buffeted him with the other. 'Talk or I'll rip your nadgers off and eat them,' he said. He radiated uncompromising malice as he said it.

'Antoninus.' There was defiance in the man's voice, but it had a brittle quality. The man was very afraid although he was trying to hide it.

'How many of you are waiting at the access conduit?' Ragnar asked.

'Go to hell, mutant lover,' said the zealot. His voice was hoarse and rasping. Eating that burning bac-stick must have hurt. There was an odd grinding sound as Haegr closed his grip and the man screamed. It sounded like bones were about to break in the man's wrists.

'How many?' said Ragnar.

'Twenty,' said the man. His scent said he was lying.

'I smell a lie,' said Haegr sounding like an evil giant from old legend. The grinding continued. The man gasped in pain. 'Fifty.' It was obvious he had reached his threshold of tolerance. Ragnar was glad. He did not enjoy torture, no matter how much the Imperium claimed some people deserved it.

'Heavy weapons?' Ragnar asked.

'Yes – covering the main approaches. Heavy bolters.'

Ragnar looked at the man. That was military hardware. He did not know why it should gall him that these zealots have access to it here on Terra but it did. It niggled at him for a moment, and then he realised why. Unless they had their own armaments manufactories they had to be getting them from somewhere. Somewhere off planet most likely. Mars was the nearest forge world, but he could not see the Adeptus Mechanicus engaging in arms smuggling within the Holy System – although stranger things had been known to happen. More likely the weapons were being brought in from somewhere further. He wondered what he would find if he searched some of the Navigator's bonded warehouses. He doubted he would ever get permission to do so, but he might attempt to find out on his own.

All these thoughts flashed through his mind in an instant and he kept his full attention on the zealot. He needed to know more. 'Who is your commander?'

'Edrik – he… he reports direct to Pantheus.'

'The merchant!' said Haegr. It seemed the fat man had been high up within the hierarchy. Perhaps this had not been such a bad lead after all.

'You have heard of him?'

'Who has not? He is rich as Mithras and twice as pious. Always giving money to good causes.'

'And one of those is your Brotherhood?' Ragnar felt like they had stumbled over something very important, if only he could get to the bottom of it.

'It sounds like he is giving more than money,' said Haegr.

'Are you sure this is true?' Ragnar demanded. The man nodded. He certainly believed it to be so. Ragnar could tell from his scent. 'How can you be so certain?'

'Edrik was at his mansion. He has also been to his palace in the belt.'

'The asteroid belt?'

'He's so fat he prefers to live in low gravity,' said the prisoner. There was a note of contempt in his voice and it shone in his wild, wide eyes. 'He likes the world to think he's holy, but he has many secret vices.'

'Not unlike yourself,' said Ragnar, indicating the man's bac-sticks. If the man saw Ragnar's point he gave no sign. The certainty of the fanatic was starting to seep back into him, the longer they let him live.

'I quite like the sound of him,' said Haegr, not letting on that Pantheus had been captured. 'Certainly more than I like the sound of you.' Antoninus's certainty was shattered by another twist of his wrist. There was more than physical pain involved here. Haegr's strength was so overwhelming that it increased his sense of helplessness and eroded his confidence. Haegr gently bashed his head off the wall a couple of times, just to make sure he got the point.

'What is your connection with House Ferracci?' Ragnar asked on the off chance that the question might dislodge a tasty nugget of information. The expression of contempt on the man's face returned, hardened, and intensified a thousand fold. 'I have no connection with those mutant bastards,' he said. 'The sooner the sacred soil of Terra is cleansed of their worthless Chaos-be-damned lives the better… And yours too,' he added as after thought. 'Only the pure blood of humanity should set foot on the sacred soil.'

There was certainty and fervour here that went bone deep. 'Why do you work for a mutant then?' he asked. The man glanced at him as if he were mad. If Ragnar had spoken Fenrisian to him, he could not have received a more blank look of incomprehension.

'Your prophet was a psyker. We killed him.'

'The prophet was blessed by the light, granted his powers by the Emperor himself so that he might continue the Emperor's work. He will rise again! Or another will rise to lead us.'

'If there are more like him then the Inquisition will be down here to scoop out your warrens like a fishwife gutting a sea bass.'

'The Inquisition blessed his work.'

Ragnar somehow doubted this, but the man seemed certain. Ragnar wondered whether the Inquisition hated the Navigators so much that they would sponsor acts of terrorism and assassination against them?

He shook his head. His mistake was thinking in terms of organisations. Organisations had rules, guidelines, principles. They did not think or feel. Only people did that. All it would take would be one man high up in the Inquisition. It would not be the Inquisition itself. He filed the thought. They were sailing in waters that were deep and murky indeed.

'This is taking too long,' said Haegr. 'His comrades will be coming back this way soon. Who knows, they might even have missed him. I say we kill him and be done.'

Ragnar shook his head. This man might have more useful information. Ragnar wanted him alive so that the Belisarians might pick his brains. Doubtless they would be better at it than he and Haegr could ever be. Antoninus lifted his head and spat at Haegr. 'Do your worst. I am not afraid to die.'

Haegr laughed. 'On second thoughts, let him live so that I can cut the blood eagle in his back. I don't

think I will even cut it, I might just break his ribs
and pull his lungs out with my bare hands.'

Antoninus's glance shifted to Haegr's gauntlets.
Both of them knew that it was no idle threat. The
huge Marine was capable of doing exactly as he
said. At that moment Haegr lifted his head and
seemed to strain to hear something.

'I think his comrades are coming back now.'

Ragnar was once again astonished by the keenness
of his senses. Only now could he make out the faint
distant sounds.

'We must away!' he said.

CHAPTER TWENTY

Antoninus smirked in triumph. Haegr caught him and said, 'You will not live to greet your friends. You might say hello to them in hell though.'

'I am not afraid to die!' said the zealot.

'That's twice you've said that,' said Haegr. 'Third time is the charm. Just remember, not all deaths are easy.'

Antoninus paused for thought. Ragnar put the muzzle of his pistol to his head. 'You can make your choice now. You can come with us or we can decorate this wall with your brain.'

It was one thing to say you feared nothing when surrounded by friends, it was another when staring at your enemies. It was one thing to defy your enemy and tell yourself you were not scared, it was another to actually make the decision whether to live or die. When the moment of crisis came most people could find reasons why they wanted to live. This was not a heroic death in battle or a glamorous martyr's doom on the flames. This was an anonymous execution. It served no purpose. And Ragnar had sensed the brittle nature of Antoninus's courage.

Antoninus swallowed. Ragnar could almost see thoughts swimming across his face. If he lived he might help his companions to bring the Wolves down. If he lived he would be able to smoke another bac-stick, and see his family if he had one. Abruptly the bravado leaked out of the man, like wine from a pricked skin. He deflated visibly. The glow remained in his eyes but they had taken on a more furtive look.

There was an almost guilty expression on his face which mixed with hatred when he looked at Ragnar. This was not a man who would thank him for making him reveal the brittle truth about himself or being there to witness it. Ragnar felt a moment of sympathy for him, even though they were enemies pure and simple. And he felt shame that was the mirror image of Antoninus's self-hate. This did not fit his heroic self-image as a Space Wolf either. He forced a snarling grin onto his lips. He would live with it.

'Shouldn't we gag him?' Linus asked.

'I could rip out his tongue,' offered Haegr hopefully.

'Gag him and bind his hands,' said Ragnar to Linus. 'Use his shirt.'

He turned to Antoninus. 'Make any sudden moves, or attempt to betray us and I will give you to Haegr.' He could tell from the man's scent, there would be no treachery, at least for the moment.

'What now?' Haegr asked. Ragnar considered their options. The men could not wait by the access conduit forever. Or could they? He cursed the lack of comm-net relays stations down here, and the shielding the layers of buildings provided. Then it dawned on him. 'You must have ways of communicating with the surface?' he said to Antoninus.

'Of course,' he said looking at Ragnar as if he were an idiot. 'There are emergency comm-net relay flexors that go all the way up, they patch into the surface grids.'

'Where is the nearest access point?'

'Anaconda Station. It's a sleep away from here. Up a level.'

'Guarded?'

'Of course. It's in our main shrine.'

'I suppose you're going to say storming it is out of the question,' said Haegr in the petulant tone of a child who knows his parents are going to deny him a treat.

Linus cleared his throat. 'There was a flexor in Imperial sprocket works number six,' he said. 'Before it was destroyed.'

'We don't have time to clear away the rubble right now.'

'There was an emergency node five hundred metres away. It patches into the grid as well.'

'How far?'

'The next level up.'

'Why didn't you say?'

'You never asked.' Ragnar suppressed his frustration. Linus was right. Haegr was not so understanding.

'Anything else you forgot to mention? You didn't also happen to have an emergency escape elevator all the way to the surface, or an aircar, or a division of Imperial Guard based there or...'

'Of course not.' Linus's tone showed how absurd he considered the suggestions. He apparently did not see the joke.

'The flexor is still functioning then.'

'It ought to be. It has worked for the last ten millennia. I don't see why it should decide to stop now.'

'If we can patch into that we can contact the surface and get some support.'

'Then let us be on our way,' said Haegr.

Ragnar nodded. He led them back out into the street. 'Lead on, Linus,' he said.

The little man glanced nervously down the street to where he thought the zealots must be. Lacking the Space Wolves' keen senses he obviously thought them a lot closer than they were. He then risked a glance at Antoninus, obviously fearing the man would give away their position. He need not have worried. The zealot was still gagged, and Haegr had one hand over the man's mouth for good measure. They headed off in the direction that Linus indicated.

'WHAT WILL YOUR friends do now?' Ragnar asked Antoninus, removing the gag. It looked for a moment like the zealot was not going to answer. Haegr growled.

'Since they have not found you yet they will split up into search parties and scour the area. They will probably request back-up from our temple. You will not be allowed to escape alive.' Antoninus could not keep the satisfaction out of his voice.

Ragnar considered their surroundings. The further they moved from the main warrens, the more run down they looked and the lower the ceilings became. More vile animals surrounded them. And yet, according to Linus, they were getting closer to his former place of work.

It was hard to imagine humans living and working in these rat holes, but according to the little scribe hundreds had. Most had moved away from the cell-like dwellings when their employment failed, although a few still haunted the rubble, eking out a pitiful existence. According to Linus they knew nothing else. They had spent their whole lives in the area, and could not conceive of moving away.

Ragnar revised his opinion of the little man. He had thought him drab and unadventurous but he could see now that by the standards of his upbringing Linus had been more dynamic than many. He had at least moved away from the area, and now he was considering moving further still. Once again Ragnar was considering the sin of relativity. Antoninus glanced around him with disdain. The people around here were low on the social scale as far as he was concerned. That much was obvious.

He realised that they had come up at least one level of the warrens in their travels. The stairwell had been long and rusting in many places. Massive spider webs had blocked it, and those must have been recently woven because Linus claimed traders and travellers still occasionally used these paths. The thought of such huge creatures did nothing for Ragnar's peace of mind, although in his heart of hearts he did not truly fear them.

As they turned another corner Ragnar noticed that Haegr was grinning. A moment later he caught a familiar scent. He could not quite believe it. It was the smell of a Wolf. 'I believe Torin is looking for us,' said Haegr. 'We will be surprising him soon.'

'Your appetite constantly surprises me,' said a soft mocking voice from the shadows. Ragnar was surprised. The scent trail was quite old and this meant that Torin must have circled round and caught them from downwind. Ragnar wondered how deliberate that was. He doubted the Wolfblade would ever tell. 'I knew you would blunder up here sooner or later.'

They were on the same level which meant that over relatively short ranges their comm-links should work. 'Why did you not try to contact us?' Ragnar asked.

'Same reason as you don't have your beacons on. Security. If the mission has been compromised who knows whether the Belisarius channels or any others are safe? The relays may be monitored and short range pulse traffic can be picked up by people with the right divinatory apparatus.' Ragnar knew his comrade was right.

'Glad to see you're still alive.' said Torin. 'I thought Haegr had gobbled down his last ox, judging from the wounds I saw.'

'Hah! It will take more than a few scratches to impede Haegr's mighty form.'

'What happened to your escort of Belisarians?' Haegr asked.

'Ambushed. I fought my way clear with half a dozen of them, and ordered them to head to the surface while I looked for you. I knew you would need help since you had to look after Haegr.'

'Mighty Haegr needs no help from cubs.'

Suddenly they were all talking at once.

'Who are your friends?'

'How did you find us?'

'Easy, I followed the trail of empty food silos and knew Haegr would be there.'

'Linus here is our friend. Antoninus is a prisoner. He has information that we may find useful.'

'There has been no time to empty silos. Chance would be a fine thing.'

'Where were you headed?'

'An emergency relay station for the Imperial sprocket autofac. We were going to contact the surface on the emergency channel.'

'Smart thinking. I am sure Haegr had no part in that.'

'A beating, Torin. Within an inch of your life…'

Ragnar was glad that their companion had been found or had found them. Torin had been searching high and low for them, stalking zealot patrols looking for clues to their whereabouts. Of course, he could not track all of them but he had learned a few things.

The zealots were far stronger down here than anyone had supposed, but they were thrashing around headless at the moment without their prophet. It appeared the dead psyker had been their leader, in this sector at least. It also appeared that they extorted food and money out of the local inhabitants in return for protection.

It was an enterprise as old as life on Terra according to Torin.

'The surprising thing is how strong the Brotherhood is down here. I suspect some sort of military build-up. I fear we could be looking at rebellion and open warfare on the surface soon.'

That did not surprise Ragnar. It followed a pattern he had seen many times before. 'We need to assemble the guards and clear this place.'

'I fear it will take more than the might of Belisarius to do that,' said Torin. 'The fanatics are numerous and well armed. We may need to forge new alliances to deal with this and soon.'

'It's just as well we found this out then,' said Ragnar.

As they talked, they followed Linus, and prodded the zealot at gunpoint. Torin and Haegr bickered cheerfully. The presence of his old sparring partner seemed to have worked wonders for Haegr's health. The ceiling became lower; the smell of dust and crumbling brickwork filled the air. There were more rats and more large spiders. Linus nodded and said they were close now.

A few moments later they turned the corner and found themselves face to face with a duralloy panel in the wall, covered in warning runes and messages in the local alphabet.

'This is it,' said Linus. 'Although I am not sure how we are going to open it without the key.'

Haegr ripped it open with one hand.

'That's against the rules,' said Linus.

'I am sure the Arbites will be along any moment to arrest me,' said Haegr.

Torin studied the ancient engine of brass cables and ceramite panels. He reached forward to tap the runes. He was making a few adjustments to the

settings to the tune of the basic engineering litanies. He ran a few test protocols on the link and
moments later, was sending pulsed communications to the surface. Apparently he got a response.
He had sealed the circuit so that not even Ragnar
and Haegr could hear what was being said.

'A pick up team will be with us within hours,' said
Torin, looking satisfied. 'And then we will be out of
here.'

'Not before time,' said Haegr. 'We should have
been gone a day ago.'

'Better late than never,' said Torin. He glanced at
Antoninus. 'Now, what about telling us a few of
your secrets?'

RAGNAR STUDIED HIS chronometer. The pick up team
was running late. It had been three hours now and
there was no sign of them. He looked at Torin who
simply shrugged. 'Maybe they ran into some unexpected problems,' he said. 'They will be here.
Valkoth himself is leading them.'

'That reassures me' said Haegr. 'If he sent out
some of those fancy dressed Belisarian clowns on
their own, they might have got lost.'

'Not everyone has your unerring sense of direction,' said Torin. 'Although I seem to recall even you
have made a few errors in your time. There was that
incident with the orks on Hera V.'

'I knew you would bring that up,' said Haegr. 'A
man can be right a thousand times, as heroic Haegr

usually is, but let him make one little mistake and…'

'Leading us into the ork boss's camp instead of the Imperial Palace was not a little mistake,' said Torin.

'I didn't notice you opening your mouth to tell me I was wrong,' said Haegr.

'I was unconscious at the time after you managed to accidentally connect with that flailing hammer of yours.'

'You always bring that up as well. One little accident and…'

'It is hard to forget such accidents when your skull is involved in them.'

At first Ragnar thought he was ignoring the remark, but then he noticed the giant was listening. So did Torin, for a cutting remark died unspoken on his lips.

'That's not Valkoth,' said Haegr. A few heartbeats later, Ragnar realised what he was talking about. He could hear stealthy sounds approaching, and could make out the faint but distinctive odour of men. The scent was a compound of meat, incense, bacstick smoke and a dozen other things. It was not the smell of Valkoth or of any Belisarian.

'They found us again,' said Haegr. He did not sound disappointed. 'It seems an unlikely coincidence,' he murmured.

Ragnar wondered if they had been betrayed again. 'Perhaps the signal was traced,' he said.

'Perhaps,' said Torin.

Antoninus had started to grin again. Ragnar was filled with a desire to wipe the smirk off his face. Torin clearly felt the same way.

'We could set a trap. Knock their friend here unconscious and rig his body up with explosives. They could all become martyrs to their holy cause together.'

Antoninus's smile turned sickly. Linus looked shocked. 'You would not really do that, would you?' he asked.

Torin shrugged. Haegr said, 'Hardly seems worth the effort. I say we just go and kill them.'

'Showing off your tactical genius again, I see,' said Torin. 'Let's at least try and find out how many of them there are and what corridors they have covered.'

'And spoil all the fun!'

'You're right. What was I thinking? Oh yes, I remember – my duty to return and protect House Belisarius and uncover the traitor who set us up.'

'Well, when you put it that way...'

A glyph blinked in Ragnar's vision. A faint chime sounded in his comm-link earbead. A moment later Valkoth's voice spoke. 'We are on the same level as you now and picking up your signal. These corridors are a maze, so it may take some time to get to you.'

'It looks like the enemy found us first,' said Torin. 'Just head for the sounds of carnage.'

'We ran into some Brotherhood boys which is why we were not there sooner,' said Valkoth. 'Just hold them off until we get there. Praise Russ.'

Torin laughed as the link dropped. 'It's nice that the old man has faith in us. I like the way he casually informs us to hold out until he gets here.'

'He knows mighty Haegr's bravery,' said Haegr. 'He knows I will keep you alive until he gets here, with a little help from Ragnar of course.'

'Well, I suppose I could always use your great bloated mass of blubber as a shield. Better than sandbags.'

'I fear I am going to have to beat you again, Torin.'

'Later,' said Ragnar, as he noticed shadowy figures appearing in the distance. Antoninus followed the direction of his gaze, but he could obviously see nothing. He looked as if he was considering running for it. Haegr flattened him with a blow of his ham-like fist. 'It would be a shame if he got away now that we have brought him all this way.'

He lifted the recumbent body and tossed it through a doorway one handed. 'We can always come back and collect him later. You'd better join him, little man. Things might get hot out here. Just make sure he does not get away.' The last was a bit of needless cruelty, Ragnar thought. Linus looked and smelled nervous enough to faint.

'Best get moving,' said Torin. Linus scuttled under cover leaving the three Wolves ready to face their onrushing foes. There appeared to be a fair number of the enemy coming in along all the approach corridors. No doubt there were more making their way from chamber to chamber. He raised his bolt pistol and snapped off a few shots into the distance. The shells could not miss the tightly packed bodies. He was rewarded with a scream.

'Spearing blowfish in a barrel,' said Haegr, leaning on the shaft of his hammer and meditating on the targets. The metal pole puffed his fat cheeks out even more. 'I could have hit that man with my hammer from here.'

Ragnar looked at him in astonishment. 'You doubt my word? The word of mighty Haegr?'

Casually, he threw the hammer down the corridor. It carried a long way, and Ragnar could smell blood and hear bones crack. 'I suppose I shall have to go and get it back now,' said Haegr and lumbered off into the distance before Ragnar could say anything. Ragnar exchanged glances with Torin. 'He is a law unto himself,' said Torin. 'But don't worry about him, somehow he always survives.'

Ragnar heard grenades going off. He could see the huge bulk of Haegr limned in the flare of their detonations. His wild laughter echoed down the corridor. He was obviously the one throwing them, and it sounded like he was enjoying himself.

'Perhaps we should go and help him,' said Ragnar.

'No, he would only object to us spoiling his fun. Besides, someone has to stay here and make sure no one gets behind us.' The two Wolves had instinctively moved to cover separate lines of approach. More of the zealots were coming both ways. Others were moving chamber to chamber.

Ragnar crouched in a doorway to make himself a smaller target and snapped off another shot. This time the response was a hail of bolter and las-rifle fire. He doubted that any of his assailants could see him. They were just firing at random, but that would make no difference if one of those shells was to connect with a vulnerable point in his armour.

How long would it take Valkoth to arrive?

CHAPTER TWENTY-ONE

THE CULTISTS KEPT coming on down the corridor and edging closer through the chambers. The bellowing of Haegr told Ragnar that the huge Marine had engaged the enemy. The cracking of skulls and splintering of bone indicated that he had regained his hammer. Bolter shells and autogun bullets chipped the plascrete around Ragnar while las-beams made it bubble and stink like hot asphalt. He considered ducking through the doorway, but it was a single chamber with no visible way out: a death trap if he were caught in it, and if the enemy had grenades or any reasonably heavy weapon. Of course, he could pick many of them off, but being pinned down was generally a recipe for disaster.

'I hate to say this, Torin, but maybe Haegr had the right idea!' said Ragnar.

'I am starting to think so myself,' bellowed Torin over the din of battle. 'Cover me!'

'I will do my best,' said Ragnar, ducking down and snapping off shots, first in one direction and then the other. As he did this Torin dived across the street and through another opening, oblivious to the hail of fire at his heels. A moment later, a hand emerged from the doorway that sent a grenade bouncing up the corridor towards their attackers. The screams told Ragnar that he had caught somebody.

It was Ragnar's turn now. Crouching low, he bounded into the corridor and moved upwards towards the attackers. Billowing smoke obscured him from sight and the hail of fire seemed to have lessened.

Ragnar felt confident that he could more than hold his own against their assailants. Once he was in their midst they would be unable to shoot at him without risking their fellows. All he would have to worry about was saving his own armoured hide. It appalled him to think that Haegr probably had done the right thing. But of course, the big man was an experienced tunnel fighter, so it was no great surprise.

Ragnar could hear the enemy babbling up ahead. A wounded man cursed and screamed alternately while his fellows told him to shut up. A commanding voice bellowed instructions. Ragnar lobbed a grenade in their direction, and the orders ceased, to be replaced by more screams and howls.

Ragnar drew his chainsword as he emerged from the smoke, and found himself face to face once again with the cowled members of the Brotherhood. He did not wait for them to recognise their peril. He leapt among them, striking right and left, slaying as he went. He showed the wounded no mercy, stamping on them as he passed, crushing hands, heads and ribs under his armoured boots. He had seen many wounded men pick up their weapons to kill again and he was not going to take any chances here.

The sheer fury of his sudden onslaught panicked the zealots. They did not know they were facing only one man. All they knew was that some furious daemon had emerged from the smoke of battle and was killing them. Ragnar passed through them like a whirlwind. Nothing withstood him. The chainsword cleaved through the barrels of lasrifles raised in hasty parries. It sent sparks scattering and made the screams of tortured metal mingle with the last wails of the dying.

He did not let up when his foes started to flee. He pursued them, despite being outnumbered scores to one. When his prey ran into their comrades from behind, he realised that he only faced the advance guard of his enemies. But that did not slow him down. As the cultists barged into each other, and tripped one another up, he followed, hacking with his chainsword, blasting with bolter shells at point-blank range, letting the wild ululating war cry of his Chapter reverberate down the corridor.

Bones broke, blood, meat and gristle got caught between the swiftly whirring blade of his chainsword. As the friction heated them, they sent up an awful stench. He kept chopping, severing limbs, opening the top of one man's skull with one blow like an islander opening a coconut with a machete. Once more he heard someone bellowing, telling the zealots to stand firm in the name of the Light. It said that they would prevail. He aimed himself towards the voice, knowing that if he slew the leader, he could create more panic and disarray.

One or two men tried to make a stand now. One of them had raised his autorifle to his shoulder and was aiming at point-blank range at Ragnar. The Space Wolf sprang to one side, as the autofire ripped past him. He brought up his own bolt pistol and slew the shooter with a single shot, silencing his weapon forever.

Someone tugged at his legs and he felt something sting the back of his knee. Looking down he saw that a wounded man had caught the weak joint at the back of his kneeguard with a combat knife. Instinct told Ragnar that the wound was neither serious nor likely to slow him down, but it was a warning to him to be more careful. He lashed out with his boot. The impact threw the wounded man's head backwards and his neck snapped. Ragnar could hear the crunch of vertebrae, but it seemed that he was losing the initiative now.

More and more fire impacted on his armour, the force of the bullets were like hammer blows. Something glanced off Ragnar's skull, drawing blood and sending waves of pain and blackness surging through his head. Perhaps he had been overconfident, he thought. There were too many of his foes for even a Space Wolf to overcome. As he reeled backwards, they continued to rally, raising weapons, drawing blades, making ready to carve him up and chop him down. Ragnar sprang back pulling the trigger of his bolt pistol repeatedly. He sent shells tearing through closely packed flesh. He howled as he fought. He was rewarded with a familiar war-cry echo close by.

Over the scent of blood and opened innards he caught the familiar smell of Fenrisian flesh and hardened ceramite. Valkoth's rescue party must be close. He need only hold on for a little longer.

He snarled defiance. He was not going to hold on, he was going to kill and kill again, dragging as many of his foes to hell as he could – like a true Fenrisian warrior. The beast within him was filled with killing lust, while the saner part of his mind turned it to his advantage. He knew that if he pressed on through his attackers he would link up with Valkoth and his force.

Guided partly by feral instinct and partly by cold calculation, he struck out again. Gathering all his strength he sprang forward, lashing left and right with his chainsword, taking off heads and limbs with every blow, leaving men to slip and fall on their own spilling intestines.

The fury of his renewed onslaught took his opponents off guard for a moment, and he hewed a bloody path through them in the direction of the oncoming Belisarians. But it did not take the fanatics long to regain their wits. Whatever their faults, a lack of desperate courage was not one of them. Some of the wounded grasped at his legs, trying to slow him. Others aimed their weapons. A wave of them threw themselves forward, trying to grapple with Ragnar, and to immobilise his arms and legs. It was a mistake; no two men were as strong as he. He threw them off, sending them flying through the air to smash into walls or into other zealots. He dashed out the brains of others with the butt of his bolt pistol. Trying to restrain his sword arm was like trying to grab the jaws of a hungry tiger.

Still they came on, and still their comrades fired. They did not care that their bullets thudded into the bodies of their fellows more often than smashing into Ragnar's armour. All were overcome by the madness and the chaos of battle. He realised that none of them had as clear a picture of what was going on as he did. The gloom and smoke confused them, as did the loud echo of their weapons. All they could see was a huge shadowy figure moving among them with almost supernatural speed. Even when they did not panic there was a natural urge to shoot, to do something – anything in the face of the threat.

Ragnar lashed out with his boot at the head of one man who was lying on his belly and shooting upward at him with a pistol. His foot connected with sickening force, sending teeth and splintered bone flying. A moment later he was through to Valkoth who was leading a line of black-garbed Belisarian guards towards him. Knowing what would come next Ragnar turned and faced the zealots. A moment later Valkoth and his men were at his side, and the fighting became close and deadly.

'By Russ, Ragnar, you might have left some for us,' said Valkoth. His gloomy aura seemed to deepen in the midst of battle. He moved his head fractionally and a lasbeam hissed by. He raised his bolter easily and fired back at his assailant. Only one shot, but it was enough. There was a precision about Valkoth's way of fighting that was very odd in a Space Wolf, but he was none-the-less deadly for it.

'I think there are a few,' said Ragnar, ducking the stab of a bayonet, then carving through weapon barrel and then man with his riposte.

'Glad to hear it,' said Valkoth, sending another man to hell with a single shot of his bolter, then laying open the forehead of an assailant closing with him with its barrel. Even as the man fell Valkoth pumped a shell into him and moved on.

They headed down the corridor towards Torin, who was holding off more zealots from behind a barrier built of corpses.

Ragnar wondered whether he really could have killed all those men on his own and then driven the others back. But when he thought of the number he had killed, he realised that it was more than possible.

'The situation here is under control. I think you should go and see what Haegr is up to,' Torin said. 'He's probably got his foot caught in a bucket.'

Even as he spoke, Valkoth was issuing a clipped order to the Belisarian guard who moved off in the direction of Torin's attackers.

'Let us all go together,' said Valkoth, leading them in the direction Haegr had taken. Within a hundred metres they found the first mauled bodies, and heard the receding sounds of slaughter. Somewhere further off they heard Haegr bellow: 'Come back and fight like men!'

'Doubtless he thinks that if he shouts loud enough they will obey him,' said Torin sardonically.

'No sign of any bucket,' said Valkoth.

'It's only a matter of time,' said Torin. 'You know that as well as I do. Well, we'd best get to him before he falls down a lift shaft trying to persuade those zealots to come back and be slaughtered.'

They advanced through scenes of awful carnage. Bruised and mangled corpses lay everywhere, their heads oddly indented or turned to jelly, broken ribs protruding through flesh. Ragnar had seen bodies run over by Land Raiders in better condition.

'I am surprised he did not stop for a snack,' said Torin, and catching the disgusted glances of his two companions, he raised an eyebrow. 'Well, he probably hasn't eaten more than a small killer whale in the past few hours.'

Ahead of them loomed the man himself. Gore covered him. Spatters of blood and brain and less recognisable substances decorated his armour and the head of his hammer. He looked around at them and said, 'You did not miss anything here. These worms were barely worth killing.'

'Your mission took a little longer than you expected,' said Valkoth sourly.

'That's the way these things go sometimes,' said Haegr, entirely unabashed. 'No plan survives contact with the enemy, as I have heard you say yourself.'

'Those are an ancient philosopher's words, not mine.'

'Well they are the first sensible words I have ever heard from any philosopher.'

'This is a first,' said Torin sardonically. 'Standing in the ruins under Earth discussing philosophy with Haegr. Whatever next?'

'We were not discussing philosophy,' said Haegr. His outraged tone made it sound as if Torin had accused him of molesting a sheep.

'Don't let me interrupt your intellectual debate,' said Torin wickedly.

Haegr lapsed into sulky silence, folded his huge arms across his chest, and snorted audibly. Valkoth looked at Torin. 'We should be going now,' he said. 'After all, I have rescued you and you have duties in the world above.'

'Rescued us!' said Torin and Haegr near simultaneously.

'The situation was under control,' said Torin.

'Mighty Haegr would have battled his way to the surface, carrying his two weak-stomached companions if need be,' said Haegr. Ragnar noticed that Valkoth's long drooping moustaches were oddly twisted around his mouth. Is he mocking us, Ragnar wondered? Was there a sense of humour at work there?

'We'd best fetch our prisoner and our guide,' said Ragnar.

'A guide?' said Valkoth. He sounded disbelieving.

'He has been of assistance,' said Ragnar innocently. 'And I believe he should be rewarded appropriately.'

RAGNAR GLANCED AROUND his chamber, glad to be back on the surface, all too aware of the comforts of the place, and the security. He lay down on the bed and stared at the ornately carved ceiling. No, that was wrong. There was no security on Earth. It was an illusion. There were traitors everywhere, even here, and soon they would need to smoke them out. There was no place in the Imperium that was truly secure, not as the ancients might have once understood the word. This was a place of intrigue and danger, of fanatics filled with burning religious hatred and self-righteous anger.

He smiled to himself. He had heard the Wolves described in those terms, and he knew that some Chapters and organisations prided themselves on zealotry and a fanatical devotion to their duty. Was there really so much difference between the Inquisition and the Brotherhood, Ragnar wondered? There was a great deal of similarity between them. Both were pledged to defend mankind from the mutant. Both were staffed by dedicated fanatics. Why single out the Inquisition, he thought? His own Chapter was as guilty of these things as the Brotherhood. Ah, but then his own Chapter was in the right. Ragnar could almost have laughed. Of course, that was what he had been taught, and that was what he believed, and in this he was no different from Antoninus.

He lay on the bed for a long time wrestling with the sin of relativity.

CHAPTER TWENTY-TWO

Two DAYS LATER, Ragnar stalked through the halls of the Belisarius Palace. Outside it was night, but inside business went on. Over one of the doors was a sign that read 'commerce never sleeps,' and the men sitting in the booths, bidding and contracting in hand sign and pidgin Gothic proved that fact. He had no idea what they might be contracting for. It could be anything from the futures in Necromundan industrial production to the shipping of a million sides of grox from the steppes of Thunder Plain.

He suspected it would not matter to these men who gathered under the shadows of the Navigators either. Their business was business. They traded where they could find a profit. The Navigators got a cut for shipping it, and possibly financing it. He had been in the palace long enough now to know that the Houses bankrolled an enormous amount of trade even though they were supposedly above such things. There were fronts over fronts over fronts. The middlemen had middlemen. It was not as it was supposed to be, but Ragnar supposed sourly that this applied to a lot of things on Terra.

He saw Linus Serpico sitting at the side of one booth frantically making notes on vellum. He looked both tired and happy, as if his only purpose in life was writing things down.

As Ragnar approached, the negotiation came to an end and both richly garbed merchants rose and shook hands before affixing their seals to the document Linus had prepared. Linus stifled a yawn, bowed to them both and flitted over to Ragnar.

Ragnar smiled at him and he smiled back happily. The Belisarians had given him work and that seemed all he required. Then a troubled look flickered over his brow. A strange edge entered his scent too. 'Excuse me, master Ragnar, but I have heard the most disturbing rumours.'

Ragnar looked at him and waited for him to say more. He was not surprised. Linus had a quick mind, and good ears, and few people seemed to pay him much notice. It was for this reason that Ragnar suspected he heard everything. 'Rumours?' he prompted.

'They say there have been riots against the Navigator Houses, and that men are massing to sweep them from the face of the planet. I mean no offence, I merely repeat what I hear.'

'I take no offence, Linus,' said Ragnar, 'but where did you hear such things?'

'The merchants talk about it. They say such things are bad for business, and the Inquisition should do something about it.'

That would suit the Inquisition, Ragnar thought. They would love to get a foothold in the navigators quarter and all they needed was a reason. If the House troops could not quell the protests and riots, the Inquisition surely would, by whatever means necessary. Disturbances to the peace of Holy Terra would only be tolerated so far. It was worrying. Ragnar himself had been involved in the suppression of several minor riots. He had been called out along with the rest of the guard to keep the peace. The mere sight of him had been enough to send many of the protesters running for their lives, which had surely been Valkoth's intention.

Still, the memory disturbed him. He had not seen so much unreasoned hatred and fear for a long time. In addition, there was something about an agitated crowd he did not like at all. Its behaviour reminded him of a Space Wolf pack, but without the guiding intelligence, or the ability to think independently when called on to do so. The people had been armed with makeshift weapons, burning and looting the stores of those they thought did business with the Navigators. In truth Ragnar suspected it had been more of an excuse for looting than anything else. They had come nowhere near the palaces, and he doubted the shopkeepers had anything more or less to do with the Navigators than anyone else in the quarter.

'These are troubled times, sir,' said Linus.

'Indeed,' said Ragnar. The little man looked up at him nervously and licked his lips.

'Is it true that the Navigator throne is vacant?' he asked.

By the Emperor, news travels fast, thought Ragnar. The Celestarch herself had only had word of old Gorki's death an hour ago. Now it was the talk of the bazaar. He did not know why he was surprised. Fortunes could be won or lost on such information. Right now factions were manoeuvring to get their representative on the throne before it was barely cold. The status and power of entire Houses would be decided. People would try and back the winner.

'As far as I know that is correct,' said Ragnar.

Linus nodded as if this confirmed what he already knew. 'There will be trouble,' he said.

Ragnar did not ask him what drove him to that conclusion. When mastodons fight, grass gets trampled. Political awareness was a basic survival skill for people around here.

Linus fell into step beside him as they made their way through the halls. He smelled tired and hungry and doubtless was returning to his cell. Ragnar was strangely glad of his presence, because he was feeling uneasy. Something did not feel right. Perhaps it was his encounter with the howling fury of the mob earlier that day, but he doubted it. Such things had never made him uneasy and restless in the past. He felt as he often did when he was hiking through the frozen peaks of Fenris. The first signs of an avalanche were often not striking. They were small meaningless things. A slight vibration underfoot, a creak of ice in the distance, an odd tone carried on the wind. He felt he was hearing such things now.

The riots, the rise of the Brotherhood, the mazy intrigues of the House surrounding him were all small signs but they hinted at a large threat. Events were occurring somewhere that boded no good for House Belisarius and his battle-brothers, he was certain. They walked a deadly path during a thaw, he thought. None of the bustling commerce that surrounded him could make him feel differently.

They left the halls of commerce behind them, passing the guards who stood vigil at the entrance to the private quarters. Ragnar returned the fist to chest salute of the House warriors and strode through. Linus made his way towards the elevators that led down to the cramped chambers of the servants' levels.

He touched Linus on the shoulder. 'Come and tell me if you hear anything suspicious, anything at all.'

'That I shall do, master Ragnar,' said the scribe before flitting off down the corridor. Ragnar gave his attention back to his surroundings. He realised that he was checking for cover, and points of ambush. He was treating these hushed, carpeted halls as if they were a battlefield he was going to have to fight on. It was a measure of his worry that he should be thinking this way.

Superficially there was no reason to be nervous; everything seemed to be fine. The guards looked alert. The people coming and going gave no sign of treachery. It was just him, he guessed. He was on edge. Terra had done that to him. That there were traitors here, and they had not been smoked out, might have something to with it too, he thought sourly.

He strode towards his chamber. He needed rest. No need to be so worried yet, he told himself. No need at all.

'You WILL STRIKE tonight,' said Cezare, stroking his upper lip with one thick finger.

Xenothan regarded the head of House Feracci warily. In his heart of hearts he loathed the man. For all his power and pride in his ancient lineage, he was nothing more than a mutant. It was an abomination that his type should sully the sacred soil of Terra. He considered these thoughts with bitter amusement. If this man is a mutant, then what are you, he asked himself? The answer came back at once. Better. And despite all the implants and all the bio-surgery, he was at least human.

'Indeed, Lord Feracci. We will strike tonight. You need have no fears. After this evening you will have far fewer enemies.'

Cezare smirked in a way that irritated Xenothan. He would have liked nothing more than to take one of his most interesting toxins and inject Feracci with it. While the man died he could have regaled him with details of which excruciating agony would strike him next. Xenothan was not naturally a cruel man, but Cezare was a mad dog, and should be treated like one.

'The Brotherhood are in place?' Cezare asked.

'Their troops are ready.'

'Your agents?'

'They know what is happening. They know tonight is the night. The death of Gorki is their signal. The way into the Belisarius Palace will be clear.'

'See that you do not fail,' said Feracci, leaning forward to sniff one of the orchids that floated in a suspensor vase before him.

The arrogance of the man is breathtaking, Xenothan thought. Still, that would be dealt with soon enough. Once the Belisarians had been brought low, his patron would want this posturing buffoon ground into the dirt as well. Let me see, thought Xenothan, what would I use on you? Something slow, and something that would ensure that your pride suffered as well as the rest of you.

Borac would make you vomit, he thought, and you would taste again all those subtle foodstuffs you so love to indulge in on your tongue, although this time they would be laced with your own stomach acid. Childish, Xenothan told himself, and not nearly subtle enough. It would be like using avierel, the victims of which voided their bowels as they died in howling agony. Perhaps something that would make him mewl and beg? Scorse suppressed certain centres of the brain that allowed decision-making, thereby reducing its victims to mindless drones.

No, he thought, that was a drug for pleasure slaves. He shook his head slightly. It was a pretty dilemma.

'You are sure the Wolfblades will give you no problem?' It was almost laughable, Xenothan thought, the way Cezare looked around furtively as he said it. It was as if he thought the accursed Fenrisians could overhear him. He felt like saying their senses are keen, but not that keen, milord. But he did not. He kept a carefully schooled look of rapt deferential attention on his face as he said, 'None, milord. If any of them get in my way, they shall die.'

'It's those who get in *their* way who tend to die,' said Cezare, the way he smiled showed it was not entirely a jest.

'With all due respect, milord, none of those others had my talents.'

'Your talents,' said Cezare with soft mockery. 'It's about time you displayed those highly lauded talents.'

Xenothan let the man's words slide off him. It would not do to let himself be baited, he thought, but he made a small note in the mental file he kept of all those upon whom he would avenge himself. The list of the living in that file was very short, the list of the dead very long. Someday soon, Cezare would make the transition from one side of the ledger to the other. Not today though, Xenothan thought. Today, he had other business. 'I believe you will find the results satisfactory, milord,' was all he allowed himself to say.

'I had better,' said Cezare. 'After all the money I have ploughed into your master's coffers.'

'Your financial arrangements are something best discussed with him,' said Xenothan smoothly. Take up that challenge if you dare, he thought. Not even Cezare Feracci would want to confront a High Lord of the Administratum without much a better reason than that. It was best to remind him that there were some things that even the head of one of the greatest of the Navigator Houses need fear. He saw Cezare pause to consider this. He knew that Xenothan's master could crush him just as easily as he was going to crush the Belisarians.

The nice thing about the Navigators was that there was always some House that wanted to do the dirty on its enemies. It was not hard to find allies among the factions, even against their own kin. It was a fact that Cezare was well aware of. Still, he was not going to allow Xenothan to get away with having scored a point.

'How do you propose to deal with the Wolf-blades? They seem remarkably adept at avoiding mortal weapons.'

'They are men, like any others, a bit faster, a bit stronger, and a bit more fierce, but believe me there are things in this universe that make even Space Marines seem feeble.'

'And you are one of those, are you?' Cezare made no attempt to hide his mockery.

'I am one, yes,' said Xenothan, with absolute certainty. 'And I have weapons against which they cannot prevail.'

'What would those be?' said Cezare. His face was smooth, but his interest was obvious. Weapons that could prevail against Imperial Space Wolves would be worth a fortune on the open market, and Cezare, for all his pretensions of being an aristocrat and a connoisseur of art, was at heart a merchant. A mutant and a merchant, thought Xenothan with some contempt. It was hardly a happy combination.

'There are certain secrets it is best not to be privy to,' said Xenothan quite truthfully. 'Secrets men have been killed for knowing.'

Cezare nodded, able to take the hint, and yet Xenothan could see the wheels moving behind his eyes. Here was a man who would never rest until he had found out what Xenothan was talking about. Not that it truly mattered. He would be dealt with long before those plans came to fruition.

It would never do for him to know what only very few in the Administratum knew. That within certain dark and almost forgotten departments of the Inquisition, there were small units of scholars and alchemists who had been working on the Adeptus Astartes problem since the time of the Heresy. It was a problem having such powerful, uncontrollable and near invulnerable groups at large within the Imperium, particularly as they were under no man's direct control. These hidden inquisitors had for millennia been working on methods of controlling or even slaying the Space Marines, and their research had borne strange fruit.

Xenothan smiled, thinking of the vial of potent toxin he carried on his person. It acted directly on the gland that the Space Marines used to neutralise poisons, temporarily overloading and confusing it. Ultimately, it turned the gland itself into a weapon against its owner. When the poison entered a Space Marine's system, he would be paralysed for a short time – not enough for an ordinary man to take advantage of – but for someone like Xenothan, a heartbeat would be more than he needed.

Of course, the poison was rare, produced only from the first blossoms of the rare Mercurian Swamp Orchid, and it was very secret. It would never do for enemies of the Imperium to acquire it, or for the Astartes to find out about all of those black research programmes. But it did exist, and Xenothan possessed some. Soon he would use it. He had to confess that he was quite looking forward to it. It had been a long time since he killed a Space Marine. Tonight, he thought, he would kill many.

'You look like a cat who just swallowed a canary,' said Cezare.

Xenothan smiled, although he was inwardly shocked by his lapse. 'I am merely thinking of your impending victory. Tonight, at one stroke., all of your enemies will be removed and the Belisarians will be your puppets.'

'Why do I find it so hard to believe the prospect of my victory makes you so happy?'

'Because it is our victory. Tonight your enemies die. Tonight I get to kill them. Tomorrow you will be *primus inter pares* – first among equals – which we both know means you will be lord of all Navigators.'

'Very well. See to it that nothing goes wrong.'

'Nothing will go wrong from my end. See that your pawn keeps his part of the deal. If he does not, many people will have cause to regret it.' Not the least you, my over-ambitious friend, thought Xenothan. It was gratifying that he did not have to speak the threat aloud for Cezare to grasp it.

* * *

RAGNAR COULD NOT sleep. It would not come. Something was not right. He could feel it in the air. The beast within him snarled, and he understood its unease, if not its source. He rose from his bed and strode through the corridors. He passed Haegr's chambers but the big man was not there. Tonight he was on duty.

He took himself off to the library. He wanted to find a book, something that would distract him. He was surprised to meet Gabriella in the corridor. She was garbed in her dress uniform and smiled at him. 'You are up late,' she said. 'Or is it true that Space Wolves never sleep?' She smiled to show him she was joking.

'I could say the same for you.'

'I have been attending the Celestarch. We were all summoned to conclave. With Gorki's death will come a great deal of horse-trading as the Houses seek to gain advantage in the negotiations for the throne.'

'You think Misha Feracci will get it?'

'Not if Lady Juliana has any say in the matter.'

'The conclave has ended?'

'The Celestarch has gone to the Vaults to consult with the Elders.'

Once more the mysterious Vaults, Ragnar thought. What is down there?

She fell into step beside him. 'Where are you going?'

'I thought I would visit the fabled library of Belisarius.'

'You have decided to become a scholar now?'

'I am hoping to find a history sufficiently tedious to bore me to sleep.'

'What is it? You look pensive.'

'I had not realised I was so easy to read.'

'You would not be had I not spent ten years in the service of Wolves. Now I can tell a thoughtful frown from an angry one.'

'I do not know. There is something in the air tonight that I do not like.'

'You sound like Valkoth. He was saying the same. He ordered the patrols redoubled before he escorted the Celestarch to the Vaults.'

'Did he now?' Ragnar was not reassured. If he were not the only Wolf to feel like this, perhaps there was something more to it than mere unease. Valkoth was a veteran. His instincts for danger would be keen.

'Yes. He has Torin and Haegr supervising the guards. He muttered something about wishing more of the Wolfblades were here but they were needed elsewhere.'

Ragnar nodded. There was a small pattern emerging here. This evening there were far fewer Wolfblades present than normal. If someone knew their schedules they could choose such a night to strike.

But it was a big if. Those were facts known to very few outside the inner circles of the Belisarius clan.

Still, he thought, what could possibly go wrong here, within the fortified stronghold of Belisarius?

SKORPEUS MOVED TOWARDS the lower entrance. The guards here were fewer and saluted him as he passed. He returned their salutes easily and nodded to those he knew. So far, so good, everything was going according to plan. He circled and stopped to speak to the two at the security console.

'Everything in order?' he asked. They nodded and saluted.

'Are you sure?'

'Yes, sir. Lord Valkoth has ordered a third order alert this evening.'

Inwardly Skorpeus cursed. The Wolves were wary indeed. Valkoth's instincts were sound. He hoped the Wolfblade had not picked up anything from his scent. No, it was impossible. They could not read him and the proof was that he was still here. If they could sense anything he would be in an interrogation cell, right now.

Calm down, he told himself. There will be no cell for you. One way or another. The poison capsule will see to that. There was no need for such thoughts. Had not the stars foretold he would become Lord of Belisarius? It would be so even if he required Cezare Feracci's help. There would be time enough afterwards to show Cezare that he would be no mere catspaw. Now all he had to do was let Cezare's tame assassin in.

He made a mental note to find out how the Lord Feracci had managed to corrupt one of the Imperium's most deadly killers. Such knowledge would be an invaluable tool.

'We know, sir, but still it's all clear.'

'Very good,' he said, striding behind the men at the console and studying the holosphere. Security in the area was indeed all clear. Except for one thing. He glanced left and right and saw no one. He slid the weapon from its holster and put it to one of the men's backs. He pulled the trigger. The man fell forward, coughing blood.

'What is going on?' he asked the other guard. The man looked at him confused. 'Is he sick?'

'I don't know, sir–' The man's words were cut off as the blast took him in the kidneys. The traitor pushed him aside and sat down in front of the holosphere. He passed his hands over the master control runes and began the cryptic invocations that would open the secured doors.

He knew that at best he would have only a few minutes. The tech-adepts would most likely assume that this was some sort of system error, and send someone to investigate. Unless those accursed Wolfblades sensed something, he thought. Well, it was too late to worry about that now. Green lights changed to red as the security doors opened. There were several of them, and their locations were known to but a few. They were meant for evacuating the palace if things went terribly wrong.

Tonight, though, they would be used for another purpose.

He rose from the command desk and moved to the security doors. They slid open to reveal a mass of black-clad masked figures led by the man he recognised as Xenothan.

'What is this?' he asked the assassin. 'You need help to kill one woman?'

'There's been a slight change of plan,' said Xenothan. Only then did Skorpeus realise that the gun in the assassin's hand was pointing directly at him. It was the last thing he ever saw.

CHAPTER TWENTY-THREE

XENOTHAN LOOKED DOWN the corridor. It was all clear, as he had expected. Already the Brotherhood men were fanning out, heading for their objectives. Some stripped off their coveralls to reveal the uniforms of Belisarius servitors, others moved towards the lower depths in full military gear. A few squads moved with feral grace into the vents overhead. Two men moved to the console and began patching themselves into the security systems.

It was amazing, Xenothan thought, just how much damage a well-motivated team could cause in a contained environment like this. The very self-sufficiency in air and water that made the palace a mighty fortress could turn into a dreadful weakness once the walls were breached. Contaminated water and air would see to that.

Don't be too sure, he told himself. There were backups for the backups and many, many layers of security. It never paid to be over-confident. Still, this mission had been planned for decades, and he was fairly sure they had accounted for all contingencies. He smiled and his facial muscles flexed, pulling his skin into a new configuration. He looked almost exactly like Skorpeus now, and he had the man's dress uniform and security talismans. There had been no blood. The poison dart had seen to that.

He doubted that anybody except another Navigator could tell that his implanted pineal eye was an artful fake, and if any Belisarian Navigator got that close, he was a dead man. Then there were the four Wolfblades, Xenothan told himself with relish – they would see through the disguise in a moment. His scent would give him away if nothing else did. Still, the same thing applied to them as applied to the Navigators. If they got that close they would be dead.

'Let's get going,' he said. The fanatics moved on with gratifying swiftness.

Sergeant Hope watched the new servants move down the corridor. One of them was very pretty, he thought, perhaps once he was off-duty he would seek her out for a chat. Just then he noticed something from the corner of his eye. He turned swiftly and saw a man he did not recognise wearing the uniform of the House. The man moved with a sense of urgency. A squad of troops followed behind him.

'What is it?' Hope asked.

'Security breach,' said the officer. 'Come with me.'

'We can't leave our posts,' said Hope. He tried not to sound as if he was keen to avoid work. He tried to sound like a man who was doing his duty. 'We have to guard the inner core.'

'Lot of precious books in that library,' said the officer. 'But the order comes straight from Valkoth.'

There was something in the man's tone Hope did not like. 'Show me the authorisation.'

'Certainly,' said the man, holding out his hand. There was something metallic in it. It was the last thing Hope noticed before his brains decorated the wall.

'WHAT WAS THAT?' Ragnar asked.

'I didn't hear anything,' said Gabriella. 'But then I do not have the keen senses of a Wolf.' There was a note of mockery in her voice and a challenging expression on her face. It vanished when she looked at Ragnar.

'Wait here,' he told her, moving down the corridor, his feet near silent on the ancient flagstones.

'I think not,' she said. 'I will be safer with you.'

Ragnar did not have time to argue. He rushed forward. There was a strange stench in the air, of death and something else. There were traces of strangers. He rounded the corner and saw that the guards who should have been there were not. He sniffed for scents and headed through a doorway into a storage chamber. There were corpses and a great deal of blood. The warmth of the scent trace told Ragnar that the killers had been here recently.

He patched himself into the comm-net. 'There are intruders within the palace,' he said. 'We have lost two warriors already, maybe more.' He added the coordinates of his position within the building. 'Inform Valkoth and the others.'

'I have already been informed,' came Valkoth's deep melancholy voice. 'I am dispatching reinforcements to your position.'

'The intruders were here very recently. I am going to investigate.'

'Be cautious, Ragnar. We do not know what we are dealing with.'

'Aye,' said Ragnar. His mind raced. This could be very big. They had no idea how these strangers got in. One thing was certain, murder had been committed here. The Belisarians had not drawn their weapons; they had been taken completely off-guard. Was this an attack? Who could be behind it? The Brotherhood, or someone else entirely. Surely it would be impossible for the fanatics to get in, he thought. Unless they had help...

'Stay here,' he told Gabriella. 'House troops will be here soon. You will be safe.'

'These men were House troops, Ragnar,' she said, pointing to the corpses. 'How safe were they?'

It was a fair point. 'Stick close and dive for cover if there is trouble. I cannot guarantee your safety.'

'I will take my chances.'

'That's what you will be doing.'

Ragnar moved swiftly and silently in the direction of the scent trace. They were coming perilously close to the entrance to the Vaults.

The scent trails became thicker. There were at least a dozen men here and they were certainly not from within the palace.

Ragnar drew his chainsword and bolt pistol. He felt his awareness expand as it always did when he approached combat. They came to one of the massive sealed doors. It was sealed no longer. Someone had over-ridden the controls, and let themselves into the Vault.

'That's not possible,' said Gabriella. 'Only the upper echelons of the family have access to these codes. And the senior Wolfblades.'

'I fear it is possible,' said Ragnar, sniffing the air. 'Someone has access to the treasures of Belisarius.'

It was then his nose caught another scent. It had the mad strangeness of Chaos. This was getting weird. Was this how the strangers had entered? Had they used Chaos sorcery to let themselves into the Vaults and then fanned out from there? That was not what the scent trails told him.

'This is worse than I thought,' he said. 'The stink of mutation is all over this place. Chaos has corrupted even the sacred soil of Terra it would seem.'

Gabriella gave him an odd look. 'Perhaps it is not Chaos you scent,' she said.

Ragnar did not have time to answer her. The sound of a weapon being fired echoed through the corridor, and there was a wild inhuman scream. At the same time, the lights flickered and failed. Total darkness. Ragnar shrugged. This was no hindrance to him. He could move by scent and touch and instinct if need be, but the girl would not be safe. He was surprised to sense her moving ahead of him.

'It is all right,' she said. 'I am a Navigator. My pineal eye can see through far worse gloom than this.' The scent of gunmetal coming from her became slightly stronger. He sensed that she too had drawn a weapon. A moment later the lights flickered once more and came on although much dimmer than before. He noticed that there was a stillness in the air that had not been there before. The palace's ventilation systems were down.

As his eyes adjusted to the new conditions Ragnar saw that Gabriella was well ahead of him, a small laspistol in one hand, her dress sabre in the other. He moved swiftly in front of her. No harm would come to the daughter of Adrian Belisarius if he could help it.

He lengthened his stride towards the sound of violence, and emerged into a large chamber in which something bloated and white and huge lay on the floor. Its legs looked more like flippers, its arms like tentacles. But the face appeared human and it had three eyes, one in the middle of the forehead that looked suspiciously like that of a Navigator. Had this creature somehow found its way in here during the attack, Ragnar wondered? Very unlikely. What then were the Navigators doing with the thing? Was it a prisoner, something they performed experiments on? Whatever it was no longer mattered. The creature was dead now. Someone had filled it full of bullets. They had taken the time to write 'Die mutant scum' on the walls in its blood as well. There was a lot of hatred there.

Gabriella entered and let out a small shriek. At first, he thought it was in horror at the sight of the monster but then he realised that she was weeping openly.

An awful suspicion entered his mind that was confirmed when she said, 'They are killing the Elders.'

'What?'

'You heard me – they are killing the Elders!'

'These things were Navigators?' said Ragnar, appalled.

'They are Navigators, very old ones, very wise ones.'

'They are mutants.'

'As are we all!'

'But you look...'

'I look more human. It makes no difference. If you live long enough and are exposed to the warp often enough, this is what happens. It's the price that we pay so that humanity can have star flight.'

Ragnar shook his head, struggling to comprehend. The logic of her words was inexorable, and he remembered the conversation he had with Ranek back on Fenris about the things he might learn on Terra. It all made more sense now. The old man must have known this, and in his own way he had tried to prepare him. But nothing could have prepared him for this reality.

'The Emperor...' he said.

'The Emperor knew, Ragnar. The Emperor knew and he granted the charters anyway.'

'But he told no one, said nothing.'

'He might have done had Horus not wounded him mortally and sentenced him to eternity in the golden throne. He was a great man, Ragnar, and he knew the truth. And while we stand here debating this, others of my kin are dying. You can hear it if you listen!'

Ragnar paused. He felt very unsettled and very unsure of himself. He was being called upon to defend mutants, real mutants. The Brotherhood was right. Was defending these mutants honourable?

'Are you going to do your sworn duty or aren't you?' Gabriella asked. 'Are you going to side with those mindless bigots or are you going to side with us?'

And there it was. It was not about the Navigators, it was about him. It was his choice. He could defend the Navigators or not. It would reflect on him. What was the difference between Gabriella whom he liked, and the corpse at his feet? Time. 'Will you…?'

'If I live long enough,' she said. 'I will look like that. Maybe not exactly but close enough. And I will still have done my duty to the Emperor. Will you?'

'It's not for you to question my loyalty to the Imperium, girl.' His decision made, he was already on the move. He had sworn to serve the Celestarch and he was going to protect her people. He would do his duty, the rest he would figure out later. The universe was more complex than he had been led to believe.

From up ahead came the butchering sounds of somebody using a chainsaw, followed by screams of pain, and then laughter.

'Hard to move without any legs, isn't it, mutant?' said a man garbed all in black, as he brandished a chainsword over the strangely altered body of someone who once surely must have been a woman.

'Yes, it is,' said Ragnar and put a bolter shell through both of the man's kneecaps. It was a cruel and unnecessary thing to do, but someone was going to feel the brunt of his anger. The man's companions turned to face him. They were quick and hyped on combat drugs and they brought their weapons to bear with astonishing speed. Ragnar did not care. He stepped to one side putting himself behind the shelter of the doorway and then snapped off shots. Every one of them was rewarded with a scream. A hail of shells answered him, tearing chunks out of the wall opposite the archway. He holstered his pistol and lobbed in a flash grenade. A moment after it exploded he stepped through the door and opened fire. He wasted no shots this time. He put a bullet through the head of every stunned man and then approached the Navigator they had been torturing.

She was skeletally thin and unnaturally tall. Her face was narrow like an eldar's, but her skin was scaled like a snake. Her stomach had been slit fully open and her innards had tumbled out. Not even the most advanced medicine would guarantee her survival, and judging by the look on her face she knew it. Terrible agony twisted her features. 'Kill me,' she said.

Ragnar turned to Gabriella who nodded. Ragnar put a bullet into the ancient woman's head, right through the pineal eye. He wished he had not felt a faint grim sense of satisfaction as he did so. He hoped for Gabriella's sake it had not shown on his face. His prejudices ran very deep.

From all around came the sounds of shooting now. It seemed that this was not the only team loose in the Vaults of the forbidden zone. There were others.

Gabriella looked very angry now. 'Navigators were behind this,' she said.

'How do you know?' he asked, ready to lunge off into the darkness once more.

'Only another Navigator House would know about these hidden Vaults and their significance.'

'Feracci?' Ragnar asked.

'The most likely candidate, don't you think?'

'If it is, he will pay.'

'Not if my House is wiped out. No one will avenge us.'

Ragnar moved on. 'The Inquisition might.'

'No. It might use this as an excuse to move against the other Navigators. But Cezare must know about this and be prepared to deal with it, or he would not have done it.'

'Then the Wolves will claim your bloodgeld for you.'

'Will they?'

'Indeed they will.' Ragnar wished he felt as sure as he sounded. Honour was one thing; the politics of the Imperium was another. Something occurred to him.

'If Cezare was behind this, then he was also behind the death of your father and Skander.'

'You could never prove that.'

Ragnar showed his fangs in a wolfish grin. 'What makes you think I require proof?'

XENOTHAN STRODE THROUGH the corridors doing his considerable best to look like the panicked folk around him. Terrible chaos had erupted right in the heart of House Belisarius. Long held plans raced to fruition. The fanatics were loose in the Navigator's precious Vaults. Assault teams were contaminating the water and air supplies. The main powercores were out.

Over the comm-net earbead he could sense panic. Word of the attack on the Vaults filtered back to the Belisarian command. They assumed that the Elders were the target of all of this and moved to defend them. Now was the time for Xenothan to strike. Misdirection was the key, he had to keep two steps ahead of his enemies. That counted for more than strength, or firepower, or wealth. It was something he was a master of. He marched on through the heart of Belisarius towards his goal.

Before this night was over the power of one of the oldest Navigator Houses would be broken, and his employer would have moved one step closer to his goal.

'HOW ARE YOU feeling?' Ragnar asked Gabriella. She looked pale and wan and filled with horror.

'I've been worse,' she said. She was bearing up well, given the number of her relatives she had seen butchered. But he could tell she was tired, scared and beginning to fray at the edges. He could not really blame her. This style of warfare was enough to test the nerves of the most seasoned warriors.

They stalked the gloomy Vaults. Massively out-numbered, their only chance was to strike from the shadows, and withdraw. If they were going to save the Elders there was no sense in courting a heroic death. Speed, savagery of attack and swiftness of flight would serve their purpose better.

Again and again, they came upon small groups of fanatics. Ragnar would open fire on the men and try to draw them away from their prey. If that failed, and it often did, he would return and snipe again, killing more and more. Overwhelmed by blood lust, the invaders brutally tortured the mutated Elders instead of proceeding with their mission. Ragnar suspected that it was only bloodlust that was preventing total eradication of the Navigators. If the Brotherhood's warriors had moved swiftly and killed quickly, they might have succeeded in their task.

Perhaps not. Here and there Ragnar came upon massive blast doors. Some had been shattered with thermal charges, but many had held. Ragnar knew that beyond them, an Elder perhaps survived. He could only hope so. At least time was on their side. More and more House troops were rushing down here, and soon they might begin to overwhelm their attackers.

The fanatics must have known this would happen, he thought. But still they came on. There was something almost admirable about the way they were prepared to throw away their lives for the cause they believed in.

Almost, he reminded himself. But they were throwing their lives away to slay people who could not fight back: crippled mutants who were incapable of holding a weapon, let alone using it.

Over the comm-net Ragnar was getting reports that they had used other weapons as well. Poisons had been introduced into the air-circulators and water supplies. The filters were being replaced and casualties were light, but it was obvious, even to Ragnar that they had come incredibly well prepared. They had staggeringly detailed knowledge of the place they were going to attack and all its weak points. Everything pointed to the presence of a traitor in their midst. It was the only way anyone could have acquired such a complete pool of intelligence data.

As he padded forward towards the scent of more fanatics, his mind continued to gnaw away at the problem. A traitor would explain how they got in too. He did not doubt that somewhere and sometime later investigators would find a security door that had been unsealed, as well as guards who had either been bribed or killed. It was the only way such a breach could be achieved.

He poked his head around the corridor and saw a group of black-garbed men. One of them was sawing the tentacles off an Elder with a chainsword, while another lay groaning and bleeding nearby. It seemed that they had encountered one mutant determined to fight back. While he was sighting the back of the chainsword wielder's head, another thought struck him.

What if the Elders were not the invaders' principle target? He was drawing conclusions from what he had seen, and in military terms that could be a dangerous and incorrect method of doing things. Presumably with the intelligence they had they were capable of striking at anyone they wanted within the House.

Why would they pick on the Elders? They were politically powerful, but from what he understood, they were mostly retired or engaged in strange research.

He pulled the trigger and the back of his target's head exploded in a cloud of red mist. His brains decorating the intruder in front of him. Ragnar sprang forward, sweeping his chainsword down at another target, and decapitated him instantly.

Gabriella too closed with the enemies. He moved swiftly to put as much distance as he could between them. He did not want to strike her accidentally in the savagery of the fray.

He lashed out with his boot, sending one invader flying into his comrade behind them. As the men went down in a tangle of limbs he pounced like a tiger on a tethered goat. He broke one man's neck with a blow from his fist, the weight of the bolt pistol clutched in it adding power to the blow. He took the other's head from his shoulders with the sword. It rolled to the ground and blinked stupidly for a moment. There was a look of utter dismay on its face.

As his body went through the motions of combat, Ragnar asked himself, why now for this attack? Perhaps it had something to do with the guards' shifts, and the presence of traitors within the defence. But it could be more complicated. What had changed with the big picture? Why would an attacker choose to roll the dice on this evening, and not some other?

Ragnar threw himself flat as a fanatic opened fire on him with a las-pistol. While the man struggled to bring his weapon to bear, Ragnar rolled and shot him, coming to his feet with a single lithe spring. Then it occurred to him: the vote for the new representative was tomorrow. This attack might well throw the Belisarians into confusion at a most critical moment. Or, he thought sombrely, it might bring a traitor to power if the Celestarch was killed. With the Elders gone or in disarray the House would have to find an alternate way of selecting its new ruler. That would take time.

But, he thought, as he lunged to put his blade through a man's heart, that could only happen if the present Celestarch was dead. A sudden dread filled Ragnar. He felt certain he had divined the enemy's plan.

CHAPTER TWENTY-FOUR

XENOTHAN PROCEEDED THROUGH the palace, following the guidance he received from the main datacore over the comm-net. In case of emergencies, he had memorised the layout from the plans the traitor had provided, but so far he had had no need to use it. Some of the area he knew from his own many trips in disguise, but these were the public places and the less secure sectors abutting them. Now he was right in the core of the palace. Behind his altered features he felt excitement, the excitement of the hunt. Tonight he stalked dangerous prey for the greatest prize of all. Tonight, he would alter the course of the Imperium for generations to come. It was a mission worthy of his talents.

A young servant strode up, with fear on her face. 'What is going on, sir?' she asked. In the stress of the moment, she had abandoned the usual protocols and spoke to him without being spoken to. 'Why the alert?'

'Intruders,' said Xenothan, injecting a note of panic into his voice. He knew that the more alarm and confusion he caused the better.

'The guards are all heading down into the Vaults,' she said. 'That is forbidden.'

Indeed it is, thought Xenothan, and we have set Belisarius a pretty conundrum. What will they tell the men who see the residents below? How will they deal with them? Perhaps they would be shipped out to some distant hellworld, and new guards would be brought in. Death was an obvious answer, but would the Celestarch have the stomach for it? Possibly. The Navigators were capable of anything when their survival depended on it.

Well, soon enough they would have other things to worry about. Xenothan headed on towards the throne room. His goal was finally within reach.

RAGNAR SPOKE QUICKLY into the comm-net. 'Is the Celestarch secure?' he asked.

'She is being guarded by Torin and a company of guards in the throne room. We never got her to the Vaults before the alert sounded.'

'Move her,' said Ragnar.

'What?' said Valkoth. Ragnar swiftly outlined his suspicions. They needed to ensure that she was not in an expected location. If there was a traitor and an attack came, they had to assume the killers would know where to strike. Ragnar had even considered suggesting she be put on a ship and lifted out into orbit, but it was likely that the invaders had considered this option and prepared for it. All around, troops had started to flow into the Vaults.

'Ragnar is right,' he heard Torin say. 'We cannot take the risk.'

Valkoth's voice returned. 'There are no signs of any breach up here.'

'That does not mean there has not been one.'

'Aye, you are correct. Explain to the Celestarch she has to move. I respectfully suggest taking her down to the Vaults.'

Very good, thought Ragnar. Not a place the enemy was likely to consider, and one already swarming with House troops. Of course, the situation down here had yet to stabilise, but it probably would before the Celestarch got here.

'Ragnar,' Valkoth continued crisply. 'Take over the fifth company and secure the nearest defensible area to the shaft nine entranceway. Let me know when you've done it. Immediately.'

'Immediately,' Ragnar agreed.

'Come with me,' he told Gabriella. 'We have work to do.'

* * *

EXPERIENCE TOLD XENOTHAN that something was wrong. There was not the density of security in the area that there should have been. He had been challenged several times but his appearance combined with the passes and rites the traitor had provided him meant that he had got through unscathed. Mostly. Those who had thought to challenge him had not lived for more than a few moments. He should now be challenged constantly but there were not many guards around.

Was it possible that the enemy had anticipated his coming and had changed their strategy? Had he been betrayed himself? Briefly he considered aborting the mission. Very briefly. His patron would not accept anything short of total success. Anyway, there was nothing so far to suggest that he had failed. He decided to push on. First, however, he needed to find a place to patch into the comm-net to let the fanatics know that there had been a change of plan. He needed to know if the Celestarch was being moved, and if she was, they were to slow that down, or stop it if possible.

He smiled. Small setbacks were part of the hunt. They would make his triumph all the sweeter once they were overcome.

RAGNAR FINISHED supervising the clearance of the holding bay. There had been more enemies than he had thought and they had fought with surprising deadliness. His force had taken more than a few

casualties before they had overcome the enemy.
Now he supervised the fortification of the area. He
had set some of his men to guard all the approaches
to their position, but held the bulk of his force in
reserve, knowing that they could be attacked from
any side.

Gabriella looked on. Her face was sooty and
marked with scratches and blood. She had taken a
few small wounds in their battles. A medic had
hastily applied a synthi-flesh plaster to them, and it
was swiftly being absorbed into the skin. 'I never
expected to have to fight here,' she said.

'There are no safe places,' said Ragnar. 'You have to
be prepared to fight anywhere.'

'Spoken like a true Space Wolf,' she said. 'But tell
me, how would you feel about fighting in the place
where you were born and grew up?'

'I have,' said Ragnar automatically, casting his
mind back to that long ago time. 'I saw my father
killed and my family enslaved.'

'Somehow that does not reassure me, Ragnar,' she
said.

'I don't suppose it would,' he said, as the realisation of what he had said sunk in.

She smiled.

'It serves me right for asking the question in the
first place.'

'No, it doesn't. This is your home. You have a right
to be upset. You still have to fight though, if you
want to keep it.'

'Those are the words of a Fenrisian.'

'The words are true no matter where they come from. In this universe there is little else we can do but fight for our place, if we want to keep it. There are plenty who would take it from us.'

'That's certainly true if you are a Navigator.'

'It's true for everybody, even a Space Marine.'

XENOTHAN MOVED THROUGH the palace, stalking his prey. Tonight, as things stood, he might not get a chance at his target, but he was not about to admit defeat. He could remain within the building, secrete himself in some hiding place and bide his time. No, that would never do. After tonight, the identity of the traitor would be revealed, and security would be redoubled. It was tonight or never, he thought. The only decision left to him was whether to abandon his mission and leave the tower or push on.

He grinned. There had never been any chance of him aborting the plan. This was the high spot of his career, a thing that would be talked about amid his secret brethren for centuries to come, if he was successful. No, he told himself, *when* he was successful.

He spoke more orders in code into the comm-net. His followers were closing in on what they thought was the Celestarch's bodyguard. He did some quick calculations. They could achieve a temporary superiority at this point, two levels down. The Belisarians were mobilising by the ramps, which was sensible. They did not want to be trapped in an elevator or dropshaft. There was far too great a possibility of something going wrong.

He gave orders for the intercept, knowing it was only a matter of time before they worked out that he and his followers were using scrambled transmissions piggy-backed onto the Belisarian net. There was plenty of time to do what was needed; all the time in the world.

TORIN KEPT HIMSELF beside the robed woman at all times, ready to interpose himself between her and danger. He sniffed the air, taking in the conflicting scents. He caught the faint traces of strangers on the recycled air, and hints of subtle toxins that had been released in miniscule amounts. He wondered what the casualties were. How many had died before that particular attack had been neutralised? Stick to your task, he told himself. He would know the worst soon enough.

He was still astonished by the boldness of this attack. Now they knew why there had been such a build-up of Brotherhood forces beneath the quarter. Every fanatic on Terra must be here. Who would have thought anyone would have dared to attack the Navigators within their own stronghold? It showed a boldness of planning and a competence of execution that he found almost admirable. But there would be hell to pay tomorrow. The Belisarians would spare no expense to find out who was behind this and avenge themselves.

Surely the attackers must have known that and
planned for it too. They would have been fools not
to, and this was not the work of fools. It was a chilling thought, that gave him pause even as he hustled
the Celestarch's crack bodyguard through the halls
of the palace. Perhaps the enemy did not expect
them to survive in any state to harm him. He would
be proved wrong.

Be careful, Torin told himself. The night is not
over yet. Who knows what other nasty surprises
are in store? Perhaps there are other traitors.
Torin felt certain that there was at least one: no
one could have penetrated the palace without
inside help from someone high up. It simply
could not have happened any other way. The
question was who? The Navigators had many
flaws but loyalty to their clan was practically bred
into them. It had to be. How could someone have
got around that?

Assuming they survived, the list of suspects could
be narrowed enormously. Very few people were in a
position to do what had been done, so one of them
was the traitor. It could not be himself, or Haegr or
Valkoth, he was sure. It could not be Ragnar. He did
not know the youth well but he had just arrived
from Fenris, and he did not seem the corruptible
type, although he had come with the wench
Gabriella. Still, she had just spent ten years with the
Wolves, so she would be in no position to be a traitor so soon. They needed to look among the high

command of the House. Torin had a few ideas about where.

Just then he caught a strange scent on the air. There were enemies coming towards them, and lots of them. 'Ready yourselves to defend the Celestarch,' he told his men as their adversaries rounded the corner and opened fire. He let his wolfish howl ring out, knowing it would frighten the foe and give heart to his own men. Moments later he lunged headlong into the swirling maelstrom of battle.

He was happy. There were few things he loved more than feeling his blade bite into the flesh of his foes.

XENOTHAN HEARD THE wolf-cry and the sound of the Brotherhood men engaging the enemy. This is it, he thought, the time he had been waiting for. He moved around the bend and saw the halls filled with the wild swirl of combat at close quarters. War raged among the tapestries and statues as the Celestarch's guard were ambushed.

From the balcony he had chosen as vantage point, he watched the Space Wolf slash away at the fanatics who came within his reach. Xenothan allowed himself a fellow professional's appreciation of the man's deadliness and then gave his attention to the target. The Celestarch was firmly behind a wall of her elite guard. They refused to give ground even in the face of ferocious attacks. The presence of their ruler and the Wolfblade seemed to stiffen their spines remarkably.

In the natural course of events things would not go well for the Brotherhood. It was only a matter of time before House reinforcements got here and they would be swept away before the storm of blades. Fortunately, Xenothan thought, that was no concern of his. His mission was all but accomplished. He took a heartbeat to savour the moment, raised his customised bolt pistol and snapped off a single shot, almost without aiming. The shell sped directly into the Celestarch's head, causing it to explode. Only Xenothan and an observer close to her side would notice that he had put the bullet right through her third eye.

The Wolfblade gave a howl of rage, and his response almost caught Xenothan off-guard. He raised his pistol and launched a snapshot. It was pure chance that caused his shell to smash into Xenothan's gun, sending it broken and spinning over the banister.

Xenothan took no chances, he lunged backwards, filled with a growing sense of triumph marred only by a faint niggling feeling that something was wrong.

He was down the stairs and almost into his extraction routine when he realised what it was. The image of the tumbling Celestarch had burned itself into his brain, and was taking its place in the gallery of his proud triumphs. It was one of those things he would savour as long as he lived. He could freeze the scene in his mind.

Replaying it now, he realised he had made a mistake. The woman had been a Navigator but she was too short and too broad to be the Celestarch. At a distance she was almost identical, and few people could have told the difference, but Xenothan was one of them. He had been made a fool of. The Wolfblades had used a decoy to distract the intruders while they hustled the real Celestarch to safety. It was a simple ploy but in the confusion of the invasion it had proven an effective one.

What to do now, Xenothan wondered? Time was running out.

RAGNAR WATCHED AS Haegr arrived. With him was a woman garbed in the dress uniform of an ordinary Navigator. Ragnar recognised her immediately as the Celestarch. Valkoth had taken a bold gamble and it had paid off. Haegr had managed to guard her all the way down into the Vaults. Somehow he had managed to stop off for food along the way. His lips and beard showed traces of fat and gravy. Ragnar could smell gammon on his breath.

'Hardly a real fight all the way here, just a few men in black to decorate my hammerhead with their brains.'

'For which I am profoundly grateful,' said the Celestarch.

'Indeed, lady,' said Ragnar leading her into the security chamber. There was only one way in and out of this place, but it was the best he could find at short notice. It might turn into a death trap if they were attacked in overwhelming numbers, but he was certain there was no other way in or out. Anyone seeking the death of the Celestarch would have to clamber over the dead bodies of Haegr, himself and a company of Belisarian guards to get her. Besides, more troops would be here as soon as they had finished clearing the Vaults of intruders. It looked like the situation was stable for the moment. The tone of the comm-net bead in his ear suddenly gave Ragnar a sense of foreboding.

'Ragnar. There is a problem,' said Torin. His voice sounded urgent.

'A problem?'

'The decoy is dead. They got to her. Is the Celestarch safe?'

'Haegr is here and so am I, and so are scores of guards. We have the Celestarch in the Vault. I don't see how he can get past us.'

The signal cut off abruptly with the sound of gunfire in the distance. A moment later a voice spoke over the comm-net. 'Ragnar, this is Torin. We have just been attacked and the decoy is dead.'

'I know, you just told me.'

'What? I have been busy killing our new guests.'

'You did not call me thirty seconds ago?'

'Thirty seconds ago I was removing my chainsword from somebody's guts.'

'Then who called me?'

'I don't know, it wasn't me. But I need to warn you about something. There is an assassin loose in the palace.'

'There are many of them but we seem to gaining the upper hand.'

'No, I mean a real Imperial assassin. He killed the decoy Valkoth sent with the Celestarch's bodyguard. When I shot at him he moved away so fast I almost could not see him. I am on his trail now, and I suspect he is heading your way.'

'An Imperial assassin? That does not seem possible. Has the Administratum turned against us?'

'I do not know, Ragnar, but I am certain that such a creature is here now. Be very careful. They are tricky and almost unstoppable once they are committed to a kill. He will try to find a way. Sit tight while I get him. Praise Russ!'

Ragnar's mind reeled. It seemed like the enemy had access to the secure codes of the Belisarian comm-net. Not only that, but he knew how to imitate Torin's voice.

How was that possible? Ragnar thought of their visit to the Feracci tower and all the machines that had been present along with all the servants. They certainly could have been eavesdropped on there.

He braced himself. It looked like the battle was not yet over. One of the deadliest creatures in the galaxy was on his way.

CHAPTER TWENTY-FIVE

XENOTHAN HURRIEDLY GAVE instructions to the last surviving Brotherhood warriors. He hoped that they would abandon their bloodletting in the Vaults long enough to converge on their great enemy, the Celestarch. By now they must realise that they were doomed, and hopefully they would be willing to give away their lives at the highest cost to the hated mutants. Killing the Celestarch would achieve that.

He quit broadcasting into the comm-net. He had to assume that by now his ruse had been discovered, and he was taking no chances of being located before his mission was complete. The Wolfblades had already proven that they were not fools. They would be doing their best to locate him. Keep moving, he told himself.

As he raced through the corridors, he checked his selection of special weapons. He had a few surprises up his sleeve. He still had the envenomed blades, the dart throwers and the grenades filled with poison gas. He had changed his appearance once more and now wore the stolen uniform of a House guard. His face was completely different – wide and flat. Sub-dermal pigmentation sacks had changed his skin colour from Navigator pale to dark brown. His scent meant he would not fool a Space Wolf, but it would fool any normal person looking for one of his previous appearance.

He was not sure the Space Wolf had caught enough of him to be able to circulate it, but again it never paid to take chances.

A guard called out to him to halt. Xenothan had no time to waste now; swiftness, not concealment was of the essence. He concentrated and his altered body responded. Time slowed as his chemically enhanced reflexes sped up. The man seemed to barely raise his weapon before Xenothan was upon him. He reached out and speared his fingers into the man's eyes, pushing them deep into their sockets. They punctured under the impact of his razor sharp fingernails.

As the guard fell, Xenothan caressed the edge of the man's throat with the edge of his hand, crushing the windpipe.

A moment later he was gone, speeding down the corridor towards his intended target. He was determined that she would not elude him a second time this night.

'THAT WAS MORE like it,' said Haegr, smacking his lips with satisfaction, as he contemplated the ruined bodies that lay everywhere on the battlefield. Ragnar rose up from behind the hastily improvised cover to survey the area in front of them. Bodies sprawled all over the entrance to the Vault. The smell of exotic woods burning filled his nostrils. The dead lay everywhere.

'I am sure you'll have plenty more entertainment in the next few minutes,' Ragnar said. 'I think I can hear more of those maniacs approaching now.'

'You can, young Ragnar. And I must admit, for feeble humans, they certainly know how to die. They fight like men possessed.'

'No doubt they will take that as a great compliment.'

'They ought to when it comes from the lips of mighty Haegr.'

Things had worsened over the past few minutes. Assembled en masse, the fanatics had attacked their position again and again. Most of the guards were wounded. None of the promised reinforcements had arrived. They were pinned down. The only consolation was that no enemies had penetrated the chamber where the Celestarch and Gabriella waited. So far they had held off all attempts to do so.

Haegr was right. The enemy did fight well. Ragnar was astonished at how well co-ordinated the fanatics were. He doubted that it was coincidence that they had suddenly started attacking this position in great numbers. A swift evil intelligence guided them. How high did the treachery within the House reach? Others would be thinking that too. Such thoughts would paralyse and demoralize their side while the enemy swept through them.

'I never thought I would have such a good fight in here of all places,' said Haegr. 'It seems these Vaults have served a useful function after all.'

Did he know about the mutants, Ragnar wondered? Did he care?

'Somebody put a lot of work into this,' said Haegr with uncharacteristic astuteness. Right again, Ragnar thought. It had to be tonight, the meeting of the Navigator Council tomorrow ensured it. If the Celestarch died, House Belisarius would be disorganised and its allies thrown into confusion.

With the House in disarray and so many of the Elders dead, it would take weeks, if not months, to choose a new Celestarch. If Cezare was behind this, he could seize the moment, promise the Navigators strong leadership in the face of this new and ominous threat, and make his son one of the High Lords of Terra. He would score a victory such as none of the great Navigator Houses had in two millennia, and his power would become insuperable. Ragnar realised that he was making a huge leap of imagination, with absolutely no proof, but it fitted the facts well. The only problem with the theory was that the power behind the attack did not have to be the Feracci; it could be any of the great ambitious Navigator Houses. There would be no way to confirm or deny the thing until the election to the throne was held tomorrow.

'We'll just have to see that they don't succeed.'

'Well said, young Ragnar. Very well said indeed.' Haegr grinned, showing his enormous tusks, and Ragnar suddenly realised why Torin respected him so. Haegr might be coarse, brutal and a diplomatic liability but, in a tight spot, the giant was just the man you wanted at your side. He showed no doubts, no fear and had no need for reassurance. He was entirely what he appeared to be – unafraid. He was quite possibly insane, but he was a truly fine warrior.

'The only way they are going to get to the Celestarch is if they climb over my dead body,' said Ragnar.

'And they'll have to climb over mine to get to yours,' said Haegr. 'Can't be having any young pups stealing the glory that is rightfully mine.'

Ragnar laughed, then glanced around at the carnage, the dead and stinking bodies, the limbless corpses, the blast marks on the marble walls. He breathed in the tainted stench of close combat in the hallways of the palace. The stench of opened guts and las-seared flesh, splattered blood and excrement. He did not see much evidence of glory here. His theories were all very well but they had to survive until the morrow. It was imperative they keep the Celestarch alive, for if they could the plot would fail, and the Belisarians would be in a position to fight another day. Perhaps they would even be able to ferret out and take vengeance on those behind their attackers.

He was surprised by his desperation. He would never have suspected things could get so bad so fast. Until this evening he had thought the power of House Belisarius unassailable. The Navigators had seemed so rich and so powerful, but not even their alliance with the Wolves had kept them from teetering on the edge of oblivion before daybreak. He realised that in the vast machine of Imperial power, the House was but one tiny cog and, by extension, so was his Chapter. It was not a pleasant thought.

'Well, it looks like we have some more visitors,' growled Haegr. 'I suppose we had better get ready to welcome them.'

XENOTHAN BOUNDED DOWN the slope and heard the roar of battle ahead. It had been a long night, but it was almost over. One last push would see this thing finished. He checked his weapons one last time, and raced headlong towards his goal. From up ahead, he heard the howling of Wolves.

* * *

RAGNAR MET THE first of the fanatics breast to breast, and sent him reeling with a punch from the hilt of his blade. Unbelievably, he had run out of bolter shells for his pistol, and the fighting was so close now, it seemed pointless to snatch up any sort of ranged weapon. Instead he grabbed a sword from a fallen guard officer and used it left handed while he wielded his chainsword with his right.

They had been forced to come out from behind the barrier and enter the battle in the chamber beyond. Now he raced through the melee butchering foes while Haegr smashed his way through more of the enemy warriors like a blood-mad bull let loose in a crowded bazaar. All around them, the enemy fell, but now it was only the two Marines who kept them at bay. Most of the guard had fallen, and still the zealots came on, reckless and fanatical.

It may have been the proscribed combat drugs they chewed on, but Ragnar suspected they would have been as bold without them. They simply would not have been so untiring and fierce and strong. Haegr did not care. He laughed as he slew. His hammer smashed skulls as if they were eggshells and snapped ribs as though they were made from dry twigs. Gore splattered his beard and his chest plate. Blood dribbled down his face giving him a daemonic look.

For all his bulk he moved so quickly that no enemy was able to draw a bead on him and few managed to land a blow. Suddenly, out of nowhere, flew a dart. It impacted on the giant's forehead and stuck there. For a moment, nothing seemed to happen, and then a look of horror came into Haegr's eyes and he stiffened and fell forward like a great oak.

If Ragnar had not known it was impossible, he would have guessed his comrade to have been laid low by some vile poison. Something flashed in his peripheral vision and he threw himself forward, smashing into the enemy warriors ahead of him. A dart whizzed past his ear, missing him narrowly.

A shriek from just beyond his position told him that somebody else had not been so lucky. A glance to his left revealed a man writhing on the floor in dreadful agony, his face turning swiftly blue, muscles writhing beneath his skin like tortured serpents.

Ragnar kept moving and more darts rattled off his armour. He caught the hint of a smell, the faintest suggestion of an unbelievably revolting mix of toxins. Wildly, he glanced around. He had yet to catch sight of the man shooting at him. No human being should have been able to evade his perceptions. He guessed that the assassin had arrived.

XENOTHAN CURSED. HE had not expected the youth to respond so swiftly. Tracking his evasive action had expended too many of the assassin's precious poisoned darts and still he had not hit. All he had done was succeed in laying low half a dozen of his own side.

What now, he wondered? There was no more time to waste. If he was going to slay the Celestarch he needed to get over the barrier and into the Vault now. He headed for the doorway.

FROM THE CORNER of his eye, Ragnar caught sight of a tall, thin, black-garbed man moving with blurring speed. He vaulted the barrier and headed towards the entrance of the inner Vault.

The stranger moved far too fast for a normal human. There was something almost insect-like in his scuttling swiftness. This was the assassin, Ragnar surmised, and in a few moments, if he wasn't stopped, he would enter the Celestarch's chamber. Ragnar did not give much for the chances of the guard keeping him from his prey. It was time for him to do his duty.

Ragnar sprang forward over the barricade, aiming for his opponent's back, ignoring all the blows that flashed towards him from the fanatics, trusting his armour to keep him from harm. He lashed out with his chainsword, hoping to catch the assassin at the top of his spine. He almost succeeded, but at the last second, the assassin threw himself forward, stretching almost bonelessly to avoid the strike. More than that, he somehow writhed out of the way, rolled forward and caught Ragnar with his foot adding to the Wolf's momentum and propelling him head over heels into the chamber.

Ragnar had to let go of the chainsword in case he fell on his own blades. He tried to control the roll and bring himself to his feet. The chainsword skated away across the marble flagstones and came to rest against a far wall. Ragnar sprang upright but the killer was ready. His boot connected with Ragnar's chin with a piledriver force that would have broken the neck of anyone other than a Space Marine. Ragnar was once more hurled off-balance, while the assassin vaulted over him. He was amazed by the speed of his foe. Never before had he encountered someone so much quicker and apparently stronger than he. There were many stronger, but none so fast. This stranger was a lethal combination of the two.

Ignoring Ragnar the assassin moved towards his target. The guards were confused by the startling speed with which events were unfolding, and were not firing because of Ragnar's presence.

'Shoot,' he bellowed, reaching up to snag the man's ankle. He just managed to grab it and once more the stranger twisted, trying to break free. The first hail of bullets filled the air around them. Several smashed into Ragnar's armour but he held his grip.

Xenothan cursed. What did it take to put this youth down? So far he had absorbed enough punishment to kill a dozen normal men and he kept coming. Worse, he managed to thwart Xenothan's every effort to get to the Celestarch. The assassin realised he had made a mistake putting down Haegr first. The giant's ferocity was legendary, and Xenothan had assumed he was the greater threat. Only now he was not sure. Another mistake, he thought, and one he had very little time to put right.

SOMEHOW, SUPERLATIVELY swiftly, the assassin avoided being hit and returned fire with a weapon he held in his left hand. More darts flew through the air and Ragnar feared the Celestarch was about to be killed. She would have died there and then had not several of her bodyguard intervened, interposing themselves between her and the assassin. They had become a human shield.

Ragnar heard the assassin curse in a strange tongue, then he bent from the waist and struck Ragnar with his hand. The blow was aimed at Ragnar's eyes. The young Space Wolf just had time to turn his head, while taloned nails sliced the skin of his forehead. He lashed out with the sword he had retained, but the man took the blow on his forearm. Ragnar expected to feel flesh slice open, but instead the blade rebounded as if it had hit solid metal. The stranger's slashed tunic was only cloth. Ragnar realised at once that he possessed some sort of subdermal armour.

The assassin brought his free foot down on the wrist of the hand with which Ragnar immobilised him. The force was irresistible and the stranger was free. A moment later the man was airborne almost as if gravity had no grip on him.

He performed an arcing backward somersault and continued to fire his darts of death into the bodies of the men protecting the ruler of Belisarius. Ragnar hoped for her sake that he did not find any chink in the wall of flesh. He assumed that the men would already be dead from the poison in their veins. He threw the sword with all his strength directly at the stranger's stomach, hoping it was not as well protected as his arms. The man twisted in the air, flailing his arm, and struck the blade away. It dropped directly into the guards, piercing one's throat. If that had been deliberate, and Ragnar had to assume it was, it was an astonishing feat of coordination.

Ragnar rolled and snatched a lasrifle from the hands of a guard. He brought it to bear on the stranger and pulled the trigger. Lacking anything to gain purchase on, and forced to follow the arc prescribed by gravity, the assassin, for once, made an easy target. Not even his reflexes were swift enough to avoid coherent light, and Ragnar hit him. The beam burned cloth and seared flesh, charring it black. Somehow the assassin managed to keep his arm in the way all the way down, and as soon as he hit the ground, he came straight at Ragnar, despite the sizzle of fat and muscle.

Too late, Ragnar noticed the knife in the killer's good hand. He caught the hint of faint deadly poison, like the stuff that had brought Haegr down. He desperately brought up his arm to try to deflect it but the stranger got the blade around it and punched it at his eye. Ragnar turned his head, and it caught him on the cheek just below the eye.

Searing agony passed through Ragnar instantly. All of his senses rearranged themselves. Sounds became colours, light became sound, touch blurred into taste, all in a way he would never be able to describe. For one who relied so much on his senses it was a sanity blasting experience. The pain flared through him in bright red and yellow waves of agony. His gasps came out in clouds of grey and green. He tasted the acid sting of the poison in his veins. Everything became roaring madness to his tortured, overloaded senses.

Desperately wondering if he was even doing what he thought he was doing, he threw himself forward, biting and rending, feeling his jaws close on something, and thinking his arms encircled his foe. He kept attempting to crush it and bite it long after the waves of red madness overwhelmed him.

CHAPTER TWENTY-SIX

HE WOKE SUDDENLY and found himself looking into the face of Gabriella. Above him he could see the ceiling of his own chamber. He breathed deeply but there seemed to be something wrong with his sense of smell. It had not seemed so dull since he had become a Wolf.

'I must be alive then,' he said. 'Else you have somehow accidentally found your way into the halls of hell.'

'Yes,' she said. 'You are alive.'

'The Celestarch?'

'She is well too, all things considered, and she prepares for the great council. It looks like there will be much else to discuss along with the selection of the new throne.'

'What happened?'

'I think I can answer that,' said a familiar voice from close by. Ragnar caught the scent now as well. 'Torin?'

'Yes, old son, I am here. I came up just as you were fanging the assassin.'

'Haegr?'

'He's too stupid to die. He is even now engaged in single combat with all the pies in the kitchen.'

'That is exactly the sort of foul slur on mighty Haegr's honour I would expect from a jealous toad like you, Torin,' said Haegr. He and his collection of meat pies found their way into Ragnar's field of vision too. 'And one that will be richly rewarded with a beating later.'

'The poison did not kill you?'

'There is no poison strong enough to kill me,' said Haegr. 'Although I admit it did slow me down a touch. Seems to have blocked my nose for the moment as well.'

'He recovered before you, because he had not taken quite the beating you did.'

'I was in the chamber before you,' said Haegr outraged.

'By one step.'

'Between us we proved more than a match for the killer despite his noxious tricks.'

'Ignore this great fat liar, Ragnar, old son, he was almost dead from the beating you gave him.'

'He was very dead after the bolter shells mighty Haegr put in him.'

'I have never fought anybody so powerful,' Ragnar said. 'He was faster than me and stronger. I never expected that from anyone, except perhaps one of the slaves of darkness.'

'No doubt he would have said the same of you.'

'What happened?'

'When I entered you were holding him all but immobile and rending his flesh with your teeth. We finished him for you, then hustled the Celestarch to safety.'

'The traitor?'

'It was Skorpeus. Or so we surmise. His dead body was found near the breached security gate.'

'Why did he betray his own clan?'

'Why does anybody? Because he wanted power and prestige and he felt he had been passed over. Doubtless Feracci promised that he would see him installed as the new Celestarch. He would do. Skorpeus probably figured better to be a puppet than a servant.' There was something false in Torin's explanation but Ragnar could not quite put his finger on it. Yet.

'Can we can prove Feracci was behind this?' asked Ragnar.

'We don't know that it was. It would be our word against his. Cezare would simply say we were lying, and that it was a plot to discredit him. Even those who disbelieved him would admire him, and fear him for being able to corrupt one of the Belisarians. It would just enhance his prestige.'

'So he will get away with it then? All those people will have died in vain.'

'I would not say that, Ragnar,' said Torin. 'He will not get to control a High Lord since the Lady Juliana will block his son's appointment and that was his dream. He has been planning for this day for decades, that much is obvious. And he failed because of you. He will be seeking vengeance for that.'

'Let him,' said Ragnar.

'Spoken like a true son of Fenris,' said Haegr with almost paternal fondness.

'Ragnar, you will either have a short career or a glorious one, possibly both,' said Torin. 'In your very brief stay on Terra you have managed to make an enemy of one of the most powerful men in the Imperium. I shudder to think what you will do as an encore.'

'What about the Imperial assassin? How is that being dealt with?'

'What Imperial assassin?' said Torin. 'If you made any inquiries I am sure you would find he was some sort of renegade.'

'That's not what you said a few hours ago…'

'No, but it's what the Administratum would say were we foolish enough to lay this matter before them.'

'That is not fair.'

'Life is not fair, Ragnar, get used to it. But again, if it's any consolation to you, I think we have ruined somebody far higher placed than Cezare tonight as well. There will be repercussions there too.'

'I would wish for something more than that.'

'Don't worry, Ragnar,' said Haegr. 'I am sure something else will come up that you can get your teeth into.'

'If that was meant to be a joke,' said Torin, 'it was not very funny.'

Haegr roared with mirth and Ragnar was forced to join him.

Valkoth appeared in the doorway. 'Still lazing about, eh?' he said gruffly. 'Well, get up off that bed and get ready for duty. You are needed in the presence room.'

RAGNAR MARCHED INTO the presence room. He felt almost fully recovered now. His senses had started to return. The place was just as he remembered. The other Wolfblades flanked him. All of them looked smug as if they knew something he did not.

The Celestarch looked down gravely from her throne. She looked older somehow, and there was a sorrow and an anger in her eyes that had not been there during their first meeting. She stretched out her arms regally.

'We are only here because of you, Ragnar, and our House would be finished were it not for your bravery.'

'I only did my sworn duty,' Ragnar replied.

'Nonetheless, Belisarius owes you a debt of gratitude, and I am prepared to show our appreciation.'

Ragnar said nothing. To do anything else would have been presumptuous.

'You lost your blade while fighting to defend us. It is up to us to replace it.' She gestured and two of the guards brought forward a massive rune-encrusted weapon. It was ancient and very beautiful and its like could not have been forged in this age. 'Take it,' she said.

Ragnar reached out and gripped the weapon. It fitted his hand as if it was made for him, and its balance was perfect. An aura of strange coldness radiated from the runes.

'I thank you,' said Ragnar. It was all he could say.

'This blade was borne in the time of the Emperor, by one of the first Wolfblades. It belonged to Skander before it belonged to you. See that you prove worthy of it.'

'I will do my best.'

'Now,' she said, 'we have other business. We must go to council and see that a new throne is correctly chosen. Gentlemen, if you would be so good as to accompany us, we will leave at once.'

Flanking the ruler of Belisarius, they strode towards a meeting that would decide the fate of Navigators for generations to come.

EPILOGUE

THE STRANGE SCENT drew Ragnar from his reverie. He looked up. It was night once more and the sounds of distant carnage filled the darkness. It seemed to Ragnar that it was coming closer. All around, warriors moved, preparing for battle. Some rushed towards the front line positions. Nearby, Urlec and the rest of the Wolves checked their weapons. They looked ready to return to the fight at a moment's notice. His nose twitched. There was a faint odour there, one that set his hackles rising.

He looked down at the blade, reluctant to let go of his memories of those long gone events and comrades and enemies. Some were dead now. Some disgraced. Some had met stranger fates. He thought of the odd twist of fortune that led him to the secret truths about the assassin on that long ago night. There was a tale that would never find its way into the Chapter's annals. He shrugged and smiled, rising to his feet. It was good to remember the past, he thought, and where he had come from, and the long distance he had travelled but now he needed to live in the present. The smell he had caught spoke of the presence of enemies. Seeing him rise, the men rose too and made their weapons ready. He gestured for them to be wary. They responded instantly, throwing themselves into cover, leaping for foxholes, glaring out into the darkness.

The earth shook as a shell impacted nearby. The impact raised a huge cloud of earth and threw several men from their feet. Counter-battery fire blazed a trail through the night. Ragnar sniffed again. He sensed sorcery. Strange energies flowed all around. It looked like the followers of Chaos were not done yet.

He concentrated hard trying to find the source of his unease. Now that he was aware of it, it was easier to pinpoint. In the woods nearby, he now saw the massive armoured figures of Space Marines who did not belong to his Chapter and were not loyal to his Emperor. They must have cloaked their approach with magic, he thought. It looked like they were intent on repaying him for his earlier surprise assault. Ragnar felt he understood. This morning was merely one small skirmish in the unending war between the Imperium and Chaos, between the Space Wolves and the Thousand Sons. That was the way of the universe – countless warring factions and unending strife. He spoke softly into the comm-net telling his men to get ready. If they acted swiftly they could turn this sneak attack on itself.

'Fire!' he shouted, and the last vestiges of his memories were whirled away by the winds of violent actions. There was a war to win. There was always another war to win.

RAGNAR BLACKMANE

DIORAMA

Exquisitely detailed miniatures and sculpted terrain base depicting Ragnar's first battle with the Chaos sorcerer Madox, as described in the novel *Space Wolf*. Limited to only 500 castings ever. Numbered collectors' certificate. Especially sculpted for the Black Library by Aly Morrison.

The Ragnar Blackmane diorama is only available by post, direct from the Black Library, so send this coupon (or a photocopy) with payment to:

Ragnar Blackmane Diorama,
The Black Library,
Games Workshop Ltd.,
Willow Road,
Nottingham NG7 2WS • UK

More Warhammer 40,000 from the Black Library

MARK OF THE WOLF!

The Space Wolf novels by William King

From the death-world of Fenris come the Space Wolves,
the most savage of the Emperor's Space Marines. Follow
the adventures of Ragnar, from his recruitment and
training as he matures into a ferocious and deadly fighter,
scourge of the enemies of humanity.

'Paints a bleak but compelling portrait
of life in the 41st century'
Publishers Weekly

SPACE WOLF

On the planet Fenris, young Ragnar is chosen to be inducted into the noble yet savage Space Wolves Chapter. But with his ancient primal instincts unleashed by the implanting of the sacred canis helix, Ragnar must learn to control the beast within and fight for the greater good of the wolf pack.

RAGNAR'S CLAW

As young Blood Claws, Ragnar and his companions go on their first off-world mission – from the jungle hell of Galt to the polluted hive-cities of hive world Venam, they must travel across the galaxy to face the very heart of evil.

GREY HUNTER

When one of their Chapter's most holy artefacts is seized by the forces of Chaos, Space Wolf Ragnar and his comrades are plunged into a desperate battle to retrieve it before a most terrible and ancient foe is set free.

WOLFBLADE

When Ragnar takes up his duties on ancient Terra, he soon becomes embroiled in an assassination plot that reaches into the very depths of Imperium!